Yellow Fairy Book

Yellow

Fairy Book

collected and edited by
ANDREW LANG
illustrated by
JANICE HOLLAND
with a foreword by
MARY GOULD DAVIS

LONGMAN

LONGMAN GROUP LIMITED
London

*Associated companies, branches and representatives
throughout the world*

THIS EDITION FIRST PUBLISHED 1949
NEW IMPRESSION 1954, 1956, 1959, 1963, 1967 AND 1971

ISBN 0 582 16250 5

PRINTED IN GREAT BRITAIN BY
LOWE AND BRYDONE (PRINTERS) LIMITED, LONDON

TO

JOAN, TODDLES, AND TINY

Books Yellow, Red, and Green and Blue,
All true, or just as good as true,
And here's the Yellow Book for you!

Hard is the path from A to Z,
And puzzling to a curly head,
Yet leads to Books—Green, Blue, and Red.

For every child should understand
That letters from the first were planned
To guide us into Fairy Land.

So labour at your Alphabet,
For by that learning shall you get
To lands where Fairies may be met.

And going where this pathway goes,
You too, at last, may find, who knows?
The Garden of the Singing Rose.

NOTE

As this edition has been set in a larger, more readable type, a few of the original stories have been omitted.

Foreword

To WRITE a few words of introduction to the first four of the Andrew Lang Fairy Books is a simple act of friendship. We are not likely to forget the pages from which the Marquis of Carabas made his first bow to us! We are eager to tell our children and our grandchildren that it was in these books that we first met 'Cinderella' and 'Jack and the Beanstalk' and 'Rumpelstiltskin.' It was in 1889 that the *Blue Fairy Book*, the first of the series, appeared. It was a period when realistic stories dominated the world of children's books. 'Novels of childhood' by Mrs. Ewing and Mrs. Molesworth and other writers were offered to the children as their only fare.

The publishers admitted that the *Blue Fairy Book* was an experiment. Its success was immediate and it turned the tide from realism to the old folk and fairy tales. After the publication of the *Blue* the children demanded others, and the *Red*, the *Green* and the *Yellow* followed. 'The children are pleased,' said Andrew Lang, 'and they are so kind as to *say* that they are pleased. The editor does not care very much for what other people may say.' More than fifty years later it is certainly safe to state that hundreds of modern women have taken their first taste of romance from these pages, hundreds of modern men their first thrill of adventure.

Andrew Lang and his staff of helpers went far afield to find the stories that are in these books. Taking the whole series, practically every literature in the world is represented. One has only to read his biography to know that it was a labour of love. Student, scholar, lover of history and romance, he left no stone unturned that might reveal a new tale for the children. Because they are ageless, they need for a new generation only the courtesy of a modern dress; clearer type, new illustrations where the old ones seem outmoded and slight editorial changes.

They have been, are and will always be, books that it is a joy to share with boys and girls, and that boys and girls are sure to find for themselves. Fathers and even grandfathers will testify that they leaped from these fairy tales to science and invention, mothers and grandmothers that in them they found the natural transition from 'The Sleeping Beauty' to the real romance. It is a part of the inheritance of childhood to have read them, and no collection of books for children is complete without them.

To Andrew Lang belongs the honour of having made a very great contribution to the preservation of the literature of the world. In bringing together from the four corners of the earth these characteristic stories, he has helped to lay the foundation stones of a united world. The love of fairy tales is common to all peoples. To English-speaking children it was Andrew Lang who opened the door of Fairyland.

MARY GOULD DAVIS

New York
March, 1948

Preface

THE EDITOR thinks that children will readily forgive him for publishing another Fairy Book. We have had the *Blue,* the *Red,* the *Green,* and here is the *Yellow.* If children are pleased, and they are so kind as to say that they are pleased, the editor does not care very much for what other people may say. Now, there is one gentleman who seems to think that it is not quite right to print so many fairy tales, with pictures, and to publish them in red and blue covers. He is named Mr. G. Laurence Gomme, and he is president of a learned body called the Folk Lore Society. Once a year he makes his address to his subjects, of whom the editor is one, and Mr. Joseph Jacobs, who has published many delightful fairy tales with pretty pictures, is another. Fancy, then, the dismay of Mr. Jacobs, and of the editor, when they heard their president say that he did not think it very nice of them to publish fairy books, above all, red, green and blue fairy books! They said that they did not see any harm in it, and they were ready to 'put themselves on their country,' and be tried by a jury of children. And, indeed, they still see no harm in what they have done; nay, like Father William in the poem, they are ready 'to do it again and again.'

Where is the harm? The truth is that the Folk Lore Society—made up of the most clever, learned, and beautiful men and women of the country—is fond of studying the history and geography of fairyland. This is contained in very old tales, such as country people tell, and savages:

> *Little Sioux and little Crow,*
> *Little frosty Eskimo.*

These people are thought to know most about fairyland and its inhabitants. But, in the *Yellow Fairy Book,* and the rest, are many tales by persons who are neither savages nor rustics, such as Madame D'Aulnoy and Herr Hans Christian Andersen. The Folk Lore Society, or its president, say that *their* tales are not so true as the rest, and should not be published with the rest. But *we* say that all the stories which are pleasant to read are quite true enough for us; so here they are, and we do not think that either the pictures or the stories are likely to mislead children.

As to whether there are really any fairies or not, that is a difficult question. Professor Huxley thinks there are none. The editor never saw any himself, but he knows several people who have seen them—in the Highlands—and heard their music. If ever you are in Nether Lochaber, go to the Fairy Hill, and you may hear the music yourself, as grown-up people have done, but you must go on a fine day.

Again, if there are really no fairies, why do people believe in them, all over the world? The ancient Greeks believed, so did the old Egyptians, and the Hindoos, and the Red Indians, and is it likely, if there are no fairies, that so many different peoples would have seen and heard them? The Rev. Mr. Baring-Gould saw several fairies when he was a boy, and was travelling in the land of the troubadours. For these reasons, the editor thinks there certainly are fairies, but they never do anyone any harm; and, in England, they have been frightened away by smoke and schoolmasters. As to giants, they have died out, but real dwarfs are common in the forests of Africa. Probably a good many stories not perfectly true have been told about fairies, but such stories have also been told about Napoleon, Claverhouse, Julius Cæsar, and Joan of Arc, all of whom certainly existed. A wise child will, therefore, remember that, if he grows up and becomes a member of the Folk Lore Society, *all* the tales in this book were not offered to him as absolutely truthful, but were printed merely for his entertainment. The exact facts he can learn later, or he can leave them alone.

There are Russian, German, French, Icelandic, and other stories here. They were translated by Miss Cheape, Miss Alma, and Miss Thyra Alleyne, Miss Sellar, Mr. Craigie (he did the Icelandic tales), Miss Blackley, Mrs. Dent, and Mrs. Lang. It is hoped that children will find the book not less pleasing than those which have already been submitted to their consideration. The editor cannot say 'good-bye' without advising them, as they pursue their studies, to read *The Rose and the Ring,* by the late Mr. Thackeray, with pictures by the author. This book he thinks quite indispensable in every child's library, and parents should be urged to purchase it at the first opportunity, as without it no education is complete.

ANDREW LANG

Contents

Illustrations

Yellow Fairy Book

The Cat and the Mouse

A CAT HAD MADE AC-
quaintance with a mouse, and had spoken so much of the great
love and friendship she felt for her, that at last the mouse consented to live in the same house with her and to go shares in
the housekeeping.

'But we must provide for the winter or else we shall suffer
hunger,' said the cat. 'You, little Mouse, cannot venture everywhere in case you ran at last into a trap.'

This good counsel was followed, and a little pot of fat was
bought. But they did not know where to put it. At length, after
long consultation, the cat said:

'I know of no place where it could be better put than in the
church. No one will trouble to take it away from there. We will
hide it in a corner, and we won't touch it till we are in want.'

So the little pot was placed in safety; but it was not long
before the cat had a great longing for it and said to the mouse:

'I wanted to tell you, little Mouse, that my cousin has a little
son, white with brown spots, and she wants me to be godmother
to it. Let me go out today, and do you take care of the house
alone.'

'Yes, go certainly,' replied the mouse, 'and when you eat

anything good, think of me. I should very much like a drop of the red christening wine.'

But it was all untrue. The cat had no cousin, and had not been asked to be godmother. She went straight to the church, slunk to the little pot of fat, began to lick it, and licked the top

VINS FINS

off. Then she took a walk on the roofs of the town, looked at the view, stretched herself out in the sun, and licked her lips whenever she thought of the little pot of fat. As soon as it was evening she went home again.

'Ah, here you are again!' said the mouse. 'You must certainly have had an enjoyable day.'

'It went off very well,' answered the cat.

'What was the child's name?' asked the mouse.

'Top Off,' said the cat drily.

'Topoff!' echoed the mouse. 'It is indeed a wonderful and curious name. Is it in your family?'

'What is there odd about it?' said the cat. 'It is no worse than Breadthief, as your godchild is called.'

Not long after this another great longing came over the cat. She said to the mouse, 'You must again be kind enough to look after the house alone, for I have been asked a second time to stand godmother, and as this child has a white ring round its neck, I cannot refuse.'

The kind mouse agreed, but the cat slunk under the town wall to the church and ate up half the pot of fat.

'Nothing tastes better,' said she, 'than what one eats by oneself,' and she was very much pleased with her day's work.

When she came home the mouse asked, 'What was this child called?'

'Half Gone,' answered the cat.

'Halfgone! What a name! I have never heard it in my life. I don't believe it is in the calendar.'

Soon the cat's mouth began to water once more, and she said to the mouse:

'All good things in threes. I have again to stand godmother. The child is quite black, and has very white paws, but not a single white hair on its body. This happens only once in two years, so you will let me go out?'

'Topoff! Halfgone!' repeated the mouse. 'They are such curious names; they make me very thoughtful.'

'Oh, you sit at home in your dark gray coat and your long tail,' said the cat, 'and you get fanciful. That comes of not going out in the day.'

The mouse had a good cleaning out while the cat was gone and made the house tidy; but the greedy cat ate up every bit of the fat.

'When it is all gone one can be at rest,' she said to herself, and at night she came home sleek and satisfied. The mouse asked at once after the third child's name.

'It won't please you any better,' said the cat. 'He was called Clean Gone.'

'Cleangone!' repeated the mouse. 'I do not believe that name has been printed any more than the others. Cleangone! What can it mean?' She shook her head, curled herself up and went to sleep.

From this time on no one asked the cat to stand godmother. But when the winter came and there was nothing to eat outside, the mouse remembered their provision and said:

'Come, Cat, we will go to our pot of fat which we have stored away; it will taste very good.'

'Yes, indeed,' answered the cat, 'it will taste as good to you as if you stretched your thin tongue out of the window.'

They started off, and when they reached it they found the pot in its place, but quite empty!

'Ah,' said the mouse, 'now I know what has happened! It has all come out! You are a true friend to me! You have eaten it all when you stood godmother; first the top off, then half of it gone, then—'

'Will you be quiet!' screamed the cat. 'Another word and I will eat you up.'

'Cleangone' was already on the poor mouse's tongue, and scarcely was it out than the cat made a spring at her, seized and swallowed her.

That is the way of the world.

The Six Swans

A KING WAS ONCE
hunting in a great wood, and he hunted the game so eagerly
that none of his courtiers could follow him. When evening
came on he saw that he had quite lost himself. He sought a
way out, but could find none. Then he saw an old woman with
shaking head coming toward him, but she was a witch.

'Good woman,' he said to her, 'can you not show me the way
out of the wood?'

'Oh, certainly, Sir King,' she replied, 'I can do that, but on
one condition, which if you do not fulfil you will never get
out of the wood and will die of hunger.'

'What is the condition?' asked the king.

'I have a daughter,' said the old woman, 'who is so beautiful
that she has not her equal in the world and she is well fitted
to be your wife. If you will make her lady queen, I will show
you the way out of the wood.'

The king in his anguish of mind consented, and the old
woman led him to her little house where her daughter was
sitting by the fire. She received the king as if she were expecting
him, and he saw that she was certainly very beautiful. But she
did not please him, and he could not look at her without a

5

secret feeling of horror. As soon as he had lifted the maiden on to his horse the old woman showed him the way, and the king reached his palace, where the wedding was celebrated.

The king had already been married once and had by his first wife seven children, six boys and one girl, whom he loved more than anything in the world. And now, because he was afraid that their stepmother might not treat them well, he put them in a lonely castle that stood in the middle of a wood. It lay so hidden, and the way to it was so hard to find, that he himself could not have found it had not a wise woman given him a reel of thread which possessed a marvellous property. When he threw it before him it unwound itself and showed him the way.

But the king went so often to his dear children that the queen was offended at his absence. She grew curious, and wanted to know what he did alone in the wood. She gave his servants a great deal of money, and they betrayed the secret to her and also told her of the reel which alone could point out the way. She had no rest now till she found out where the king guarded the reel. Then she made some little white shirts and, as she had learned from her witch mother, sewed an enchantment in each of them.

And when the king had ridden off she took the little shirts and went into the wood, and the reel showed her the way. The children, who saw someone in the distance, thought it was their dear father coming to them and sprang to meet him joyfully. Then she threw over each one a little shirt which, when it had touched their bodies, changed them into swans, and they flew away over the forest. The queen went home quite satisfied and thought she was well rid of her stepchildren. But of the girl she knew nothing, and fortunately the child had not run to meet her with her brothers.

The next day the king came to visit his children, but he found no one but his daughter.

'Where are your brothers?' asked the king.

'Alas, dear Father!' she answered. 'They have gone away and left me all alone.' And she told him that looking out of her little window she had seen her brothers flying over the wood in the shape of swans. The king mourned, but he did not think of the queen. As he was afraid of losing the maiden also, he wanted to take her with him. But she was afraid of the stepmother, and begged the king to let her stay just one night more in the castle in the wood.

The poor maiden thought, My home is no longer here, I will go and seek my brothers. And when night came she fled away into the forest. She ran all through the night and the next day, till she could go no farther for weariness. Then she saw a little hut, went in and found a room with six little beds. She crept under one of them, lay on the hard floor, and was going to spend the night there.

But when the sun had set she heard a noise and saw six swans flying in at the window. They stood on the floor and blew all their feathers off, and their swanskins came off like a shirt. Then the maiden recognized her brothers, and overjoyed she crept out from under the bed. Her brothers were no less delighted than she to see their little sister again, but their joy did not last long.

'You cannot stay here,' they said to her. 'This is a den of robbers.'

'Could you not protect me?' asked the little sister.

'No,' they answered, 'for only a quarter of an hour every evening do we regain our human forms; then we are changed into swans again.'

Then the little sister cried and said, 'Can you not be freed?'

'Oh, no,' they said, 'the conditions are too hard. You must not speak or laugh for six years and must make in that time six shirts for us out of star flowers. If a single word comes out of your mouth, all your labour is in vain.'

When the brothers had said this the quarter of an hour came to an end, and they flew away out of the window as swans. But the maiden had determined to free her brothers even if it should cost her her life. She left the hut, went into the forest, climbed a tree and spent the night there. The next morning she went out, collected star flowers, and began to sew. She could speak to no one, and she had no wish to laugh, so she sat there, looking only at her work.

When she had lived there some time, it happened that the king of the country was hunting in the forest, and his hunters came to the tree on which the maiden sat. They called to her and asked, 'Who are you?'

But she gave no answer.

'Come down to us,' they said, 'we will do you no harm.'

But she shook her head silently. As they pressed her further with questions, she threw them the golden chain from her neck. But they did not leave off, and she threw them her girdle, and when this was no use, her garters and then her dress. The huntsmen would not leave her alone, but climbed the tree, lifted the maiden down, and led her to the king. The king asked:

'Who are you? What are you doing up in that tree?'

But she answered nothing.

He asked her in all the languages he knew, but she was as silent as a fish. Because she was so beautiful, however, the king's heart was touched, and he was seized with a great love for her. He wrapped her up in his cloak, placed her before him on his horse and brought her to his castle. There he had her

'What are you doing up in that tree?'

dressed in rich clothes, and her beauty shone out as bright as day, but not a word could be drawn from her. He seated her at table by his side, and her modest ways and behaviour pleased him so much that he said:

'I will marry this maiden and none other in the world.' And after some days he married her. But the king had a wicked mother who was displeased with the marriage, and said wicked things of the young queen.

'Who knows who this girl is?' she said. 'She cannot speak and is not worthy of a king.'

After a year, when the queen had her first child, the old mother took it away from her. Then she went to the king and said that the queen had killed it. The king would not believe it, and would not allow any harm to be done her. But she sat quietly sewing at the shirts and troubling herself about nothing. The next time she had a child the wicked mother did the same thing, but the king could not make up his mind to believe her. He said:

'She is too sweet and good to do that. If she were not dumb and could defend herself, her innocence would be proved.'

But when the third child was taken away, and the queen was again accused and could not utter a word in her own defence, the king was obliged to give her over to the law, which decreed that she be burned to death. When the day came on which the sentence was to be executed, it was the last day of the six years in which she must not speak or laugh. The six shirts were done, except for the left sleeve of the last.

When she was led to the stake, the queen laid the shirts on her arm, and as she stood on the pile and the fire was about to be lighted, she looked around her and saw six swans flying through the air. Then she knew that her release was at hand

and that she could free her dear brothers from enchantment. Her heart danced for joy.

The swans fluttered round her and hovered low so that she could throw the shirts over them. The swanskins fell off, and her brothers stood before her living, well and beautiful. Only the youngest had a swan's wing instead of his left arm. They embraced and kissed each other, and the queen went to the king, who was standing by in great astonishment.

'Dearest Husband, now I can speak and tell you openly that I am innocent and have been falsely accused.'

She told him of the old woman's deceit and how she had taken the three children away and hidden them. Then they were fetched, to the great joy of the king, but his wicked mother came to no good end.

But the king and the queen with their six brothers lived many years in happiness and peace.

The Dragon of the North

VERY LONG AGO, THERE
lived a terrible monster, who came out of the North, and laid
waste whole tracts of country, devouring both men and beasts.
It was feared that unless help came no living creature would
be left on the face of the earth. The monster had a body like
an ox and legs like a frog, two short forelegs and two long
ones behind, and besides that it had a tail like a serpent, ten
fathoms in length. When it moved it jumped like a frog, and
with every spring it covered half a mile of ground. Its habit
was to remain for several years in the same place and not to
move on till the whole neighbourhood was eaten up.

Nothing could hunt it, because its whole body was covered
with scales, which were harder than stone or metal. Its two
great eyes shone by night, and even by day, like the brightest
lamps; and anyone who had the ill luck to look into those
eyes became bewitched and was obliged to rush into the
monster's jaws. In this way the dragon was able to feed upon
both men and beasts without the least trouble to itself, as it
did not need to move from the spot where it was lying.

All the neighbouring kings had offered rich rewards to anyone
who should destroy the monster, either by force or enchant-

ment. Many had tried their luck, but all had miserably failed.
Once a great forest in which the dragon lay had been set on
fire; the forest was burned down, but the fire did not do the
monster the least harm.

However, there was a tradition amongst the wise men of the
country that the dragon might be overcome by one who
possessed King Solomon's signet ring, upon which a secret
writing was engraved. Anyone wise enough to interpret it
could find out how the dragon could be destroyed. Only no
one knew where the ring was hidden.

At last a young man, with a good heart and plenty of
courage, set out to search for the ring. He took his way toward
the sunrise, because he knew that all the wisdom of old time
came from the East. After some years he met a famous Eastern
magician, and asked for his advice. The magician answered:

'Mortal men can give you no help. Birds of the air would
be better guides if you could learn their language. I can help
you if you will stay with me a few days.'

The youth thankfully accepted the magician's offer and said,
'I cannot now offer you any reward for your kindness, but
should my undertaking succeed your trouble shall be richly
repaid.'

The magician brewed a powerful potion out of nine herbs
which he had gathered by moonlight. And he gave the youth
nine spoonfuls of it daily for three days, which made him able
to understand the language of birds.

At parting, the magician said to him, 'If you ever find
Solomon's ring come back to me, for there is no one else in
the whole world who can explain the inscription on the ring
to you.'

From that time the youth always had company, because he
understood the language of birds. In this way he learned many

things, but time went on, and he heard nothing about the ring.
It happened one evening, when he was hot and tired with
walking and had sat down under a tree in a forest to eat his
supper, that he saw two gaily-plumaged birds, sitting at the
top of the tree, talking to one another. The first bird said:

'I know that wanderer under the tree there, who has come
so far without finding what he seeks. He is trying to find
King Solomon's lost ring.'

The other bird answered, 'He will have to seek help from the
witch maiden. If she does not have the ring herself, she knows
well enough who has it.'

'But where is he to find the witch maiden?' said the first
bird. 'She is here today and gone tomorrow. He might as well
try to catch the wind.'

The other replied, 'I do not know, certainly, where she is at present, but in three nights she will come to the spring to wash her face, as she does every month when the moon is full, so she may never grow old nor wrinkled, but always keep the bloom of youth.'

'Well,' said the first bird, 'the spring is not far from here. Shall we go and see how she does it?'

'Willingly, if you like,' said the other.

The youth resolved to follow the birds to the spring. Two things made him uneasy: first, he might be asleep when the birds went, and secondly, he might lose sight of them, since he had no wings to carry him along swiftly. He was too tired to keep awake all night, yet his anxiety prevented him from sleeping soundly. When, with the earliest dawn, he looked up to the treetop, he was glad to see his feathered companions still asleep with their heads under their wings. He ate his breakfast and waited until the birds should start, but they did not leave the place all day. They hopped about from one tree to another looking for food until the evening, when they went back to their old perch to sleep. The next day the same thing happened, but on the third morning one bird said to the other, 'Today we must go to the spring to see the witch maiden wash her face.'

They remained on the tree till noon; then they flew away toward the south. The young man's heart beat with anxiety but he kept the birds in view until they again perched upon a tree. The young man ran after them until he was quite exhausted and out of breath. Three times they flew on and he followed. At length they reached a small open space in the forest, on the edge of which they placed themselves on the top of a high tree. When the youth had overtaken them, he saw a clear spring in the middle of the space. He sat down at the foot of the tree upon which the birds were perched and listened attentively to what they were saying to each other.

'The sun is not down yet,' said the first bird. 'We must wait yet a while till the moon rises and the maiden comes to the spring. Do you think she will see that young man sitting under the tree?'

'Nothing is likely to escape her eyes, certainly not the young man,' said the other bird. 'Will the youth have the sense not to let himself be caught in her toils?'

'We will wait,' said the first bird, 'and see how they get on together.'

The evening light had faded, and the full moon was already shining down upon the forest, when the young man heard a slight rustling sound. After a few moments out of the forest a maiden came, gliding over the grass so lightly that her feet seemed scarcely to touch the ground, and stood beside the spring. The youth could not turn away his eyes from the maiden, for he had never seen a woman so beautiful. Without seeming to notice anything, she went to the spring, looked up to the full moon, then knelt down and bathed her face nine times. Then she looked up to the moon again and walked nine times round the well, and as she walked she sang this song:

> 'Full-faced moon with light unshaded,
> Let my beauty ne'er be faded.
> Never let my cheek grow pale!
> While the moon is waning nightly,
> May the maiden bloom more brightly,
> May her freshness never fail!'

Then she dried her face with her long hair and was about to go away, when she turned toward the tree. The youth rose and stood waiting. Then the maiden said:

'You ought to have a heavy punishment because you have presumed to watch me in the moonlight. But I will forgive you this time, because you are a stranger and knew no better. But you must tell me truly who you are and how you came to this place, where no mortal has ever set foot before.'

The youth answered humbly, 'Forgive me, beautiful maiden. I chanced to come here after long wandering and found a good place to sleep under this tree. At your coming I did not know what to do, but stayed where I was, because I thought my silent watching could not offend you.'

The maiden answered kindly, 'Come and spend this night with me. You will sleep better on a pillow than on damp moss.'

The youth hesitated, but presently he heard the birds saying from the top of the tree, 'Go where she calls you, but take care to give no blood, or you will sell your soul.' So the youth went with her, and soon they reached a beautiful garden, where stood a splendid house, glittering in the moonlight as if it were built of gold and silver.

When the youth entered he found many splendid chambers, each one finer than the last. Hundreds of tapers burned in golden candlesticks and shed a light like the brightest day. At length they reached a chamber where a table was spread with the most costly dishes. At the table were placed two chairs, one of silver, the other of gold. The maiden seated herself upon the golden chair, and offered the silver one to her companion. They were served by maidens dressed in white, whose feet made no sound as they moved about, and not a word was spoken during the meal. Afterward the youth and the witch maiden conversed pleasantly together, until a woman came in to remind them it was bedtime. The youth was now shown into another room, containing a silken bed with down cushions, where he slept delightfully.

The next morning the maiden asked him whether he would not like to stay with her always in this beautiful place. As he did not answer immediately, she continued, 'You see how I always remain young and beautiful. I am under no one's orders, but can do just what I like, so I have never thought of marrying before. But from the moment I saw you I took a fancy to you. If you agree, we might be married and live together like princes, because I have great riches.'

The youth could not but be tempted with the beautiful maiden's offer, but he remembered how the birds had called her the witch, and their warning always sounded in his ears. Therefore he answered, 'Do not be angry, dear maiden, if I cannot decide immediately, on this important matter. Give me a few days to consider.'

'Why not?' answered the maiden. 'Take as long as you like, and take counsel with your own heart.'

To make the time pass pleasantly, she took the youth over every part of her beautiful dwelling and showed him all her splendid treasures. The maiden could make anything she wished appear by the help of King Solomon's signet ring. Only none of these things remained fixed, they passed away like the wind without leaving a trace behind.

One day the maiden took him into a secret chamber, where a little gold box was standing on a silver table. Pointing to the box, she said:

'Here is my greatest treasure, its like is not to be found in the whole world. It is a precious gold ring. I will give you this ring as a marriage gift, and it will make you the happiest of mortal men. But that our love may last forever, you must give me for the ring three drops of blood from the little finger of your left hand.'

When the youth heard these words a cold shudder ran over

him, for he remembered that his soul was at stake. However, he concealed his feelings and made no direct answer, only asking the maiden, as if carelessly, what was remarkable about the ring?

She answered, 'No mortal is able entirely to understand the power of this ring, because no one thoroughly understands the secret signs engraved upon it. But even with my half-knowledge I can work great wonders. If I put the ring upon the little finger of my left hand I can fly like a bird through the air wherever I wish to go. If I put it on the third finger of my left hand I am invisible, but I can see everything that passes around me, though no one can see me. If I put the ring upon the middle finger of my left hand neither fire nor water nor any sharp weapon can hurt me. If I put it on the forefinger of my left hand, with its help I can produce whatever I wish. In a single moment I can build houses or anything I desire. Finally, as long as I wear the ring on the thumb of my left hand that hand is so strong it can break down rocks and walls. Besides these, the ring has other secret signs which, as I said, no one can understand. The ring belonged to King Solomon, the wisest of kings, during whose reign the wisest men lived. It is supposed that an angel gave it to the wise king.'

When the youth heard all this he determined to get possession of the ring, though he did not quite believe in all its wonderful gifts. He wished the maiden would let him have it in his hand, but he did not like to ask her for it, and after a while she put it back into the box. A few days later they were again speaking of the magic ring, and the youth said, 'I do not think the ring can have all the power you say it has.'

Then the maiden opened the box and took the ring out, and it glittered like the clearest sunbeam. She put the ring on her third finger, and in an instant she had vanished from his eyes.

Presently she was beside him again, laughing, and holding the ring between her fingers.

'Do let me try,' said the youth, 'whether I can do these wonderful things.'

The maiden, suspecting no treachery, gave him the magic ring. The youth pretended to have forgotten what to do and asked which finger he must put the ring on so no sharp weapon could hurt him?

'Oh, the middle finger of your left hand,' the maiden answered, laughing.

She took the knife and tried to strike the youth, and he even tried to cut himself with it, but found it impossible. Then she led him into a courtyard where stood a great boulder.

'Now,' she said, 'put the ring upon the thumb of your left hand, and you will see how strong that hand has become.'

The youth did so and found to his astonishment that with a single blow the stone flew into a thousand pieces. Then the youth bethought him that he who does not use his luck when he has it is a fool; this was a chance which once lost might never return. So while they stood laughing at the shattered stone he placed the ring, as if in play, upon the third finger of his left hand.

'Now,' said the maiden, 'you are invisible to me until you take the ring off again.'

But the youth had no mind to do that; on the contrary, he went farther off. Then he put the ring on the little finger of his left hand and soared into the air like a bird.

When the maiden saw him flying away she thought at first that he was still in play, and cried, 'Come back, Friend, for now you see I have told you the truth.' But the young man never came back. Then the maiden saw she was deceived and bitterly repented that she had ever trusted him with the ring.

With a single blow the stone flew into a thousand pieces

The young man never halted in his flight until he reached the dwelling of the wise magician who was delighted to find that his search had been successful and at once set to work to interpret the secret signs engraved upon the ring, but it took him seven weeks to make them out clearly. Then he gave the youth the following instructions to overcome the Dragon of the North:

'You must have an iron horse cast, with little wheels under each foot. You must also have a spear two fathoms long. You will be able to wield it by means of the magic ring on your left thumb. The spear must be as thick as a large tree, with both its ends sharp. In the middle of the spear you must have two strong chains ten fathoms in length. As soon as the dragon has made himself fast to the spear, which you have thrust through his jaws, you must spring quickly from the iron horse and fasten the ends of the chains firmly to the ground with iron stakes. After two or three days the monster's strength will be so far exhausted that you will be able to come near him. Then you can put Solomon's ring upon your left thumb and give him the finishing stroke, but keep the ring upon your third finger until you have come close to him, so that the monster cannot see you, else he might strike you dead with his long tail. But when all is done, take care you do not lose the ring and that no one takes it from you by cunning.'

The young man thanked the magician and promised, should he succeed, to reward him. But the magician answered, 'I have profited so much by the wisdom of the ring that I desire no other reward.'

Then they parted, and the youth quickly flew home through the air. After remaining in his own home for some weeks, he heard people say that the terrible Dragon of the North was not far off and might shortly be expected. The king announced publicly that he would give his daughter in marriage, as well as a large part of his kingdom, to whosoever should free the country from the monster. The youth then went to the king and told him that he had good hopes of subduing the dragon, if the king would grant him all he needed for the purpose. The king willingly agreed, and the iron horse, the great spear and the chains were prepared as the youth requested.

When all was ready, it was found that the iron horse was so heavy a hundred men could not move it, so there was nothing for it but to move it with his own strength by means of the magic ring. The dragon was now so near that in a couple of springs he would be over the frontier. The youth was puzzled, for if he had to push the iron horse from behind he could not ride upon it as the sorcerer had said he must. But a raven unexpectedly gave him this advice:

'Ride upon the horse and push the spear against the ground, as if you were pushing off a boat from the land.'

The youth did so and found that in this way he could easily move forward. The dragon had his monstrous jaws wide open, all ready for his expected prey. A few paces nearer, and man and horse would certainly have been swallowed up! The youth trembled with horror, and his blood ran cold, yet he did not lose his courage. Holding the iron spear upright in his hand, he brought it down with all his might, right through the monster's lower jaw.

Then quick as lightning he sprang from his horse before the dragon had time to shut his mouth. The youth now hastened to fasten down the chains to the ground by means of the enormous iron pegs which he had provided.

The death struggle of the monster lasted three days and three nights; in his writhing he beat his tail so violently against the ground, that at ten miles' distance the earth trembled as if with an earthquake. When he at length lost power to move his tail, the youth with the help of the ring took up a stone, which twenty ordinary men could not have moved, and very soon the monster lay lifeless before him.

How great was the rejoicing when the news was spread abroad that the terrible monster was dead! His conqueror was received with as much pomp as if he had been the mightiest of kings. The old king did not need to urge his daughter to marry the slayer of the dragon; he found her willing to bestow her hand upon this hero. In a few days a magnificent wedding was celebrated. The rejoicings lasted four whole weeks, for all the neighbouring kings came to thank the man who had freed the world from their common enemy.

But everyone forgot amid the general joy that they ought to have buried the dragon's monstrous body. Before long the whole air was poisoned, and a pestilence broke out which destroyed many hundreds of people. In this distress, the king's son-in-law resolved to seek help once more from the Eastern magician, to whom he at once travelled through the air like a bird by the help of the ring. But there is a proverb which says that ill-gotten gains never prosper, and the prince found that the stolen ring brought him ill luck after all.

The witch maiden never rested night or day until she found out where the ring was. As soon as she discovered by means of her magical arts that the prince in the form of a bird was on his way to the Eastern magician, she changed herself into an eagle and watched until he came in sight, for she knew him at once by the ring which was hung round his neck by a ribbon. Then the eagle pounced upon the bird and tore the ring from his neck before he had time to prevent her. The eagle flew down to the earth with her prey, and the two stood face to face in human form once more.

'Now, villain, you are in my power!' cried the witch maiden. 'I favoured you and you repaid me with treachery and theft. You stole my most precious jewel; and do you expect to live happily as the king's son-in-law? Now the tables are turned and I will be revenged on you for your crimes.'

'Forgive me, forgive me!' cried the prince. 'I know well how deeply I have wronged you and most heartily do I repent it.'

The maiden answered, 'Your prayers and your repentance come too late, and if I were to spare you everyone would think me a fool. First you scorned my love, and then you stole my ring, and you must bear the punishment.'

With these words she put the ring upon her left thumb, lifted the young man with one hand and walked away with him under her arm. This time she did not take him to a splendid palace, but to a deep cave in a rock. The maiden now chained the young man's hands and feet so he could not escape; then she said, 'Here you shall remain. I will bring you every day enough food to prevent your dying of hunger, but you need never hope for freedom any more.' With these words she left him.

The old king and his daughter waited anxiously for many weeks for the prince's return, but no news of him arrived. The king's daughter often dreamed that her husband was going through some great suffering; she therefore begged her father to summon all the enchanters and magicians, that they might try to find out where the prince was and how he could be set free. At last a celebrated magician from Finland was brought before the king, who had found out that the king's son-in-law was imprisoned in the East.

The king now sent messengers to look for his son-in-law, and they by good luck met with the old magician who had interpreted the signs on King Solomon's ring and thus possessed more wisdom than anyone else in the world. The magician soon found out what he wished to know, and pointed out the place where the prince was imprisoned, but said:

'He is kept there by enchantment and cannot be set free without my help. I will therefore go with you myself.'

So they all set out and after some days came to the cave where the unfortunate prince had been chained up for nearly seven years. He recognized the magician immediately, but the old man did not know him, he had grown so thin. However, the magician undid the chains by the help of magic, and took care of the prince until he recovered and became strong enough to travel.

When the prince reached home he found that the old king had died, so he was raised to the throne. And now after his long suffering came prosperity, which lasted to the end of his life; but he never got back the magic ring, nor has it ever again been seen by mortal eyes.

["Der Norlands Drache," from *Esthnische Mährchen*. Kreutzwald.]

The Emperor's New Clothes

M

ANY YEARS AGO
there lived an emperor who was so fond of new clothes that
he spent all his money on them. He did not care about his
soldiers, he did not care about the theatre; he only liked to go
out walking to show off his new clothes. He had a coat for
every hour of the day; and just as they say of a king, 'He is in
the council chamber,' they always said here, 'The emperor is
in the wardrobe.'

In the great city in which the emperor lived there was
always something going on; every day many strangers came
there. One day two impostors arrived who announced they
were weavers, and said they knew how to manufacture the
most beautiful cloth imaginable. Not only were the texture and
pattern uncommonly beautiful, but the clothes which were
made of the stuff possessed this wonderful property, they were
invisible to anyone who was not fit for his office or who was
unpardonably stupid.

'My, oh, my,' said the people. 'Think of that!'

'Those must indeed be splendid clothes,' said the emperor to
himself. 'If I had them on I could find out which men in my
kingdom are unfit for the offices they hold; I could distinguish

the wise from the stupid! Yes, this cloth must be woven for me at once.'

And he gave both the impostors money that they might begin their work.

They placed two weaving looms and pretended they were working, but they had not the least thing on them. They also demanded the finest silk and the best gold, which they put in their pockets, and worked at the empty looms till late into the night.

I should like very much to know how much they have woven, thought the emperor. But he remembered, when he thought about it, that whoever was stupid or not fit for his office would not be able to see it. Now he certainly believed that he had nothing to fear for himself, but he wanted first to send somebody else in order to see how he stood with regard to his office. Everybody in the whole town knew what a wonderful power the cloth had, and all were curious to see how bad or how stupid their neighbour was.

'I will send my old and honoured minister to the weavers,' said the emperor. 'He can judge best what the cloth is like, for he has intellect, and no one understands his office better than he.'

Now the good old minister went into the hall where the two impostors sat working at the empty looms.

Dear me! thought he, opening his eyes wide. I can see nothing! But he did not say so.

Both the impostors begged him to be so kind as to step closer, and asked him if it were not of beautiful texture and lovely colours. They pointed to the empty loom, and the poor old minister went forward rubbing his eyes. But he could see nothing, for there was nothing there.

'Dear, dear,' he said to himself, 'can I be stupid? I have never thought that, and nobody must know it! Can I be unfit for my office? No, I must certainly not say I cannot see the cloth!'

'Have you nothing to say about it?' asked one of the men who was weaving.

'Oh, it is lovely, most lovely!' answered the old minister, looking through his spectacles. 'What a texture! What colours! Yes, I will certainly tell the emperor that it pleases me very much.'

'Now we are delighted to hear that,' said both the weavers, and thereupon they named the colours and explained the making of the pattern.

4

The old minister paid great attention so he could tell it all to the emperor when he came back to him, which he did.

The impostors now wanted more money, more silk and more gold to use in their weaving. They put it all in their own pockets, and there were no threads on the looms but they went on as they had before, working at the empty looms. The emperor soon sent another worthy statesman to see how the weaving was progressing and whether the cloth would soon be finished. It was the same with him as with the first one; he looked and looked, but because there was nothing on the empty looms he could see nothing.

'Is it not a beautiful piece of cloth?' asked the two impostors, as they described the splendid material which was not there.

Stupid I am not, thought the man, so it must be my good office for which I am not fitted. It is strange, certainly, but no one must be allowed to notice it. And so he praised the cloth which he did not see, and expressed his delight at the beautiful colours and the splendid texture.

'Yes, it is quite beautiful,' he said to the emperor.

Everybody in the town was talking of the magnificent cloth.

Now the emperor wanted to see it himself while it was still on the loom. With a great crowd of select followers, among whom were both the worthy statesmen who had already been there before, he went to the cunning impostors, who were now weaving with all their might, but without fibre or thread, of course.

'Is it not splendid!' said both the old statesmen who had already been there. 'See, Your Majesty, what a texture! What colours!' And they pointed to the empty looms, for they believed that the others could see the cloth quite well.

'What!' said the emperor to himself. 'I can see nothing! This is indeed horrible! Am I stupid? Am I not fit to be emperor?

'Oh, very beautiful,' he said. 'It has my gracious approval.' And he nodded pleasantly and examined the empty looms, for he would not say he could see nothing.

His whole court round him looked and looked and saw no more than the others; but they said like the emperor, 'Oh, it is beautiful!' And they advised him to wear the new and magnificent clothes to be made of it for the first time at the great procession which was soon to take place. 'Splendid! Lovely! Most beautiful!' went from mouth to mouth. Everyone seemed delighted and the emperor gave to the impostors the title of Court Weavers to the Emperor.

Throughout the whole of the night before the morning on which the procession was to take place, the impostors were up and were working by the light of more than sixteen candles. The people could see that they were very busy making the emperor's new clothes ready. They pretended they were taking the cloth from the loom, were cutting with huge scissors in the air and were sewing with needles without thread, and then they said at last, 'Now the clothes are finished!'

The emperor came himself with his most distinguished knights, and each impostor held up his arm just as if he were holding something, and said, 'See, here are the breeches! Here is the coat! Here the cloak!' and so on.

'These clothes are so comfortable that one would imagine one had nothing on at all; but that is the beauty of it!'

'Yes,' said all the knights, but they could see nothing, for there was nothing there.

'Will it please Your Majesty graciously to take off your clothes,' said the impostors, 'then we will dress you in the new clothes, here before the mirror.'

The emperor took off all his clothes, and the impostors placed themselves before him as if they were putting on each part of his new clothes which was ready, and the emperor turned and bent himself in front of the mirror.

'How beautifully they fit! How well they sit!' said everybody. 'What material! What colours! Such a gorgeous suit!'

'They are waiting outside with the canopy which Your Majesty is wont to have borne over you in the processions,' announced the Master of Ceremonies.

'Look, I am ready,' said the emperor. 'Doesn't it sit well!' And he turned himself again to the mirror to see if his finery was on all right.

The chamberlains put their hands near the floor as if they were lifting up the train. Then they acted as if they were holding something in the air. They would not have it noticed that they could see nothing.

So the emperor went along in the procession under the splendid canopy, and all the people in the streets and at the windows said, 'How matchless are the emperor's new clothes! The train fastened to his dress, how beautifully it hangs!'

No one wished it to be noticed that he could see nothing, for then he would have been unfit for his office or else very stupid. None of the emperor's clothes had met with such approval as had these.

'But he has nothing on!' said a little child at last.

'Just listen to the innocent child!' said the father, and each one whispered to his neighbour what the child had said.

'But he has nothing on!' the whole of the people called out at last.

The emperor heard and it seemed to him they were right; but he thought, I must go on with the procession now. And the chamberlains walked along still more uprightly, holding up the train which was not there at all.

[Hans Christian Andersen.]

The Golden Crab

O NCE UPON A TIME
there was a fisherman who had a wife and three children.
Every morning he used to go out fishing, and whatever fish
he caught he sold to the king. One day, among the other
fishes, he caught a golden crab. When he came home he put
all the fishes together into a great dish, but he kept the crab
separate, because it shone so beautifully, and placed it upon a
high shelf in the cupboard. Now while his wife was cleaning
the fish she tucked up her gown so that her feet were visible.
Suddenly she heard a voice, which said:

> *'Let down, let down your petticoat*
> *That lets your feet be seen.'*

She turned round in surprise, and then she saw the little
golden crab.

'What! You can speak, can you, you ridiculous crab?' she
said, for she was not pleased at the crab's remarks. Then she
took him up and placed him on a dish.

When her husband came home to dinner, they presently
heard the crab's little voice saying, 'Give me some too.' They

were much surprised, but they gave him something to eat. When the old man came to take away the plate which had contained the crab's dinner, he found it full of gold, and as the same thing happened every day he soon became very fond of the crab.

One day the crab said to the fisherman's wife, 'Go to the king and tell him I wish to marry his younger daughter.'

The old woman went accordingly and laid the matter before the king, who laughed at the notion of his daughter marrying a crab, but did not decline the proposal altogether, because he was a prudent monarch and knew that the crab was likely a prince in disguise. He said, therefore, to the fisherman's wife:

'Go, and tell the crab I will give him my daughter if by tomorrow morning he can build a wall in front of my castle much higher than my tower, upon which all the flowers of the world must grow and bloom.'

The fisherman's wife went home and gave this message. Then the crab gave her a golden rod, and said:

'Go and strike with this rod three times upon the ground on the place which the king showed you, and tomorrow morning the wall will be there.'

The old woman did so and went away again.

The next morning, when the king awoke, what do you think he saw? The wall stood there before his eyes, exactly as he had bespoken it! Then the old woman went back to the king and said to him, 'Your Majesty's orders have been fulfilled.'

'That is all very well,' said the king, 'but I cannot give away my daughter until there stands in front of my palace a garden in which there are three fountains, of which the first must play gold, the second diamonds, and the third brilliants.'

So the old woman had to strike again three times upon the

ground with the rod, and the next morning the garden was there. The king now gave his consent, and the wedding was fixed for the very next day.

Then the crab said to the old fisherman:

'Now take this rod; go and knock with it on a certain mountain. Then a black man will come out and ask you what you wish for. Answer him thus: "Your master, the king, has sent me to tell you that you must send him his golden garment that is like the sun." Make him give you, besides, the queenly robes of gold and precious stones which are like the flowery meadows, and bring them both to me. And bring me also the golden cushion.'

The old man went and did his errand. When he had brought the precious robes, the crab put on the golden garment and then crept upon the golden cushion, and in this way the fisherman carried him to the castle, where the crab presented the other garment to his bride. Now the ceremony took place, and when the married pair were alone together the crab made himself known to his young wife and told her how he was the son of the greatest king in the world, and how he was enchanted. He became a crab by day and was a man only at night; and he could also change himself into an eagle as often as he wished.

No sooner had he said this than he shook himself and immediately became a handsome youth, but the next morning he was forced to creep back again into his crab shell. And the same thing happened every day. But the princess's affection for the crab, and the polite attention with which she behaved to him, surprised the royal family very much. They suspected some secret, but though they spied and spied they could not discover it.

Thus a year passed away, and the princess had a son, whom

she called Benjamin. But her mother still thought the whole matter very strange. At last she said to the king that he ought to ask his daughter whether she would not like to have another husband instead of the crab? But when the daughter was questioned she answered:

'I am married to the crab, and him only will I have.'

Then the king said to her, 'I will appoint a tournament in your honour, and I will invite all the princes in the world to it, and if any one of them pleases you, you shall marry him.'

In the evening the princess told this to the crab, who said to her, 'Take this rod, go to the garden gate and knock with it. Then a black man will come out and say to you, "Why have you called me, and what do you require of me?" Answer him thus, "Your master, the king, has sent me hither to tell you to send him his golden armour and his steed and the silver apple." And bring them to me.'

The princess did so and brought him what he desired.

The following evening the prince dressed himself for the tournament. Before he went he said to his wife:

'Now mind you do not say when you see me that I am the crab. For if you do this, evil will come of it. Place yourself at the window with your sisters; I will ride by and throw you the silver apple. Take it in your hand, but if they ask you who I am, say that you do not know.' So saying, he kissed her, repeated his warning once more and went away.

The princess went with her sisters to the window and looked on at the tournament. Presently her husband rode by and threw the apple up to her. She caught it in her hand and went with it to her room, and by-and-by her husband came back to her. But her father was much surprised that she did not seem to care about any of the princes; he therefore appointed a second tournament.

Her husband threw the apple up to her

The crab then gave his wife the same directions as before, only this time the apple which she received from the black man was of gold. But before the prince went to the tournament he said to his wife, 'Now I know you will betray me today.'

But she swore to him that she would not tell who he was. He then repeated his warning and went away.

In the evening, while the princess, with her mother and sisters, was standing at the window, the prince suddenly galloped past on his steed and threw her the golden apple.

Then her mother flew into a passion, gave her a box on the ear, and cried out, 'Does not even that prince please you, you fool?'

The princess in her fright exclaimed, 'That is the crab himself!'

Her mother, who was more angry because she had not been told sooner, ran into her daughter's room where the crab shell was still lying, took it up and threw it into the fire. Then the poor princess cried bitterly, but it was of no use; her husband did not come back.

One day an old man went to a stream to dip in a crust of bread which he was going to eat, when a dog came out of the water, snatched the bread from his hand and ran away. The old man ran after him, but the dog reached a door, pushed it open and ran in, the old man following him. He did not overtake the dog, but found himself on a staircase, which he descended. Then he saw before him a stately palace and, entering, he found himself in a large hall where a table was set for twelve persons. He hid himself in the hall behind a great picture and waited to see what would happen.

At noon he heard such a great noise that he trembled with fear. When he took courage to look out from behind the picture, he saw twelve eagles flying in. At this sight his fear became still greater. The eagles flew to the basin of a fountain that was there and bathed themselves, when suddenly they were changed into twelve handsome youths. Now they seated themselves at the table, and one of them took up a goblet filled with wine, and said, 'A health to my father!' Another said, 'A health to my mother!' and so the toasts went round. Then one of them said:

> *'A health to my dearest lady,*
> *Long may she live and well!*
> *But a curse on the cruel mother*
> *Who burned my golden shell!'*

And so saying he wept bitterly. Then the youths rose from the table, went back to the great stone fountain, turned themselves into eagles again, and flew away.

Then the old man went away too, returned to the light of day and went home. Soon afterward he heard that the princess was ill and the only thing that did her good was having stories told her. He therefore went to the royal castle, obtained an audience of the princess, and told her about the strange things he had seen in the underground palace. No sooner had he finished than the princess asked him whether he could find the way to that palace.

'Yes,' he answered, 'certainly.'

And now she desired him to guide her thither at once. The old man did so, and when they came to the palace he hid her behind the great picture and advised her to keep silence, and he placed himself behind the picture also. Presently the eagles came flying in and changed themselves into young men, and in a moment the princess recognized her husband among them and tried to come out of her hiding place; but the old man held her back. The youths seated themselves at the table; and now the prince said again, while he took up the cup of wine:

> *'A health to my dearest lady,*
> *Long may she live and well!*
> *But a curse on the cruel mother*
> *Who burned my golden shell!'*

Then the princess could restrain herself no longer, but ran forward and threw her arms round her husband. And immediately he knew her again and said:

'Do you remember how I told you that day you would betray me? Now you see that I spoke the truth. But all that bad time is past. Now listen to me: I must still remain enchanted for three months. Will you stay here with me till that time is over?'

So the princess stayed with him and said to the old man, 'Go back to the castle and tell my parents that I am staying here.'

Her parents were very much vexed when the old man came back and told them this, but as soon as the three months of the prince's enchantment were over, he ceased to be an eagle and became once more a man, and they returned home together. And then they lived happily, and we who hear the story are happier still.

["Prinz Krebs," from *Griechische Mährchen*. Schmidt.]

The Iron Stove

ONCE UPON A TIME, when wishes came true, there was a king's son who was enchanted by an old witch, and he was obliged to sit in a large iron stove in a wood. There he lived for many years, and no one could free him. At last a king's daughter came into the wood. She had been wandering round and round for nine days and came at last to the iron stove. A voice came from within and asked her:

'Where do you come from and where do you want to go?'

She answered, 'I have lost my way to my father's kingdom, and I shall never find my way home again.'

Then the voice from the iron stove said, 'I will help you find your home again in a very short time, if you will promise to do what I ask. I am a greater prince than you are a princess, and I will marry you.'

Then she grew frightened, and thought, What can a young lassie do with an iron stove? But as she wanted very much to go home to her father, she promised to do what he wished. The prince said:

'You must come again and bring a knife with you to scrape a hole in the iron.'

Then someone walked near her and said nothing, but he brought her in two hours to her home. There was great joy in the castle when the princess returned, and the old king fell on her neck and kissed her. But she was very much troubled, and said:

'Dear Father, listen to what has befallen me! I should never have found the way home again had I not come to an iron stove. I have had to promise I will go back to free him and marry him!'

The old king nearly fainted, for she was his only daughter. They determined that the miller's daughter, who was very beautiful, should take her place. They gave the girl a knife and took her to the wood, and said she must scrape at the iron stove. She scraped for twenty-four hours, but did not make the least impression. When day broke, a voice called from the iron stove:

'It seems to me that it is day outside.'

Then she answered, 'It seems so to me; I think I hear my father's mill rattling.'

'So you are a miller's daughter! Then go away at once, and tell the king's daughter to come.'

Then she went away and told the old king the thing inside the iron stove would not have her but wanted the princess. The king was frightened, and his daughter wept. But they had a swineherd's daughter who was even more beautiful than the miller's daughter, and they gave her a piece of gold to go instead of the princess. Then she scraped for four-and-twenty hours, but she could make no impression. As soon as day broke the voice from the stove called out:

'It seems to be daylight outside.'

Then she answered, 'It seems so to me; I think I hear my father blowing his horn.'

'So you are a swineherd's daughter! Go away at once, and let the king's daughter come. And say to her that what I foretell shall come to pass, and if she does not come everything in the kingdom shall fall into ruin and not one stone shall be left upon another.'

When the princess heard this she began to cry, but it was no good; she had to keep her word. She took leave of her father, put a knife in her belt, and went to the iron stove in the wood. As soon as she reached it she began to scrape and the iron gave way. Before two hours had passed she had made a little hole. Then she peeped in and saw such a beautiful youth, all shining with gold and precious stones, that she fell in love with him on the spot. So she scraped away harder than ever and made the hole so large that he could get out.

Then he said, 'You are mine, and I am thine; you are my bride and have set me free!' He wanted to take her with him to his kingdom, but she begged him to let her go just once more to her father. And the prince let her go, but told her not to say more than three words to her father, then to come back again.

So she went home, but alas! She said more than three words; and immediately the iron stove vanished and went away over a mountain of glass and sharp swords. But the prince was free and was no longer shut up in it.

The princess said good-bye to her father and went again into the great wood to look for the iron stove. She sought it for nine days, but she could not find it, and then her hunger became so great she did not know how she could live any longer. And when it was evening she climbed into a little tree and wished that the night would not come, because she was afraid of the wild beasts.

When midnight came she saw afar off a little light, and

thought, Ah, if only I could reach that! Then she climbed
down from the tree and went toward the light. She came to a
little old house, with grass growing all round, and stood in
front of a little heap of wood. She thought, Alas, what am I
coming to? and peeped through the window. But she saw
nothing inside except big and little toads and a table beautifully spread with roast meats and wine, and all the dishes and
drinking cups were of silver. Then she took heart and knocked.
A fat toad called out:

> *'Little green toad with leg like crook,*
> *Open wide the door, and look*
> *For the latch shook and shook.'*

And a little toad came forward and let her in.

When the princess entered they all bade her welcome and

made her sit down. They asked how she came there and what she wanted. Then she told them everything that had happened to her and how, because she had exceeded her permission to speak only three words, the stove had disappeared with the prince; and how she had searched a very long time, and must wander over mountain and valley till she found him.

Then the old toad said:

> *'Little green toad whose leg doth twist,*
> *Go to the corner of which you wist,*
> *And bring to me the large old kist.'*

And the little toad brought out a great chest. Then they gave her food and drink, and led her to a beautifully made bed of silk and samite, on which she lay down and slept soundly.

When day dawned the princess rose, and the old toad gave her three things out of the huge chest to take with her. She would have need of them, for she had to cross a high glass mountain, three cutting swords and a great lake. When she had passed these she would find her lover again. So she was given three large needles, a plough wheel and three nuts, which she was to take great care of. She set out with these things and when she came to the glass mountain, which was so slippery, she stuck the three needles behind her feet and then in front and so got over it, and when she was on the other side put them carefully away.

Then she reached the three cutting swords and sat on her plough wheel and rolled over them. At last she came to a great lake and, when she had crossed that, arrived at a beautiful castle. The princess went in and asked for a place as a servant, a poor maid who would gladly be engaged, for she knew that the prince whom she had freed from the iron stove was in the castle. So she was taken on as a kitchenmaid for very small wages. Now the prince was about to marry another princess, for he thought his love had died long ago.

In the evening, when she had washed up and was ready, the maid felt in her pocket and found the three nuts which the old toad had given her. She cracked one and was going to eat the kernel, when behold! There was a beautiful royal dress inside it! When the bride heard of this, she came and begged for the dress and wanted to buy it, saying that it was not a dress for a serving maid. Then the princess said she would not sell it unless she was granted one favour— to sleep by the prince's door. The bride granted her this, because the dress was so beautiful and she had none like it. When it was evening she said to her bridegroom, 'That stupid maid wants to sleep by your door.'

'If you are contented, I am,' he said. But the bride gave him a glass of wine in which she had poured a sleeping draught. Then the prince went to his room, but he slept so soundly that the maid could not wake him. She wept all night long, and said:

'I freed you in the wild wood out of the iron stove. I have sought you and have crossed a glassy mountain, three sharp swords and a great lake before I found you. Will you not hear me now?'

The servants outside heard how she cried the whole night, and they told their master in the morning.

When she had washed up the next evening she bit the second nut, and there was a still more beautiful dress inside. When the bride saw it she wanted to buy it also. But the maid did not want money and asked that she should sleep again by the prince's door. The bride, however, gave him a sleeping draught, and he slept so soundly that he heard nothing. But the kitchen maid wept the whole night long, and said:

'I have freed you in a wood from an iron stove. I sought you and have crossed a glassy mountain, three sharp swords and a great lake to find you, and now you will not hear me!'

The servants outside heard how she cried the whole night, and in the morning they told their master. When she had washed up on the third night she bit the third nut, and there was a still more beautiful dress inside made of pure gold. When the bride saw it she wanted to have it, but the maid would only give it to her on condition that she should sleep for the third time by the prince's door. But this time the prince took care not to drink the sleeping draught. When she began to weep, and to say:

'Dearest sweetheart, I freed you in the horrible wild wood from an iron stove,' he jumped up and said, 'You are right. You are mine, and I am thine.'

Though it was still night, he took her with him in a carriage and when they came to the great lake they rowed across, and when they reached the three sharp swords they sat on the plough wheel, and on the glassy mountain they used the three needles to help them across.

So they arrived at last at the little old house, but when they stepped inside it turned into a large castle. The toads were all freed and were beautiful king's children, running about for joy. There the prince and the princess were married, and they remained in the castle, which was much larger than her father's. But because the old king did not like being left alone, they went and fetched him. So they had two kingdoms and lived in great happiness.

A mouse has run,
My story's done.

[Jakob and Wilhelm Grimm.]

The Dragon and His Grandmother

THERE WAS ONCE A
great war, and the king who was waging it gave his soldiers
so little pay they could not live upon it. Then three of them
took counsel together and determined to desert.

One of them said to the others, 'If we are caught, we shall be
hanged on the gallows. How shall we set about it?'

Another said, 'Do you see that large cornfield there? If we
hide ourselves in that, no one could find us. The army cannot
come into it and tomorrow it is to march on.'

They crept into the corn, but the army remained encamped
close around them. The three soldiers sat for two days and two
nights in the corn and grew so hungry they nearly died. But
if they were to venture out, it was certain death.

They said at last, 'What use was our deserting? We must
perish here miserably.'

While they were speaking a fiery dragon came flying by.
It hovered near them and asked why they were hidden there.

They answered, 'We are three soldiers and have deserted
because our pay was so small. Now if we remain here we shall

die of hunger, and if we move out we shall be strung up on the gallows.'

'If for seven years you will serve me,' said the dragon, 'I will lead you through the midst of the army so no one shall catch you.'

'We have no choice and must take your offer,' said they.

Then the dragon seized them in his claws, took them through the air over the army, and set them down again a long way from it.

He gave them a little whip, saying, 'Whip and slash with this, and as much money as you want will jump up before you. You can live as great lords, keep horses and drive about in carriages. But after seven years you are mine. I will then give you a riddle,' he said; 'if you guess it, you shall be free and out of my power.' Then he put a book before them, which he made all three of them sign.

The dragon then flew away, and the three soldiers journeyed on with their little whip. They had as much money as they wanted, wore grand clothes, and made their way into the world. Wherever they went they lived in merrymaking and splendour, drove about with horses and carriages, ate and drank, but did nothing wrong.

The time passed quickly away, and when the seven years were nearly ended two of them grew anxious and very frightened, but the third made light of it, saying, 'Don't be afraid, brothers, I wasn't born yesterday. I will guess the riddle.'

They went into a field, sat down, and two of them pulled long faces. An old woman passed by, and asked them why they were so sad.

'Alas, what have you to do with it? You cannot help us.'

'Who knows?' she answered. 'Only confide your trouble to me.'

Then they told her how the dragon had given them money as plentifully as blackberries for seven long years, and that as they had signed their names they were his, unless when the time had passed they could guess a riddle.

The old woman said, 'If you would help yourselves, one of you must go into the wood, where he will come upon a tumble-down building of rocks. He must go in, and there he will find help.'

The two melancholy ones thought, That won't save us, and they remained where they were. But the third and merry one jumped up and went into the wood till he found the rock hut. In it sat a very old woman, who was the dragon's grandmother. She asked him how he came, and what his business there was. He told her all that had happened, and because she was pleased she took compassion on him and said she would help him.

She lifted up a large stone which lay over the cellar, saying, 'Hide yourself there and you can hear all that is spoken in this room. Only sit still and don't stir. When the dragon comes, I will ask him what the riddle is; listen carefully to what he answers.'

At midnight the dragon flew in and asked for his supper. His grandmother laid the table and brought out food and drink, and they ate and drank together. Then in the course of the conversation she asked him what he had done that day.

'I haven't had much luck today,' he said, 'but I have a tight hold on three soldiers.'

'Indeed! Three soldiers!' said she. 'Who cannot escape you?'

'They are mine,' answered the dragon scornfully, 'for I shall give them one riddle which they will never be able to guess.'

'What riddle is it?' she asked.

'I will tell you. In the North Sea lies a dead sea cat that shall be their roast meat; and the rib of a whale that shall be their silver spoon; and the hollow hoof of a dead horse that shall be their wineglass.'

When the dragon had gone to bed, his old grandmother pulled up the stone and let the soldier out.

'Did you pay attention to everything?'

'Yes,' he replied, 'I know enough and can help myself splendidly.'

Then he went secretly by way of the window and in all haste back to his comrades. He told them how he had heard from the dragon's own lips the answer to the riddle.

Then they were all delighted and in high spirits, took out their whip and cracked so much money that it came jumping up from the ground. When the seven years had quite gone, the dragon came with his book and, pointing to the signatures, said:

'I will take you underground with me; you shall have a meal there. If you can tell me what you will have for your roast meat, you shall be free and shall also keep the whip.'

Then said the first soldier, 'In the North Sea lies a dead sea cat; that shall be the roast meat.'

The dragon was much annoyed and hummed and hawed a good deal. Then he asked the second, 'But what shall be your spoon?'

'The rib of a whale shall be our silver spoon.'

The dragon made a face and growled three times, 'Hum, hum, hum. Do you know what your wineglass shall be?' he asked the third soldier.

'A dead horse's hoof shall be our wineglass.'

Then the dragon flew away with a loud shriek and had no more power over them. But the three soldiers took the little whip, always had as much money as they wanted, and lived happily to their lives' end.

The Donkey Cabbage

HERE WAS ONCE A
young hunter who went boldly into the forest. He had a merry
and light heart, and as he went whistling along there came an
ugly old woman, who said to him:

'Good day, dear hunter! You are very merry and contented,
but I suffer hunger and thirst, so give me a trifle.'

The hunter was sorry for the poor old woman, and he felt
in his pocket and gave her all he could spare. The old woman
said:

'Listen, dear hunter, because of your kind heart I will make
you a present. Go on your way; in a short time you will come
to a tree where nine birds sit quarrelling over a cloak in their
claws. Take aim with your gun and shoot into the middle of
them. They will let the cloak fall, but one of the birds will be
hit and will drop down dead. Take the cloak with you; it is
a wishing cloak, and when you throw it on your shoulders you
have only to wish yourself at a certain place, and in the
twinkling of an eye you are there. Take the heart out of the
dead bird and swallow it whole, and early every morning you
will find a gold piece under your pillow.'

The hunter thanked the wise woman and said to himself,

'These are splendid things she has promised me, if only they come to pass!' So he walked on about a hundred yards, and then he heard above him in the branches such a screaming and chirping that he looked up, and there he saw a number of birds tearing a cloth with their beaks and feet, shrieking, tugging and fighting, as if each wanted it for himself, as indeed everyone did.

'Well,' said the hunter, 'this is wonderful! It is just as the old woman said.' And he took his gun on his shoulder, pulled the trigger and shot into the midst of them, so that their feathers flew about. Then the flock took flight with much screaming, but one fell dead and the cloak fluttered down. Then the hunter did as the old woman had told him. He cut open the bird, found its heart and swallowed it, and took the cloak home with him.

The next morning when he awoke he remembered the promise and wanted to see if it had come true. When he lifted up his pillow there sparkled the gold piece, and the next morning he found another, and so on every time he rose. He collected a heap of gold, but at last he thought, What good is all my gold to me if I stay at home? I will travel and look a bit about me in the world. So he took leave of his parents, slung his hunting knapsack and his gun round him, and journeyed into the world.

It happened that one day he went through a thick wood, and when he came to the end of it there lay in the plain before him a great castle. At one of the windows in it stood an old woman with a most beautiful maiden by her side, looking out. But the old woman was a witch, and she said to the girl:

'There comes one out of the wood who has a wonderful treasure in his body which we must manage to possess ourselves of, darling daughter. We have more right to it than he.

He has a bird's heart in him, and so every morning there lies a gold piece under his pillow.'

She told her how she was to coax it from him and at last threatened her angrily, saying, 'And if you do not obey me, you shall repent it!'

When the hunter came nearer he saw the maiden, and said to himself, 'I have travelled so far now that I will rest and turn into this beautiful castle; money I have in plenty.' But the real reason was that he had caught sight of the girl's lovely face.

He went into the house and was kindly received and hospitably entertained. It was not long before he was so much in love with the witch maiden that he thought of nothing else and only looked in her eyes, and whatever she wanted he gladly did.

Then the old witch said, 'Now we must have the bird heart: he will not feel when it is gone.' She prepared a drink, and when it was ready she poured it in a goblet and gave it to the maiden, who had to hand it to the hunter.

'Drink to me now, my dearest,' she said. Then he took the goblet, and when he had swallowed the drink the bird heart came out of his mouth. The maiden had to get hold of it secretly and then swallow it herself, for the old witch wanted to have it. Thenceforward he found no more gold under his pillow, and it lay under the maiden's. But he was so much in love and so much bewitched that he thought of nothing except spending all his time with her.

Then the old witch said, 'We have the bird heart, but we must also get the wishing cloak from him.'

The maiden answered, 'We will leave him that, he has already lost his wealth!'

The old witch grew angry, and said, 'Such a cloak is a wonderful thing; it is seldom to be had in the world, and have it I must and will.' She beat the maiden and said that if she did not obey it would go ill with her.

So she did her mother's bidding and, standing one day by the window, she looked away into the far distance as if she were very sad.

'Why are you standing there looking so sad?' asked the hunter.

'Alas, my love,' she replied, 'over there lies the granite mountain where the costly precious stones grow. I have such great longing to go there that when I think of it I am very sad. For who can fetch them? Only the birds who fly; a man, never.'

'If you have no other trouble,' said the hunter, 'that one I can easily remove from your heart.'

Then he wrapped his cloak round her too and wished to fly to the granite mountain, and in an instant there they were, sitting on it! The precious stones sparkled so brightly on all sides that it was a pleasure to see them, and they collected the most beautiful and costly together. But now the old witch had through her witchcraft caused the hunter's eyes to become heavy.

He said to the maiden, 'We will sit down for a little while and rest. I am so tired that I can hardly stand on my feet.'

So they sat down, and he laid his head on her lap and fell asleep. As soon as he was sound asleep she unfastened the cloak from his shoulders, threw it round her own, left the granite and stones and wished herself home again.

When the hunter had finished his sleep and awoke, he found that his love had betrayed him and left him alone on the wild mountain. 'Oh,' said he, 'why is faithlessness so great in the world?' And he sat down in sorrow and trouble, not knowing what to do.

But the mountain belonged to fierce and huge giants, who lived on it and traded there, and he had not sat long before he saw three of them striding toward him. So he lay down as if he had fallen into a deep sleep.

The giants came up, and the first pushed him with his foot, and said, 'What sort of earthworm is that?'

The second said, 'Crush him dead.'

But the third said contemptuously, 'It is not worth the trouble! Let him live; he cannot remain here, and if he goes higher up the mountain the clouds will take him and carry him off.'

Talking thus they went away. But the hunter had listened to their talk, and as soon as they had gone he rose and climbed to the summit. When he had sat there a little while a cloud swept by and, seizing him, carried him away. It travelled for a time in the sky, and then it sank down and hovered over a large vegetable garden surrounded by walls, and the hunter came safely to the ground amidst cabbages and lettuces.

Then he looked about him, saying, 'If only I had something to eat! I am so hungry, and it will go badly with me in the future, for I see here not an apple or pear or fruit of any kind—nothing but vegetables everywhere. At a pinch I can eat a salad; it does not taste particularly nice, but it will refresh me.'

So he looked about for a good head of cabbage and ate it, but no sooner had he swallowed a couple of mouthfuls than he felt very strange, and found himself to be wonderfully changed Four legs began to grow on him, a thick head and two long ears, and he saw with horror that he had changed into a donkey. But as he was still very hungry, and this juicy salad tasted very good to his present nature, he went on eating with a still greater appetite. At last he ate another kind of cabbage but had scarcely swallowed it when he felt another change, and he once more regained his human form.

The hunter now lay down and slept off his weariness. When he awoke the next morning he broke off a head of the bad and a head of the good cabbage, thinking, This will help me to regain my own and to punish faithlessness. Then he put the heads in his pockets, climbed the wall and started off to seek the castle of his love. When he had wandered about for a couple of days, he found it quite easily. He then browned his face quickly, so that his own mother would not have known him, and went into the castle, where he begged for a lodging.

'I am so tired,' he said, 'I can go no farther.'

The witch asked, 'Countryman, who are you, and what is your business?'

He answered, 'I am a messenger of the king and have been sent to seek the finest salad that grows under the sun.

I have been so lucky as to find it and am bringing it with me, but the heat of the sun is so great that the tender cabbage threatens to grow soft, and I do not know if I shall be able to bring it any farther.'

When the old witch heard of the fine salad she wanted to eat it, and said, 'Dear countryman, just let me taste the wonderful salad.'

'Why not?' he answered. 'I have brought two heads with me and I will give you one.'

So saying, he opened his sack and gave her the bad one. The witch suspected no evil, and her mouth watered to taste the new dish, so she went into the kitchen to prepare it herself. When it was ready she could not wait till it was served at the table but immediately took a couple of leaves and put them in her mouth. No sooner, however, had she swallowed them than she lost her human form and ran into the courtyard in the shape of a donkey.

Now the servant came into the kitchen, and when she saw the salad standing there ready to eat she was about to carry it up, but on the way, according to her old habit, she tasted it and ate a couple of leaves. Immediately the charm worked, and she became a donkey and ran out to join the old witch, and the dish with the salad in it fell to the ground. In the meantime, the messenger was sitting with the lovely maiden, and as no one came with the salad, and she wanted very much to taste it, she said, 'I don't know where the salad is.'

Then thought the hunter, The cabbage must have already begun to work. And he said, 'I will go to the kitchen and fetch it myself.'

When he came there he saw the two donkeys running about in the courtyard, but the salad was lying on the ground.

'That's all right,' said he; 'two have had their share!' And lifting the remaining leaves up, he laid them on the dish and brought them to the maiden.

'I am bringing you the delicious food my own self,' he said, 'so that you need not wait any longer.'

Then she ate and, as the others had done, at once lost her human form and ran as a donkey into the yard.

When the hunter had washed his face, so that the changed ones might know him, he went into the yard, saying, 'Now you shall receive a reward for your faithlessness.'

He tied them all three with a rope and drove them before him till he came to a mill. He knocked at the window, and the miller put his head out and asked what he wanted.

'I have three tiresome animals,' he answered, 'which I don't want to keep any longer. If you will take them, give them food and stabling and do as I tell you with them, I will pay you as much as you want.'

The miller replied, 'Why not? What shall I do with them?'

Then the hunter said that he was to give to the old donkey, which was the witch, three beatings and one meal; to the younger one, which was the servant, one beating and three meals; and to the youngest one, which was the maiden, no beating and three meals, for he could not find it in his heart to let the maiden be beaten.

Then he went back into the castle, and he found there all that he wanted. After a couple of days the miller came and said he must tell him that the old donkey, which was to have three beatings and only one meal, had died. 'The two others,' he added, 'are certainly not dead, and get their three meals every day, but they are so sad that they cannot last much longer.'

Then the hunter took pity on them, laid aside his anger, and told the miller to drive them back again. And when they came he gave them some of the good cabbage to eat, and they became human again. Then the beautiful maiden fell on her knees before him, saying, 'Oh, my dearest, forgive me the ill I have done you! My mother compelled me to do it. It was against my will, for I love you dearly. Your wishing cloak is hanging in a cupboard, and as for the bird heart I will make a drink and give it back to you.'

But he changed his mind, and said, 'Keep it; it makes no difference, for I will take you to be my own dear true wife.' And the wedding was celebrated, and they lived happily together.

The Little Green Frog

ONCE UPON A TIME there lived two kings, called Peridor and Diamantino. They were cousins as well as neighbours, and both were under the protection of the fairies; though it is only fair to say the fairies did not love them half so well as their gentle, lovely wives did.

Now princes can generally manage to have their own way so it is harder for them to be good. So it was with Peridor and Diamantino; but of the two, the fairies declared Diamantino was the worse. Indeed, he behaved so badly to his wife Aglantine, that the fairies would not allow him to live any longer. The dowager queen was wise and good and tried to make her people happy. She was lonely because the fairies, for reasons of their own, determined to bring up her daughter, the little Princess Serpentine, among themselves.

As for the other king, he was really fond of his wife, Queen Constance, but he often grieved her by his thoughtless ways, and in order to punish him for his carelessness, the fairies caused her to die suddenly. When she was gone the king felt how much he had loved her, and his grief was so great (though he never neglected his duties) that his subjects called him

6

Peridor the Sorrowful. Most likely he would have died too if it had not been for the fairies.

The one comfort the poor king had was his son, Prince Saphir, who was only three years old at the time of his mother's death, and great care was given to his education. By the time he was fifteen Saphir had learned everything a prince should know, and he was, besides, charming and agreeable.

It was about this time that the fairies suddenly took fright lest his love for his father should interfere with the plans they had made for the young prince. So, to prevent this, they placed in a pretty room of which Saphir was very fond a little mirror in a black frame, such as were often brought from Venice.

The prince did not notice for some days anything new in the room, but at last he perceived it and went up to look more closely. What was his surprise to see reflected in the mirror, not his own face, but that of a young girl as lovely as the morning! And, better still, every movement of the girl, just growing out of childhood, was also reflected in the wonderful glass.

As might have been expected, the young prince lost his heart completely to the beautiful image, and it was hard to get him to leave the room, so busy was he in watching the lovely unknown. It was delightful to see his beloved at any moment he chose. But his spirits sank when he wondered what was to be the end of this adventure.

The magic mirror had been in the prince's possession for about a year when, one day, a new disquiet seized him. As usual, he was looking at the girl, when suddenly he thought he saw a second mirror reflected in the first, exactly like his own and with the same power. And in this he was right. The young girl had only possessed her mirror for a short time and, ne-

He saw a lovely young girl in the mirror

glecting all her duties, spent her time gazing in the mirror.

Now it was not difficult for Saphir to guess why the new mirror was consulted so often; but try as he would he could never see the face reflected in it, for the young girl's figure always came between. All he knew was that the face was a man's, and this was quite enough to make him madly jealous. Perhaps the wise fairies had their reasons for acting as they did.

When these things happened Saphir was about eighteen years old, and fifteen years had passed away since the death of his mother. King Peridor had grown more and more unhappy as time went on, and at last he fell so ill it seemed his days were numbered. He was so much beloved by his subjects that this sad news was heard with despair by the nation, and the prince was beside himself.

During his whole illness the king never spoke of anything but the queen, his sorrow at having grieved her and his hope of one day seeing her again. All the doctors and all the water cures in the kingdom had been tried, and nothing did him any good. At last he persuaded them to let him lie quietly in his room, where no one came to trouble him.

Perhaps the worst pain he had to bear was one which made it very hard for him to breathe. He commanded his servants to leave the windows open that he might get air. One day, when he had been left alone for a few minutes, a bird with brilliant plumage fluttered round the window and finally rested on the sill. Her feathers were sky-blue and gold, her feet and beak of such glittering rubies that no one could bear to look at them, her eyes made the brightest diamonds seem dull, and on her head she wore a crown. As for her voice, the bird never sang at all. In fact, she did nothing but gaze steadily at the

king, and as she gazed, the king felt his strength come back
to him.

Filled with joy at his cure, the king tried to seize the bird but,
swifter than a swallow, she managed to avoid him.

In vain he described the bird to his attendants, who rushed in
at his first call. They sought the wonderful creature both on
horse and foot and summoned the fowlers to their aid, but the
bird could nowhere be found. The love the people bore King
Peridor was so strong, and the reward he promised was so
large, that in the twinkling of an eye every man, woman and
child had fled into the fields, and the towns were quite empty.

All this bustle, however, ended in nothing but confusion
and, what was worse, the king soon fell ill as before. Prince
Saphir, who loved his father very dearly, hoped he might
succeed where the others had failed and at once prepared himself for a more distant search. In spite of loving protests, he
rode away, followed by his household, trusting to chance to
help him. He had formed no plan, and there was no reason
he should choose one path more than another. His only idea
was to make straight for the favourite haunts of birds. But in
vain he examined all the hedges and all the thickets, in vain
he questioned everyone he met along the road. The more he
sought the less he found.

At last he came to one of the largest forests in all the world,
composed entirely of cedars. But in spite of the deep shadows
cast by the wide-spreading branches of the trees, the grass
underneath was soft and green and covered with the rarest
flowers. It seemed to Saphir exactly the sort of place where
such a bird would live, and he determined not to quit the wood
until he had searched it from end to end. And he did more.
He ordered some nets painted the same colours as the bird's

plumage, thinking that all are easily caught by what is like ourselves. In this he had the help not only of the fowlers by profession, but also his attendants, who excelled in this art. For a man is not a courtier unless he can do everything.

After searching as usual for nearly a whole day Prince Saphir was overcome with thirst. He was too tired to go farther, when happily he discovered a bubbling fountain of the clearest water. Being an experienced traveller, he drew from his pocket a little cup and was just about to dip it in the spring, when a lovely little green frog jumped into the cup. Far from admiring its beauty, Saphir shook it off impatiently; but quick as lightning the frog jumped back again. Saphir, who was raging with thirst, was just about to shake it off anew, when the little creature fixed upon him the most beautiful eyes in the world, and said:

'I am a friend of the bird you are seeking, and when you have quenched your thirst listen to me.'

So the prince drank his fill and then lay down on the grass to rest himself.

'Now,' the frog began, 'be sure you do in every respect exactly what I tell you. First you must order your attendants to remain in a little hamlet close by until you want them. Then go, quite alone, down a road that you will find on your right hand, looking southward. This road is planted all the way with cedars of Lebanon, and after going down it a long way you will come at last to a magnificent castle. And now,' she went on, 'attend carefully to what I am going to say. Take this tiny grain of sand and put it into the ground as close as you can to the gate of the castle. It has the virtue both of opening the gate and also of sending to sleep all the inhabitants. Then go at once to the stable, paying no heed to anything except what I tell you. Choose the handsomest of all the horses, leap quickly on its back, and come to me as fast as you can. Farewell, Prince; I wish you good luck,' and with these words the little frog plunged into the water and disappeared.

The prince, who felt more hopeful than he had since he left home, did as he had been told. He left his attendants in the hamlet, found the road the frog had described to him and followed it all alone, and at last he arrived at the gate of the castle, which was even more splendid than he had expected, for it was built of crystal and all its ornaments were of massive gold. However, he had no thoughts to spare for its beauty and quickly buried his grain of sand in the earth. In one instant the gates flew open, and all inside fell sound asleep.

Saphir flew straight to the stable and already had his hand on the finest horse it contained, when his eye was caught by a suit of magnificent harness hanging close by. It occurred to him directly that the harness belonged to the horse and, without ever thinking of harm, he hastily placed it on the animal's back.

Suddenly the people in the castle became broad awake and rushed to the stable. They flung themselves on the prince and dragged him before their lord. But luckily for the prince, who could only find very lame excuses for his conduct, the lord of the castle took a fancy to him and let him depart without further questions.

Very sad, and very much ashamed of himself, Saphir crept back to the fountain, where the frog was awaiting him with a good scolding.

'Whom do you take me for?' she exclaimed angrily. 'Do you really believe that it was just for the pleasure of talking that I gave you the advice you have neglected so abominably?'

But the prince was so deeply grieved and apologized so very humbly that after some time the heart of the good little frog was softened, and she gave him another tiny grain, but instead of being sand as before it was now a grain of gold. She directed him to do just as he had done before, with only this difference, that instead of going to the stable which had been the ruin of his hopes, he was to enter right into the castle itself and go as fast as he could down the passages till he came to a room filled with perfume, where he would find a beautiful maiden asleep on a bed. He was to wake the maiden instantly and carry her off and not to pay any heed to whatever resistance she might make.

The prince obeyed the frog's orders one by one, and all went well for this second time also. The gate opened, the inhabitants fell sound asleep, and he walked down the passage till he found the girl on her bed, exactly as he had been told he would. He woke her, and begged her firmly but politely to follow him quickly. After a little persuasion the maiden consented, but only on condition that she was allowed first to put on her dress. This sounded so reasonable and natural that it did not enter the prince's head to refuse her request.

But the maiden's hand had hardly touched the dress when the palace suddenly awoke from its sleep, and the prince was seized and bound. He was so vexed with his own folly, and so taken aback at the disaster, that he did not attempt to explain his conduct, and it would have gone badly with him if his friends the fairies had not softened the hearts of his captors so once more they allowed him to leave quietly.

However, what troubled him most was the idea of having to meet the frog who had been his benefactress. How was he ever to appear before her with this tale? Still, after a long struggle with himself, he made up his mind that nothing else was to be done and he deserved whatever she might say to him. And she said a great deal, for she had worked herself into a terrible passion; but the prince humbly implored her pardon, and ventured to point out that it would have been very hard to refuse the young lady's reasonable request.

'You must learn to do as you are told,' was all the frog would reply. But Saphir was so unhappy and begged so hard for forgiveness that at last the frog's anger gave way, and she held up to him a tiny diamond stone.

'Go back,' she said, 'to the castle and bury this little diamond close to the door. But be careful not to return to the stable or to the bedroom; they have proved too fatal to you. Walk straight to the garden and enter through a portico into a small green wood, in the midst of which is a tree with a trunk of gold and leaves of emeralds. Perched on this tree you will see the beautiful bird you have been seeking so long. You must cut the branch on which it is sitting and bring it back to me without delay. But I warn you solemnly that if you disobey my directions, as you have done twice before, you have nothing more to expect either of me or anyone else.'

With these words she jumped into the water, and the prince, who had taken her threats much to heart, departed, firmly resolved not to deserve them. He found it all just as he had been told: the portico, the wood, the magnificent tree, and the beautiful bird sleeping soundly on one of the branches. He speedily lopped off the branch, and though he noticed a splendid golden cage hanging close by, he left it alone and came back to the fountain, holding his breath and walking on tiptoe all the way, for fear lest he should awake his prize. But what was his surprise, when instead of the fountain, he saw in

its place a little rustic palace and standing in the doorway a charming maiden. It was the lady of the mirror!

'What, madam!' he cried, hardly knowing what he said. 'What! Is it you?'

The maiden blushed and answered, 'Ah, my lord, it is long since I first beheld your face, but I did not think you had ever seen mine.'

'Oh, madam,' replied he, 'you can never guess the days and the hours I have passed lost in admiration of you.'

And after these words they each related all the strange things that had happened. After some time spent in the most tender conversation, the prince asked the lovely unknown by what lucky chance she was wandering in the forest, where the fountain had gone, and if she knew anything of the frog to whom he owed all his happiness and to whom he must give the bird which was still sound asleep.

'Ah, my lord,' she replied, 'the frog stands before you. Let me tell you my story; it is not a long one. I know neither my country nor my parents, and the only thing I can say for certain is that I am called Serpentine. The fairies have taken care of me ever since I was born, have looked after my education, and have bestowed on me endless kindness. I have always lived in seclusion, and for the last two years I have wished for nothing better. I had a mirror'—here shyness and embarrassment choked her words—but regaining her composure, she added:

'Fairies insist on being obeyed without question. They changed the little house into the fountain and, having turned me into a frog, they ordered me to say to the first person who came to the fountain exactly what I repeated to you. But, my lord, when you stood before me, it was agony to my heart, filled as it was with thoughts of you, to appear to your eyes under so monstrous a form. However, there was no help for it and, painful as it was, I had to submit. I could not get back my proper form till you had become master of the beautiful bird, though I am quite ignorant of your reason for seeking it.'

Then Saphir explained about his father's health, and on hearing this story Serpentine grew very sad, and her lovely eyes filled with tears.

'Ah, my lord,' she said, 'you know nothing of me but what you have seen in the mirror and I, who cannot even name my parents, learn that you are a king's son.'

In vain Saphir declared that love made them equal. Serpentine would only reply:

'I love you too much to allow you to marry beneath your rank. I shall be very unhappy, of course, but I shall never alter my mind. If I do not find from the fairies that my birth is worthy of you, then, whatever my feelings, I will never accept your hand.'

The conversation was at this point when one of the fairies appeared in her ivory car, accompanied by a beautiful woman. At this moment the bird suddenly awakened and, flying on to Saphir's shoulder (which it never afterwards left), began fondling him as well as a bird can. The fairy told Serpentine that she was pleased with her and made herself very agreeable. She presented Saphir to the lady with her, who was no other than his Aunt Aglantine, widow of Diamantino.

They all fell into each other's arms, then the fairy mounted her chariot, placed Aglantine by her side, and Saphir and Serpentine on the front seat. She also sent a message to the prince's attendants that they might travel slowly back to the court of King Peridor, and that the beautiful bird had really been found. Then they all started off in her chariot. But in spite of the swiftness with which they flew through the air, the time passed even quicker for Saphir and Serpentine, who had so much to think about.

They were still confused with the pleasure of seeing each other, when the chariot arrived at King Peridor's palace. He had been carried to a room on the roof, where his nurses thought he would die at any moment. Directly the chariot drew within sight of the castle the beautiful bird took flight and, making straight for the dying king, at once cured him of his sickness.

Then she resumed her natural shape, for the bird was no other than Queen Constance, whom he had long believed dead. Peridor was rejoiced to embrace his wife and his son once more, and with the help of the fairies began to make preparations for the marriage of Saphir and Serpentine, who turned out to be the daughter of Aglantine and Diamantino, and as much a princess as he was a prince. The people of the kingdom were delighted, and everybody lived happy and contented to the end of their lives.

[*Cabinet des Fées.*]

The Grateful Beasts

THERE WAS ONCE UPON
a time a man and woman who had three fine-looking sons,
but they were so poor they had hardly enough food for themselves, let alone their children. So the sons determined to set
out into the world and try their luck. Before starting, their
mother gave them each a loaf of bread and her blessing, and
having taken a tender farewell of her and their father, the
three set forth on their travels.

Ferko, the youngest of the brothers, was a beautiful youth,
with a splendid figure, blue eyes, fair hair, and a complexion
like milk and roses. His two brothers were as jealous of him
as they could be, for they thought that with his good looks he
would be sure to be the more fortunate.

One day all three were sitting at ease under a tree, for the
sun was hot and they were tired of walking. Ferko fell fast
asleep, but the other two remained awake, and the eldest said
to the second brother:

'Our brother Ferko is so beautiful that everyone takes a fancy
to him, which is more than they do to us. If we could only get
rid of him we might succeed better.'

The second brother answered, 'My advice is to eat his loaf

of bread, and then to refuse to give him a bit of ours until he has promised to let us put out his eyes or break his legs.'

His eldest brother agreed to this wicked proposal, and the two wretches seized Ferko's loaf and ate it all, while the poor boy was still asleep.

When he did awake he felt very hungry and turned to eat his bread, but his brothers cried out, 'You ate your loaf in your sleep, you glutton! Starve as long as you like, you won't get a scrap of ours.'

Ferko was at a loss to understand how he could have eaten the bread in his sleep, but he said nothing, and fasted all that day and the next night. But on the following morning he was so hungry that he burst into tears and implored his brothers to give him a bit of their bread. Then the cruel creatures laughed. But when Ferko continued to beg and beseech them, the eldest said at last, 'If you will let us put out one of your eyes and break one of your legs, then we will give you a bit of our bread.'

At these words poor Ferko wept more bitterly than before, and bore the torments of hunger till the sun was high in the heavens. Then he could stand it no longer and consented to allow his left eye to be put out and his left leg to be broken. When this was done he stretched out his hand eagerly for the piece of bread, but his brothers gave him such a tiny scrap that the starving youth finished it in a moment and besought them for a second bit. But the more Ferko wept and told his brothers that he was dying of hunger, the more they laughed and scolded him for his greed.

So he endured the pangs of starvation all that day, but when night came his endurance gave way, and he let his right eye be put out and his right leg broken for a second piece of bread. After his brothers had thus successfully maimed and disfigured

him for life, they left him groaning on the ground and continued their journey without him.

Poor Ferko ate the scrap of bread they had left him and wept
bitterly, but no one heard him or came to his help. Night came
on, and the poor blind youth could only crawl along the
ground, not knowing where he was going. But when the sun
was once more high in the heavens, Ferko felt the blazing
heat scorch him and sought for some cool shady place to rest
his aching body. He climbed a hill and lay down in the grass,
as he thought, under the shadow of a big tree. Now it was no
tree he leaned against, but a gallows on which two ravens were
seated. The one was saying to the other:

'Is there anything the least wonderful or remarkable about
this neighbourhood?'

'I should think there was!' replied the other. 'Anyone who
bathes in the lake down below us, though he were at death's
door, becomes sound and well on the spot, and those who wash
their eyes with the dew on this hill become as sharp-sighted
as the eagle, even if they have been blind from youth.'

'Well,' answered the first raven, 'my eyes are in no want of
this healing bath, for Heaven be praised, they are as good as
ever they were. But my wing has been very feeble since it was
shot by an arrow years ago, so let us fly at once to the lake
that I may be restored to health and strength again.' And so
they flew away.

Their words rejoiced Ferko's heart, and he waited impatiently till evening should come and he could rub the precious
dew on his sightless eyes.

At last it began to grow dusk, and the sun sank behind the
mountains. Gradually it became cooler on the hill, and the
grass was wet with dew. Then Ferko bathed his face in it till
his eyes were damp with dewdrops, and in a moment he saw

'Be of good cheer, for I can soon heal your leg.'

clearer than ever he had before. The moon was shining brightly and lighted him to the lake where he could bathe his poor broken legs.

Then Ferko crawled into the lake and, no sooner had he done so, than his legs felt as sound and strong as they had been before, and he thanked the kind fate that had led him to the hill where he heard the ravens' conversation. Ferko filled a bottle with the healing water and then continued his journey in the best of spirits.

He had not gone far before he met a wolf limping disconsolately along on three legs. On perceiving Ferko the wolf began to howl dismally.

'My good friend,' said the youth, 'be of good cheer, for I can soon heal your leg.' And with these words he poured some of the precious water over the wolf's paw, and in a moment the animal was springing about sound and well on all fours. The grateful creature thanked his benefactor warmly and promised Ferko to do him a good turn if he should ever need it.

Ferko continued his way till he came to a ploughed field. Here he noticed a little mouse creeping wearily along on its hind paws, for its front paws had both been broken in a trap.

Ferko felt so sorry for the little beast that he spoke to it in the most friendly manner, and washed its small paws with the healing water. In a moment the mouse was sound and whole and, after thanking the kind physician, it scampered away over the ploughed furrows.

Again Ferko proceeded on his journey, but he hadn't gone far before a queen bee flew against him, trailing one wing behind her, which had been cruelly torn by a big bird. Ferko was no less willing to help her than he had been to help the wolf and the mouse, so he poured some healing drops over the wounded wing. On the spot the queen bee was cured and, turning to Ferko, she said, 'I am most grateful for your kindness and shall reward you some day.' And with these words she flew away humming gaily.

Then Ferko wandered on for many a long day and at length reached a strange kingdom. He thought he might as well offer his services to the king of the country, for he had heard that the king's daughter was as beautiful as the day.

So he went to the royal palace and, as he entered the door, the first people he saw were his two brothers who had so shamefully ill-treated him. They had managed to obtain places in the king's service, and when they recognized Ferko with his eyes and legs sound and well they were greatly frightened, for they feared he would tell the king of their conduct.

No sooner had Ferko entered the palace than all eyes were turned on the handsome youth, and the king's daughter herself was lost in admiration, for she had never seen anyone so handsome before. His brothers noticed this, and envy and jealousy were added to their fear so they determined once more to destroy him. They went to the king and told him that Ferko was a wicked magician, who had come to carry off the princess.

Then the king had Ferko brought before him, and said, 'You are a magician who wishes to rob me of my daughter, and I condemn you to death. If you can fulfil three tasks your life shall be spared, on condition you leave the country. But if you cannot perform what I demand you shall be hanged on the nearest tree.'

And, turning to the two wicked brothers, he said, 'Suggest something for him to do, no matter how difficult. He must succeed in it or die.'

They replied, 'Let him build Your Majesty in one day a more beautiful palace than this.'

The king was pleased with this proposal and commanded

Ferko to set to work. The two brothers were delighted, for they thought they would now be rid of Ferko forever. The poor youth himself was heartbroken and cursed the hour he had crossed the boundary of the king's domain. As he was wandering disconsolately about the meadows near the palace, a little bee flew past. Settling on his shoulder she whispered in his ear:

'What is troubling you, my kind benefactor? Can I be of any help to you? I am the bee whose wing you healed and would like to show my gratitude.'

Ferko recognized the queen bee, and said, 'Alas! How could you help me? I have been set to do a task which no one in the whole world could do. Tomorrow I must build a palace more beautiful than the king's, and it must be finished before evening.'

'Is that all?' asked the bee. 'Then you may comfort yourself, for before the sun goes down tomorrow night a palace shall be built unlike any a king has dwelt in before. Just stay here till I come again.'

She flew merrily away, and Ferko, reassured by her words, lay down on the grass and slept peacefully till morning.

Early on the following day the whole town was on its feet, and everyone wondered how and where the stranger would build the wonderful palace. The princess alone was silent and sorrowful. She had cried all night till her pillow was wet, so much did she take the fate of the beautiful youth to heart.

Ferko spent the whole day in the meadows, and when evening came, the queen bee flew by. She said, 'The wonderful palace is ready. Be of good cheer, and lead the king to the hill just outside the city walls.' And humming gaily she flew away again.

Ferko went at once and told the king the palace was finished. The whole court went out to see the wonder, and their astonishment was great at the sight of a splendid palace on the hill just outside the walls of the city. It was made of the most exquisite flowers that ever grew in mortal garden. The roof was all of crimson roses, the windows of lilies, the walls of white carnations, the floors of glowing auriculas and violets, the doors of gorgeous tulips and narcissi, with sunflowers for knockers, and all round hyacinths and other sweet-smelling flowers bloomed in masses so that the air was perfumed far and near and enchanted all. This splendid palace had been built by the grateful queen bee, who had summoned all the bees in the kingdom to help her.

The king's amazement knew no bounds, and the princess's eyes beamed with delight as she turned them from the wonderful building to the smiling Ferko. But the two brothers had grown green with envy, and only declared the more that Ferko was nothing but a wicked magician.

The king, although he had been surprised and astonished at the way his commands had been carried out, was vexed that the stranger should escape with his life. Turning to the two brothers, he said:

'He has certainly accomplished the first task, with the aid, no doubt, of his diabolical magic. What shall we give him to do now? Let us make it as difficult as possible.'

Then the eldest brother replied, 'The corn has all been cut, but it has not yet been put into barns. Let the knave collect all the grain in the kingdom into one big heap before tomorrow night, and if so much as a stalk of corn is left let him be put to death.'

The princess grew white with terror when she heard these words. Ferko felt much more cheerful now than he had the first time and wandered out into the meadows again, but he could think of no way of escape. The sun sank to rest and night came on, when a little mouse started out of the grass at Ferko's feet, and said to him:

'I'm delighted to see you, my kind benefactor. But why are you looking so sad? Can I be of any help to you and thus repay your great kindness to me?'

Then Ferko recognized the mouse whose front paws he had healed, and replied, 'Alas! How can you help me in a matter that is beyond any human power? Before tomorrow night all the grain in the kingdom must be gathered into one big heap, and if as much as one stalk of corn is wanting I must pay for it with my life.'

'Is that all?' answered the mouse. 'That needn't distress you much. Just trust in me, and before the sun sets again you shall hear that your task is done.' And with these words the little creature scampered away into the fields.

Ferko, who never doubted that the mouse would be as good as its word, lay down comforted on the soft grass and slept soundly till next morning. The day passed slowly, and with the evening came the little mouse, who said:

'Now there is not a single stalk of corn left in any field. They are all collected in one big heap on the hill out there.'

Then Ferko went joyfully to the king and told him that all he demanded had been done. And the whole court went out to see the wonder and were no less astonished than they had been the first time. For in a heap higher than the king's palace lay all the grain of the country, and not a single stalk of corn had been left behind in any of the fields. And how had all this been done? The little mouse had summoned every other mouse to its help, and together they had collected all the grain in the kingdom.

The king could not hide his amazement, but at the same time his wrath increased and he was more ready than ever to believe the two brothers. Only the beautiful princess rejoiced over Ferko's success, and looked on him with friendly glances, which the youth returned.

The cruel king turned once more to the two brothers and said, 'His diabolical magic has helped him again. Now what third task shall we set him to do? No matter how impossible it is, he must do it or die.'

The eldest answered quickly, 'Let him drive all the wolves of the kingdom onto this hill before tomorrow night. If he does this he may go free, otherwise he shall be hanged as you have said.'

At these words the princess burst into tears, and when the king saw this he ordered her to be shut up in a high tower and carefully guarded till the dangerous magician should either have left the kingdom or been hung on the nearest tree. Ferko wandered out into the fields again and sat down on the stump of a tree, wondering what he should do next. Suddenly a big wolf ran up to him, and said:

'I'm very glad to see you again, my kind benefactor. What are you thinking about all alone by yourself? If I can help you in any way, only say the word, for I would like to give you a proof of my gratitude.'

Ferko at once recognized the wolf he had healed, and told him what he had to do the following day. 'But how in the world am I to collect all the wolves of the kingdom?'

'If that's all you want done,' answered the wolf, 'you needn't worry yourself. I'll undertake the task, and you'll hear from me again before sunset tomorrow. Keep your spirits up.' And with these words he trotted quickly away.

Then the youth rejoiced greatly, for now he felt that his life was safe. But he grew very sad when he thought of the beautiful princess and that he would never see her again if he left the country. He lay down once more on the grass and soon fell fast asleep.

All the next day he spent wandering about the fields, and toward evening the wolf came running to him in a great hurry and said, 'I have collected together all the wolves in the kingdom, and they are waiting for you in the wood. Go quickly to the king, and tell him to go to the hill that he may see the wonder with his own eyes. Then return at once and get on my back. I will help you to drive all the wolves together.'

Ferko went straight to the palace and told the king that he was ready to perform the third task if he would come to the hill and see it done. Ferko then returned to the fields and, mounting on the wolf's back, he rode to the wood close by.

Quick as lightning the wolf flew round the wood, and in an instant many hundred wolves rose up before him, increasing in number every moment, till they could be counted by thousands. He drove them all before him onto the hill, where the king and his whole court and Ferko's two brothers were standing. Only the lovely princess was not present, for she was shut up in her tower weeping bitterly.

The wicked brothers foamed with rage when they saw the failure of their wicked designs. But the king was overcome by a sudden terror when he saw the enormous pack of wolves approaching nearer and nearer. Calling out to Ferko, he said, 'Enough, enough! We don't want any more.'

But the wolf, on whose back Ferko sat, said to its rider, 'Go on! Go on!' And at the same moment many more wolves ran up the hill, howling horribly, and showing their white teeth.

The king in his terror called out, 'Stop a moment! I will give you half my kingdom if you will drive all the wolves away.'

But Ferko pretended not to hear, and drove some more

thousands before him so that everyone quaked with horror and fear. Then the king raised his voice again and called out:

'Stop! You shall have my whole kingdom, if you will only drive these wolves back to the places they came from.'

But the wolf kept on encouraging Ferko, and said, 'Go on! Go on!' So he led the wolves on, till at last they fell on the king and the wicked brothers and ate them and the whole court up in a moment.

Then Ferko went straight to the palace and set the princess free, and on the same day he married her and was crowned king of the country. The wolves all went peacefully back to their own homes, and Ferko and his bride lived for many years in peace and happiness together and were much loved by great and small in the land.

[From the Hungarian. Kletke.]

The Giants and the Herdboy

THERE WAS ONCE UPON a time a poor boy who had neither father nor mother. In order to gain a living he looked after the sheep of a great lord. Day and night he spent out in the open fields, and only when it was very wet and stormy did he take refuge in a little hut on the edge of a big forest. Now one night, when he was sitting on the grass beside his flocks, he heard not very far from him the sound as of someone crying. He rose up and followed the direction of the noise. To his dismay and astonishment he found a giant lying at the entrance of the wood; he was about to run off as fast as his legs could carry him, when the giant called out:

'Don't be afraid, I won't harm you. On the contrary, I will reward you handsomely if you will bind up my foot. I hurt it when I was trying to root up an oak tree.'

The herdboy took off his shirt and bound up the giant's wounded foot with it. Then the giant rose up and said very kindly and politely:

'Now come and I will reward you. We are going to celebrate a marriage today, and I promise you we shall have plenty of fun. Come and enjoy yourself but, in order that my brothers may not see you, put this band round your waist and then you'll be invisible.'

With these words he handed the herdboy a belt, and walking on in front he led him to a fountain where hundreds of giants and giantesses were assembled preparing to hold a wedding. They danced and played different games till midnight; then one of the giants tore up a plant by its roots, and all the giants and giantesses made themselves so thin that they disappeared into the earth through the hole made by the uprooting of the plant. The wounded giant remained behind to the last and called out:

'Herdboy, where are you?'

'Here I am, close to you,' was the reply.

'Touch me,' said the giant, 'so that you too may come with us underground.'

The herdboy did as he was told and, before he could have believed it possible, found himself in a great hall, where even the walls were made of pure gold. Then to his astonishment he saw that the hall was furnished with the tables and chairs that belonged to his master. In a few minutes the company began to eat and drink. The banquet was a gorgeous one, and the poor youth fell to and ate and drank heartily. When he had eaten as much as he could he said to himself, 'Why shouldn't I put a loaf of bread in my pocket? I shall be glad of it tomorrow.' So he seized a loaf when no one was looking and stowed it away under his tunic. No sooner had he done so than the wounded giant limped up to him and whispered softly:

'Herdboy, where are you?'

'Here I am,' replied the youth.

'Then hold on to me,' said the giant, 'so that I may lead you up above again.'

So the herdboy held on to the giant and in a few moments

he found himself on the earth once more, but the giant had vanished. The herdboy returned to his sheep and took off the invisible belt which he hid carefully in his bag.

The next morning the lad felt hungry and thought he would cut off a piece of the loaf he had carried away from the giants' wedding feast and eat it. But although he tried with all his might, he could not cut off the smallest piece. Then in despair he bit the loaf, and what was his astonishment when a piece of gold fell out of his mouth and rolled at his feet. He bit the bread a second and a third time, and each time a piece of gold fell out of his mouth, but the bread remained untouched. The herdboy was delighted over his stroke of good fortune and, hiding the magic loaf in his bag, he hurried off to the nearest village to buy himself something to eat, and then he returned to his sheep.

Now the lord whose sheep the herdboy looked after had a very lovely daughter, who always smiled and nodded to the youth when she walked with her father in his fields. For a long time the herdboy had made up his mind to prepare a surprise for this beautiful creature on her birthday. So when the day approached he put on his invisible belt, took a sack of gold pieces with him, and slipping into her room in the middle of the night he placed the bag of gold beside her bed and returned to his sheep. The girl's joy was great, and so was her parents', next day when they found the sack full of gold pieces.

The herdboy was so pleased to think what pleasure he had given that the next night he placed another bag of gold beside the girl's bed. And this he continued to do for seven nights, and the girl and her parents made up their minds that it must be a good fairy who brought the gold every night. But one night they determined to watch and see from their hiding place who the bringer of the sack of gold really was.

On the eighth night a fearful storm of wind and rain came on while the herdboy was on his way to bring the beautiful girl another bag of gold. Then for the first time he noticed, just as he reached his master's house, that he had forgotten the belt which made him invisible. He didn't like the idea of going back to his hut in the wind and wet, so he just stepped as he was into the girl's room, laid the sack of gold beside her and was turning to leave the room, when his master confronted him and said:

'You young rogue, so you were going to steal the gold that a good fairy brings every night, were you?'

The herdboy was so taken aback by his words, that he stood trembling before him, and did not dare to explain his presence. Then his master spoke:

'As you have hitherto always behaved well in my service I will not send you to prison. But leave your place instantly and never let me see your face again.'

So the herdboy went back to his hut and, taking his loaf and belt with him, went to the nearest town. There he bought himself some fine clothes and a beautiful coach with four horses, hired two servants, and drove back to his master. How astonished he was to see his herdboy returning to him in this manner! Then the youth told him of the piece of good luck that had befallen him and asked him for the hand of his beautiful daughter. This was readily granted, and the two lived in peace and happiness to the end of their lives.

[From the *Bukowinaer*. Von Wliolocki.]

The Invisible Prince

ONCE UPON A TIME
there lived a fairy who had power over the earth, the sea, fire
and the air; and this fairy had four sons. The eldest, who was
quick and lively with a vivid imagination, she made Lord of
Fire, which was in her opinion the noblest of all the elements.
To the second son, whose wisdom and prudence made amends
for his being rather dull, she gave the government of the earth.
The third was wild and savage and of monstrous stature; and
the fairy, his mother, who was ashamed of his defects, hoped
to hide them by creating him King of the Seas. The youngest,
who was the slave of his passions and of a very uncertain
temper, became Prince of the Air.

Being the youngest, he was naturally his mother's favourite;
but this did not blind her to his weaknesses, and she foresaw
that some day he would suffer much pain through falling in
love. So from his earliest childhood he heard nothing but stories
of princes who had fallen into all sorts of troubles through love.

All the time that his mother could spare she passed in giving
him a love of the chase, which henceforth became his chief joy.
For his amusement she had made a new forest, planted with
the most splendid trees, and turned loose in it every animal

that could be found anywhere on the globe. In the midst of this forest she built a palace which had not its equal for beauty in the whole world, and then she considered that she had done quite enough to make any prince happy.

Now this was all very well, but a man cannot struggle against his fate. In his secret heart the prince got tired of his mother's constant talk on this subject; and when one day she quitted the palace to attend to some business, begging him never to go beyond the grounds, he at once jumped at the chance of disobeying her.

Left to himself the prince, feeling very much bored with his own company, ordered some of his spirits of the air to carry him to the court of a neighbouring sovereign. This kingdom was the Island of Roses, where the climate is so delicious the grass is always green and the flowers always sweet. The waves, instead of beating on the rocks, seemed to die gently on the shore; clusters of golden bushes covered the land, and the vines were bent low with grapes.

The king of this island had a daughter named Rosalie, more lovely than any girl in the whole world. No sooner had the eyes of the Prince of the Air rested on her than he instantly thought how best to make himself happy, and the shortest way that occurred to him was to have Rosalie carried off by his attendant spirits.

It is easy to imagine the feelings of the king when he found his daughter had vanished. He mourned her loss night and day, and his only comfort was to talk it over with a young and unknown prince, who was then staying at the court. Alas, he did not know what a deep interest the stranger had in Rosalie, for he too had seen her, and had fallen a victim to her charms.

One day the king, more sorrowful than usual, was walking

sadly along the seashore. After a long silence the unknown prince, who was his only companion, suddenly spoke.

'There is no evil without a remedy,' he said to the unhappy father; 'and if you will promise me your daughter in marriage, I will undertake to bring her back to you.'

'You are trying to soothe me by vain promises,' answered the king. 'Did I not see her caught up into the air, in spite of cries which would have softened the heart of anyone but the barbarian who has robbed me of her? The unfortunate girl is pining away in some unknown land, and I shall see her no more. But go, generous stranger; bring back Rosalie if you can, and live happily with her ever after in this country, of which I now declare you heir.'

Although the stranger's name was unknown to Rosalie's father, he was really the only son of the King of the Golden Isle, which had for its capital a city that extended from one sea to another. The walls, washed by the quiet waters, were covered with gold, which made one think of the yellow sands. Above them was a rampart of orange and lemon trees, and all the streets were paved with gold.

A life of adventure had been foretold at the prince's birth. This so frightened his father and mother that a fairy produced a little pebble which she told them to keep for the prince till he grew up. By putting it in his mouth he would become invisible so long as he did not try to speak. In this way the good fairy hoped the prince would be protected against all dangers.

No sooner did the prince begin to grow out of boyhood than he longed to see if the other countries of the world were as splendid as the one in which he lived. So he set out, but a frightful storm drove his ship onto unknown shores, where

'I will undertake to bring your daughter back to you.'

most of his followers were put to death by savages, and the prince himself only escaped by using his magic pebble. He passed through the midst of them unseen and wandered on till he reached the coast, where he re-embarked on board his ship.

The first land he had sighted was the Island of Roses, and he went at once to the court of the king. The moment his eyes had beheld the Princess Rosalie he fell in love with her like everyone else.

He had already spent several months in this condition when the Prince of the Air whirled her away, to the grief and despair of every man on the island. But sad though everybody was, the Prince of the Golden Isle was inconsolable, and he passed both days and nights in bemoaning his loss.

'Alas!' he cried. 'Shall I never see my lovely princess again? Who knows where she may be; what fairy may have her in his keeping? I am only a man, but I am strong in my love, and I will seek the whole world through till I find her.'

So saying, he left the court and travelled many weary days without hearing a single word of the lost princess. One morning, as he was walking through a thick forest, he suddenly perceived a magnificent palace standing at the end of a pine avenue. He quickly arrived at the gate of the palace, which was formed of a single agate. The gate swung open to let him through, and he next passed successively three courts, surrounded by deep ditches filled with running water, with birds of brilliant plumage flying about the banks. Everything around was rare and beautiful, but the prince scarcely raised his eyes to all these wonders, for he thought only of the princess and where he should find her. In vain he opened every door and searched in every corner; he neither saw Rosalie nor anyone else.

At last there was no place left for him to search but a little wood, which contained in the centre a sort of hall built entirely of orange trees, with four small rooms opening out of the corners. Three of these were empty except for statues and wonderful things, but in the fourth the invisible prince caught sight of Rosalie. His joy at beholding her again was, however, somewhat lessened by seeing the Prince of the Air kneeling at her feet and pleading his own cause. But it was in vain that he implored her to listen; she only shook her head.

'No, you snatched me from my father whom I loved, and all the splendour in the world can never console me. Go! I can never feel anything toward you but hate and contempt.' With these words she turned away and entered her own apartments.

The invisible prince followed her but, fearing to be discovered by the princess in the presence of others, he made up his mind to wait quietly till dark and employed the long hours in writing a poem to the princess, which he laid on the bed beside her. This done, he thought of nothing but how best to rescue Rosalie. He resolved to wait until the Prince of the Air paid a visit to his mother and brothers, in order to strike the blow.

One day Rosalie was sitting alone in her room thinking of her troubles when she suddenly saw a pen get up from the desk and write by itself on a sheet of white paper. She was greatly astonished and instantly went over to the table. She found some lovely verses, telling her that another shared her distress and loved her with all his heart, and that he would never rest until he had delivered her from the hands of the man she hated. Thus encouraged, the princess, feeling sure there was some magic, told her story and of the arrival of a young stranger in her father's palace, whose looks had so charmed her that since that day she had thought of no one else.

At these words the prince could contain himself no longer.

He took the pebble from his mouth and flung himself at Rosalie's feet.

When they had got over the first rapture of meeting they began to make plans to escape from the power of the Prince of the Air. But this did not prove easy, for the magic stone would only serve for one person at a time, and in order to save Rosalie the Prince of the Golden Isle would have to expose himself to the fury of his enemy. Rosalie would not hear of this.

'No, Prince,' she said, 'since you are here this island no longer seems a prison. Besides, you are under the protection of a fairy, who always visits your father's court at this season. Go instantly and seek her and implore the gift of another stone with similar powers. Once you have that, there will be no further difficulty in the way of escape.'

The invisible prince set out. He had, however, entirely forgotten the road by which he had come, and lost himself for so long in the forest that when he reached home the fairy had already left. In spite of all his grief, there was nothing for it but to wait till the fairy's next visit and allow Rosalie to wait three months longer. One day, as he was strolling along an alley in the woods, he saw a huge oak open its trunk, and out of it step two princes in earnest conversation. As the Prince of the Golden Isle had the magic stone in his mouth, they imagined themselves alone and did not lower their voices.

'What!' said one. 'Are you always going to allow yourself to be tormented by hopeless love? In your whole kingdom can you find nothing else to satisfy you?'

'What is the use,' replied the other, 'of being Prince of the Gnomes if I cannot win the love of the Princess Argentine? From the moment I first saw her, sitting in the forest surrounded by flowers, I have never ceased to think of her night and day. Although I love her so much I am convinced she will never care for me. You know that I have in my palace the cabinets of the years. In the first, great mirrors reflect the past; in the second, we contemplate the present; in the third, the future can be read. I consulted the cabinets, after I had gazed on the Princess Argentine, but instead of her returning my love, I only saw scorn and contempt. Think how great must be my devotion when, in spite of my fate, I still love on!'

Now the Prince of the Golden Isle was interested by this conversation, for the Princess Argentine was his sister, and he hoped, by means of her influence over the Prince of the Gnomes, to obtain the release of Rosalie. So he returned to his father's palace, where to his joy he found his friend the fairy, who at once presented him with a magic pebble like his own.

He lost no time in setting out to deliver Rosalie, and travelled so fast that he soon arrived at the forest. But though he found the palace he did not find Rosalie. He hunted high and low, but there was no sign of her, and his despair was great.

At last he remembered the conversation of the two princes about the cabinets of the years; if he could manage to reach the oak tree, he might discover what had become of Rosalie. Happily, he soon found out the secret and entered the cabinet of the present, where he saw reflected in the mirrors the unfortunate Rosalie sitting in a castle, weeping bitterly, and surrounded with genii, who never left her night or day.

This sight increased the misery of the prince, for he did not know where the castle was; however, he resolved to seek the whole world through. He began by setting sail in a favourable wind, but his bad luck followed him even on the sea. He had scarcely lost sight of the land when a violent storm arose, and after several hours of beating about, his vessel was driven on to some rocks, on which it dashed itself to bits.

The prince was able to catch a floating spar and to keep himself afloat. After a long struggle with the winds and waves, he was cast upon a strange island. What was his surprise, on reaching the shore, to hear sounds of the most heartrending distress, mingled with the sweetest songs which had ever charmed him! His curiosity was instantly roused, and he advanced cautiously till he saw two huge dragons guarding the gate of a wood. They were terrible indeed to look upon. Their bodies were covered with glittering scales; their curly tails extended far over the land; flames darted from their mouths and noses; and their eyes would have made the bravest shudder. But as the prince was invisible they did not see him, and he could slip past them into the wood.

The prince went on his way, thinking, however, that great prudence was necessary or he might become the victim of some enchantment; and he was thankful to slip past the dragons and enter a beautiful park, with clear streams and sweet flowers, and a crowd of men and maidens.

The sight of all these happy couples only made the prince grieve the more, and he spent his days wandering along the seashore. But one day he was sitting on a rock bewailing his fate when all in a moment the sea appeared to raise itself nearly to the skies, and the caves echoed with hideous screams. As he looked a woman rose from the depths of the sea, flying madly before a furious giant.

Her cries softened the heart of the prince, and drawing his sword, he rushed after the giant, so as to give the lady time to escape. But hardly had he reached the enemy when the giant touched him with a ring and the prince was fixed immovable where he stood. Then the giant, hastily seizing the woman in his arms, plunged with her into the sea. He sent some tritons to bind chains about the Prince of the Golden Isle, and he too was borne to the depths of the ocean, without the hope of seeing the princess.

Now the giant whom the invisible prince had so rashly attacked was the King of the Seas, the third son of the Queen of the Elements, and he had touched the youth with a magic ring which enabled a mortal to live under water. So the Prince of the Golden Isle found when, bound in chains by the tritons, he was carried through immense seaweed forests filled with strange monsters, till he reached a vast sandy space surrounded by huge rocks. On the tallest of the rocks sat the giant as on a throne.

'Rash mortal,' said he, when the prince was dragged before him, 'you have deserved death, but you shall live only to suffer more cruelly. Go, and add to the number of those whom it is my pleasure to torture.'

At these words the unhappy prince found himself tied to a rock; but he was not alone in his misfortunes, for all round him were chained princes and princesses, whom the giant held captive. Indeed, it was his chief delight to create a storm, in order to add to his prisoners.

As his hands were fastened, it was impossible for the Prince of the Golden Isle to make use of his magic stone, and he passed his nights and days dreaming of Rosalie. But at last the giant took it into his head to amuse himself by arranging fights among his captives. Lots were drawn, and one fell upon the prince, whose chains were immediately loosened. The moment he was set free, he snatched up his stone and became invisible.

The astonishment of the giant at the sudden disappearance of the prince may well be imagined. He ordered the passages to be watched, but it was too late, for the prince had already glided between two rocks. He wandered for a long while through the forests where he met nothing but fearful monsters. He climbed rock after rock, steered his way from tree to tree, till at length he arrived at the edge of the sea, where rose a mountain, and behold! It was the one he had seen in the cabinet of the present.

Filled with joy, he made his way to the top of the mountain, which pierced the clouds, and there he found a palace. He entered, and in the middle of a long gallery he discovered a crystal room, in which sat Rosalie, guarded night and day by genii. There was no door anywhere, nor any window. At this sight the prince became more puzzled than ever, for he did not know how he was to warn Rosalie of his return. Yet it broke his heart to see her weeping from dawn till dark.

One day, as Rosalie was walking up and down her room, she was surprised to see that the crystal which served for a wall had grown cloudy, as if some one had breathed on it, and what was more, wherever she moved the brightness of the crystal always became clouded. This was enough to cause the princess to suspect that the Prince of the Golden Isle had returned. She began by being very gracious to the Prince of the Air, so when she begged that her captivity might be lightened a little she should not be refused.

At first she asked to be allowed to walk for one hour every day up and down the long gallery. This was granted, and the invisible prince speedily handed her the stone, which she at once slipped into her mouth. No words can paint the fury of her captor at her disappearance. He ordered the spirits of the air to fly through all space and to bring back Rosalie wherever she might be. They instantly flew off to obey his commands, and spread themselves over the whole earth.

Meantime Rosalie and the invisible prince had reached, hand in hand, a door of the gallery which led through a terrace into the gardens. In silence they glided along and thought themselves already safe, when a furious monster dashed itself by accident against Rosalie and the invisible prince and in her fright she let go his hand. No one can speak as long as he is invisible, and besides, they knew that the spirits were all around them, and at the slightest sound they would be recognized. So all they could do was to feel about in the hope that their hands might once more meet.

But, alas, the joy of liberty lasted but a short time. The princess, having wandered in vain up and down the forest, stopped at last on the edge of a fountain. As she walked she wrote on the trees:

'If ever the prince, my lover, comes this way, let him know that it is here I dwell, and that I sit daily on the edge of this fountain, mingling my tears with its waters.'

These words were read by one of the genii, who repeated them to his master. The Prince of the Air, in his turn making himself invisible, was led to the fountain and waited for Rosalie. When she drew near he held out his hand, which she grasped eagerly, taking it for that of her lover. Seizing his opportunity, the Prince of the Air passed a cord round her arms and, throwing off his invisibility, cried to his spirits to take her into the lowest pit.

It was at this moment that the invisible prince appeared, and, at the sight of the Prince of the Air mounting into the air holding a silken cord, he guessed instantly that he was carrying off Rosalie.

'Can I survive my misfortunes?' he cried. 'I fancied I had come to an end of my troubles, and now they are worse than ever. What will become of me? Never can I discover the place where this monster will hide Rosalie.' Indeed his sorrow was enough to kill him, when the thought that by means of the cabinets of the years he might find out where the princess was imprisoned gave him a little comfort. So he walked on through the forest and, after some hours, arrived at the gate of a temple, guarded by two huge lions. Being invisible, he was able to enter unharmed. In the middle of the temple was an altar, on which lay a book and behind the altar hung a great curtain. The prince approached the altar and opened the book, which contained the names of all the lovers in the world: and in it he read that Rosalie had been carried off by the Prince of the Air to an abyss which had no entrance except by way of the Fountain of Gold.

Now, as the prince had no idea where this fountain was to be found, it might be thought he was not much nearer Rosalie than before. However, the prince did not despair.

'Though every step that I take may perhaps lead me farther from her,' he said to himself, 'I am still thankful to know that she is alive.'

On leaving the temple the invisible prince saw six paths lying before him, each of which led through the wood. He was hesitating which to choose, when he beheld two people coming toward him, down the path which lay most to his right. They turned out to be Prince Gnome and his friend, and the sudden desire to hear of his sister, Princess Argentine, caused the invisible prince to follow them and to listen to their conversation.

'Do you think,' Prince Gnome was saying, 'do you think that I would not break my chains if I could? I know the Princess Argentine will never love me, yet each day I feel her dearer still. As if this were not enough, I have the horror of feeling she probably loves another. So I have resolved to put myself out of my pain by means of the Golden Fountain. A single drop of its water falling on the sand will trace the name of my rival in her heart. I dread the test, and yet this very dread convinces me of my misfortune.'

The invisible prince followed Prince Gnome like his shadow and, after walking some time, they arrived at the Golden Fountain. The unhappy prince stooped down with a sigh and dipping his finger in the water let fall a drop on the sand. Instantly appeared the name of Prince Flame, his brother. The shock of this discovery was so real that Prince Gnome sank fainting into the arms of his friend.

Since he had been touched by the giant's ring, the invisible prince had the power to live in the water as well as on land, so he at once dived into the fountain. He perceived in one corner a door leading into the mountain, and at the foot of the mountain was a high rock on which was fixed an iron ring with a cord attached. The prince promptly guessed that the cord was used to chain the princess and drew his sword to cut it. In a moment he felt the princess's hand in his. She had always kept her magic pebble in her mouth, in spite of the prayers and entreaties of the Prince of the Air to make herself visible.

So hand in hand the invisible prince and Rosalie crossed the mountain; but as the princess had no power of living under water, she could not pass the Golden Fountain. Speechless and invisible they clung together on its brink, trembling at the frightful tempest the Prince of the Air had raised in his fury. The storm had already lasted many days when tremendous heat began to make itself felt. The lightning flashed, the thunder rolled, and fire bolts fell from heaven, burning up the forests and even the fields of corn.

In one instant the very streams were dried up, and the prince, seizing his opportunity, carried the princess over the Golden Fountain. It took them a long time to reach the Golden Isle, but at last they did, and they never wanted to leave it any more.

The Crow

ONCE UPON A TIME
there were three princesses who were all young and beautiful;
but the youngest, although she was not fairer than the other
two, was the most lovable of them all. About half a mile from
the palace in which they lived stood a castle. It was uninhabited
and almost a ruin, but the garden was a mass of blooming
flowers, and in this garden the youngest princess used often
to walk.

One day, when she was pacing to and fro under the lime
trees, a black crow hopped out of a rosebush in front of her.
It was torn and bleeding, and the kind little princess was quite
unhappy about it. When the crow saw this it turned to her
and said:

'I am not really a black crow, but an enchanted prince who
has been doomed to spend his youth in misery. If you only
liked, Princess, you could save me. But you would have to say
good-bye to all your own people and be my constant companion
in this ruined castle. There is one habitable room in it, in which
there is a golden bed. There you will have to live all by yourself
and don't forget that, whatever you may see or hear in the

night, you must not scream out, for if you give so much as a
single cry my sufferings will be doubled.'

The good-natured princess at once left her home and her
family and hurried to the ruined castle and took possession of
the room with the golden bed. When night approached she lay
down, but though she shut her eyes tight sleep would not come.

At midnight she heard to her great horror someone coming
along the passage, and in a moment her door was flung wide
open and a troop of strange beings entered the room. They at
once proceeded to light a fire in the huge fireplace; then they
placed a great cauldron of boiling water on it. When they had
done this, they approached the bed on which the trembling
girl lay and, screaming and yelling, they dragged her toward
the cauldron. She nearly died with fright, but she never uttered
a sound. Then of a sudden the cock crew, and all the evil spirits
vanished.

At the same moment the crow appeared and hopped round
the room with joy. It thanked the princess most heartily for
her goodness and said that its sufferings had already been
greatly lessened.

Now one of the princess's elder sisters, who was very inquisi-
tive, had found out about everything and went to pay her
youngest sister a visit in the ruined castle. She implored her so
urgently to let her spend the night with her that at last the
little princess consented. But at midnight, when the odd folk
appeared, the elder sister screamed with terror, and from this
time on the youngest princess insisted always on keeping watch
alone.

So she lived in solitude all the daytime, and at night she
would have been frightened had she not been so brave. But
every day the crow came and thanked her for her endurance

and assured her that his sufferings were far less than they had been. And so two years passed away, when one day the crow came to the princess and said:

'In another year I shall be freed from the spell I am under, because then the seven years will be over. But before I can resume my natural form and take possession of the belongings of my forefathers, you must go out into the world and take service as a maidservant.'

The young princess consented at once, and for a whole year she served as a maid. In spite of her youth and beauty she was very badly treated and suffered many things. One evening, when she was spinning flax and had worked until her little hands were weary, she heard a rustling beside her and a cry of joy. Then she saw a handsome youth standing beside her, who knelt down at her feet and kissed the little weary hands.

'I am the prince,' he said, 'whom in your goodness, when I was wandering about in the shape of a black crow, you freed from the most awful torments. Come now to my castle with me, and let us live there happily together.'

So they went to the castle where they had both endured so much. But when they reached it, it was difficult to believe that it was the same, for it had all been magnificently rebuilt. And there they lived for a hundred years, a hundred years of joy and happiness.

[From the Polish. Kletke.]

How Six Travelled the Wide World

THERE WAS ONCE UPON a time a man who understood all sorts of arts. He served in the war and bore himself bravely and well, but when the war was over, he got his discharge, and set out on his travels with three farthings of his pay in his pocket. 'Wait,' he said, 'that does not please me. Only let me find the right people and the king shall yet give me all the treasures of his kingdom.'

He strode angrily into the forest, and there he saw a man standing by six trees he had uprooted as if they were straws. He said to him, 'Will you be my servant and travel with me?'

'Yes,' the man answered, 'but first of all I will take this little bundle of sticks home to my mother.' And he took one of the trees and wound it round the other five, raised the bundle to his shoulders and bore it off. Then he came back and went with his master, who said, 'We two ought to be able to travel through the wide world!'

And when they had gone a little way they came upon a

hunter, who was on his knees, his gun on his shoulder, aiming at something. The master said to him:

'Hunter, what are you aiming at?'

He answered, 'Two miles from this place sits a fly on a branch of an oak. I want to shoot out its left eye.'

'Oh, go with me,' said the man. 'If we three are together we shall easily travel through the wide world.'

The hunter agreed and went with him, and they came to seven windmills whose sails were going round quite fast, and yet there was not a breath of wind, nor was a leaf moving. The man said, 'I don't know what is turning those windmills; there is not the slightest breeze blowing.' So he walked on with his servants, and when they had gone two miles they saw a man sitting on a tree, holding one of his nostrils and blowing out of the other.

'Fellow, what are you puffing at up there?' asked the man.

He replied, 'Two miles from this place are standing seven windmills. See, I am blowing to drive them round.'

'Oh, go with me,' said the man. 'If we four are together we shall easily travel through the wide world.'

So the blower went with him, and after a time they saw a man who was standing on one leg and had unstrapped the other and laid it near him.

Then said the master, 'You have made yourself very comfortable to rest!'

'I am a runner,' answered he, 'and so that I shall not go too quickly, I have unstrapped one leg. When I run with two legs, I go faster than a bird flies.'

'Oh, go with me. If we five are together, we shall easily travel through the wide world.' So he went with him and, not long afterward, they met a man who wore a little hat, but he had it slouched over one ear.

The king's daughter emptied his pitcher

9

'Manners, manners!' said the master to him. 'Don't hang your hat over one ear; you look like a madman!'

'I dare not,' said the other, 'for if I were to put my hat on straight, there would come such a frost that the very birds in the sky would freeze and fall dead on the earth.'

'Oh, go with me,' said the master. 'If we six are together, we shall easily travel through the wide world.'

Now the six came to a town in which the king had proclaimed that whoever should run with his daughter in a race, and win, should become her husband; but if he lost, he must lose his head. This was reported to the man, who declared he would compete. 'But,' he said, 'I shall let my servant run for me.'

The king replied, 'Then both your heads must be staked, and your head and his must be guaranteed for the winner.'

When this was agreed upon and settled, the man strapped the other leg on the runner, saying to him, 'Now be nimble, and see that we win!'

It was arranged that whoever should first bring water out of a stream a long way off should be the victor. Then the runner took a pitcher, and the king's daughter another, and they began to run at the same time. But in a moment, when the king's daughter was only just a little way off, no spectator could see the runner, and it seemed as if the wind had whistled past. In a short time he reached the stream, filled his pitcher with water, and turned round again. But, half way home, a great drowsiness came over him; he put down his pitcher, lay down, and fell asleep. He had, however, put a horse's skull which was lying on the ground, for his pillow, so that he should not be too comfortable and might soon wake up.

In the meantime the king's daughter, who could also run well, better than an ordinary man could, reached the stream and hastened back with her pitcher full of water. When she saw the runner lying there asleep, she was delighted, and said, 'My enemy is given into my hands!' She emptied his pitcher and ran on.

Everything now would have been lost, if by good luck the hunter had not been standing on the castle tower and had seen everything with his sharp eyes.

'Ah,' said he, 'the king's daughter shall not overreach us,' and, loading his gun, he shot so cleverly that he shot away the horse's skull from under the runner's head, without hurting him. Then the runner awoke, jumped up, and saw that his pitcher was empty and the king's daughter far ahead. But he did not lose courage and ran back to the stream with his pitcher, filled it once more with water, and was home ten minutes before the king's daughter arrived.

'Look,' said he, 'I have only just exercised my legs. That was nothing of a run.'

But the king was angry, and his daughter even more so, that she should be won by a common, discharged soldier. They consulted together how they could destroy both him and his companions.

Then the king said to her, 'I have found a way. Don't be frightened. They shall not come home again.'

So the king said to the soldier, 'You must now make merry with your companions and eat and drink' And he led them into a room with a floor of iron, the doors were also of iron, and the windows were barred. In the room was a table spread with delicious food. The king said to them, 'Go in and enjoy yourselves,' and as soon as they were inside he had the doors shut and bolted. Then he made the cook come and ordered him to keep a large fire burning under the room until the iron was red hot. The cook did so, and the six sitting round the table felt very warm, and they thought this was because of their good fare. But when the heat became still greater and they wanted to go out, but found the doors and windows fastened, then they knew that the king was trying to bake them.

'But he shall not succeed!' cried he of the little hat. 'I will make a frost come which shall make the fire ashamed and die out!'

So he put his hat on straight, and at once there came such a frost that all the heat disappeared and the food on the dishes began to freeze. When a couple of hours had passed, and the king thought they must be quite dead from the heat, he had the doors opened and went in himself to see. But when the doors were opened, there stood all six, alive and well, saying they were glad they could come out to warm themselves, for the great cold in the room had frozen all the food hard in the dishes. Then the king went angrily to the cook and scolded him and asked him why he had not done what he was told. But the cook answered, 'There is heat enough there; see for yourself.' Then the king saw a huge fire burning under the iron room and understood that he could do no harm to the six in this way. The king now began again to think how he could free himself from his unwelcome guests. He commanded the master to come before him, and said:

'If you will take gold and give up your right to my daughter, you shall have as much as you like.'

'Oh, yes, Your Majesty,' answered he, 'give me as much as my servant can carry, and I will give up your daughter.

The king was delighted, and the man said, 'I will come and fetch it in fourteen days.'

Then the master called all the tailors in the kingdom to-gether and made them sit down for fourteen days sewing a

sack. When it was finished, he made the strong man who had
uprooted the trees take the sack on his shoulder and go with
him to the king.

The king said, 'What a powerful fellow that is, carrying on
his shoulder a bale of linen as large as a house!' He was much
frightened, and thought, What a lot of gold he will make
away with! Then he had a ton of gold brought, which sixteen
of the strongest men had to carry; but the strong man seized
it with one hand and put it in the sack, saying, 'Why don't
you bring me more? That scarcely covers the bottom!' The
king had to send again and again to fetch his treasures. The
strong man shoved it all into the sack, and the sack was only
half full.

'Bring more,' he cried, 'these crumbs don't fill it!' So seven
thousand wagons filled with all the gold of the whole kingdom
were driven up, and these the strong man shoved into the
sack, oxen and all.

'I will no longer be particular,' he said, 'and will take what
comes so the sack shall be full.'

When everything was put in and there was not yet enough,
he said, 'I will make an end of this; it is easy to fasten a sack
when it is not full.' Then he threw it on his back and went
with his companions.

Now, when the king saw how a single man was carrying
away the wealth of the whole country he was very angry. He
made his cavalry mount and pursue the six and bring back
the strong man with the sack. Two regiments soon overtook
them, and called, 'You are prisoners! Lay down the sack of
gold or you shall be cut down.'

'What do you say?' said the blower. 'We are prisoners?
Before that, you shall dance in the air!'

And he held one nostril and blew with the other. The two regiments were separated and blown away in the blue sky over the mountains, one this way, and the other that. A sergeant-major cried for mercy, saying he had nine wounds, and was a brave fellow, and did not deserve this disgrace. So the blower let him off, and he came down without hurt. Then he said to the sergeant-major:

'Now go home to the king, and say that if he sends any more cavalry I will blow them all into the air.'

When the king received the message, he said, 'Let the fellows go, they are bewitched.'

Then the six brought the treasure home, shared it among themselves, and lived contentedly till the end of their days.

The Wizard King

Ⅰ N VERY ANCIENT TIMES
there lived a king whose power lay not only in the vast extent
of his dominions, but also in the magic secrets of which he
was master. After spending the greater part of his early youth
in pleasure, he met a princess of such remarkable beauty that
he at once asked her hand in marriage and, having obtained it,
considered himself the happiest of men.

After a year's time a son was born, worthy in every way, and
much admired by the whole court. As soon as the queen
thought him strong enough for a journey she set out with him
secretly to visit her fairy godmother, because the fairy had
warned the queen that the king was a magician. As from time
immemorial there had been a standing feud between the fairies
and the wizards, the king might not have approved of his
wife's visit.

The fairy godmother took the deepest interest in all the
queen's concerns and was much pleased with the little prince.
She endowed him with the power of pleasing everybody, as
well as with a wonderful ease in learning everything to make
him a perfectly accomplished prince. Accordingly, he was
the delight of his teachers, surpassing everyone's expectations.

Before he was many years old, however, he had the great sorrow of losing his mother. Her last words advised him never to undertake anything of importance without consulting the fairy.

The prince's grief at the death of his mother was great, but it was nothing compared to that of the king, his father. Neither time nor reason seemed to lighten his sorrow, and the sight of all the familiar faces and things about him only served to remind him of his loss. The king therefore resolved to travel for change. By means of his magic he was able to visit every country he came to see under different shapes, returning every few weeks to the place where he had left a few followers.

Having travelled from land to land in this fashion, it occurred to him to take the form of an eagle. In this shape he flew across many countries and came at length to a lovely spot, where the air seemed filled with the scent of jessamine and orange flowers with which the ground was thickly planted. Attracted by the sweet perfume he flew lower and perceived some large and beautiful gardens filled with the rarest flowers and with fountains throwing up their clear waters into the air in a hundred different shapes. A wide stream flowed through the garden, and on it floated richly ornamented barges and gondolas filled with people dressed in the most elegant manner and covered with jewels.

In one of these barges sat the queen of that country with her only daughter, a maiden more beautiful than the day star, and attended by the ladies of the court. No more exquisitely lovely mortal was ever seen than this princess, and it needed all an eagle's strength of sight to prevent the king being hopelessly dazzled. He perched on the top of a large orange tree, whence he was able to survey the scene and to gaze at pleasure on the princess's charms.

An eagle with a king's heart is apt to be bold

Now, an eagle with a king's heart in his breast is apt to be bold, and accordingly he made up his mind to carry off the lovely damsel, feeling sure that having once seen her he could not live without her.

He waited till he saw her in the act of stepping ashore when, suddenly swooping down, he carried her off before her equerry in attendance had advanced to offer her his hand. The princess on finding herself in an eagle's talons uttered the most heart-breaking shrieks and cries. But her captor, though touched by her distress, would not abandon his lovely prey and continued to fly through the air too fast to allow of his saying anything to comfort her.

At length, when he thought they had reached a safe distance, he began to lower his flight and gradually descending to earth deposited his burden in a flowery meadow. He then entreated her pardon for his violence and told her that he was about to carry her to a great kingdom over which he ruled and where he desired she should rule with him, adding many tender and consoling expressions.

For some time the princess remained speechless; but recovering herself a little, she burst into a flood of tears. The king, much moved, said:

'Adorable Princess, dry your tears. I implore you. My only wish is to make you the happiest person in the world.'

'If you speak truth, my lord,' replied the princess, 'restore me to my home. Otherwise I can only look on you as my worst enemy.'

The king retorted that her opposition filled him with despair, but he hoped to carry her to a place where all would respect her, and give her every pleasure. So saying, he seized her once more and, in spite of all her cries, rapidly bore her off to the neighbourhood of his capital. Here he gently placed her on a lawn, and as he did so she saw a magnificent palace spring up at her feet. The architecture was imposing, the interior of the rooms handsome and furnished in the best possible taste.

The princess was pleased to find herself surrounded by a number of pretty girls, all anxious to wait on her, while a brilliantly coloured parrot said the most agreeable things in the world.

The king resumed his own form and might well have pleased any other than this princess, who could only regard him with feelings of hatred, which she was at no pains to conceal. The king hoped, however, that time would soften her anger. He took the precaution of surrounding the palace with a dense cloud, and then hastened to his court, where his prolonged absence was causing much anxiety.

The prince and all the courtiers were delighted to see their beloved king again, but they had to submit to more frequent absences than ever on his part. He made business a pretext for shutting himself up in his study, but it was really in order to fly off and spend the time with the princess, who remained obdurate.

The king began to fear that in spite of all his precautions, she might have heard of the prince his son, whose goodness, youth and beauty made him adored at court. This idea made him uneasy, and he resolved to send the prince on his travels escorted by a magnificent retinue.

The prince, after visiting several courts, arrived at the one where the lost princess was still deeply mourned. The king and queen received him most graciously, and some festivities were revived to do him honour.

One day when the prince was visiting the queen in her own apartments he was much struck by a beautiful portrait. He eagerly inquired whose it was, and the queen, with many tears, told him it was all that was left her of her beloved daughter, who had suddenly been carried off, she knew neither where nor how.

The prince was deeply moved and vowed that he would search the world for the princess. The queen assured him of her eternal gratitude and promised, should he succeed, to give him her daughter in marriage, together with all the estates she herself owned.

The prince, far more attracted by thoughts of possessing the princess than her promised dower, set forth on his quest after taking leave of the king and queen, who gave him a miniature of their daughter. His first act was to seek the fairy under whose protection he had been placed, and implore her assistance and counsel in this important matter.

After listening attentively to the whole adventure, the fairy asked for time to consult her books. She informed the prince that the object of his search was not far distant but it was too difficult for him to enter the enchanted palace where she was, as the king his father had surrounded it with a thick cloud, and that they must gain possession of the princess's parrot. This, she added, did not appear impossible, as it often flew about in the neighbourhood.

The fairy went out and soon returned with the bird in her hand. She promptly shut it up in a cage and, touching the prince with her wand, transformed him into an exactly similar parrot; after which, she instructed him how to reach the princess.

The prince reached the palace in safety, but was so dazzled at first by the princess's beauty, which far surpassed her portrait, that he was quite dumb. The princess was surprised and anxious, and fearing the parrot, who was her greatest comfort, had fallen ill, she took him in her hand and caressed him.

This soon reassured the prince and encouraged him to play his part well.

Presently the king appeared, and the parrot noticed with joy how much he was disliked. As soon as the king left, the princess retired to her dressing room; the parrot flew after her and overheard her lamentations at the continued persecutions of the king, who had pressed her to consent to their marriage. The parrot said so many clever and tender things to comfort her that she began to doubt whether this could indeed be her own parrot. When he saw her well-disposed toward him, he exclaimed:

'Madam, I have a most important secret to confide to you, and I beg you not to be alarmed by what I am about to say. I am here on behalf of the queen your mother, and to deliver Your Highness. Behold this portrait the queen, your mother, gave me.'

The princess's surprise was great, but after what she had seen and heard it was impossible not to hope, for she had recognized the likeness of herself which her mother always wore.

When he found her listening attentively to him, he implored the princess to allow him to resume his natural shape. She did not speak, so he drew a feather from his wing, and she beheld before her a prince of such surpassing beauty it was impossible not to hope she might owe her liberty to so charming a person.

Meantime the fairy had prepared a chariot, to which she harnessed two powerful eagles. Then placing in it the cage, with the parrot, she charged the bird to conduct the chariot to the window of the princess's dressing room. This was done in a few minutes, and the princess, stepping into the chariot with the prince, was delighted to find her parrot again.

As they rose through the air the princess remarked a figure

mounted on an eagle's back flying in front of the chariot. She was rather alarmed, but the prince reassured her, telling her it was the good fairy to whom she owed so much and who was now conducting her in safety to her mother.

That same morning the king awoke suddenly from a troubled sleep. He had dreamed the princess was being carried off and, transforming himself into an eagle, he flew to the palace. When he failed to find her he flew into a terrible rage and hastened home to consult his books, by which means he discovered that it was his son who had deprived him of this precious treasure. Immediately he took the shape of a harpy and, filled with rage, was determined to devour his son and the princess too, if only he could overtake them.

He set out at full speed; but he started too late and was further delayed by a strong wind which the fairy raised behind the young couple so as to baffle any pursuit.

With what rapture the queen received the daughter she had given up for lost, as well as the amiable prince who had rescued her! The fairy entered with them and warned the queen that the wizard king would shortly arrive, infuriated by his loss, and that nothing could preserve the prince and princess from his rage and magic unless they were actually married.

The queen hastened to inform the king, her husband, and the wedding took place on the spot.

As the ceremony was completed the wizard king arrived. His despair at being too late so bewildered him that he appeared in his natural form and attempted to sprinkle a black liquid over the bride and bridegroom, which was intended to bewitch them, but the fairy stretched out her wand on the magician himself. He fell down senseless, and the princess's father, deeply offended, ordered him removed and locked up in prison.

Now as magicians lose all their power as soon as they are in prison, the king felt himself much embarrassed at being thus at the mercy of those he had so greatly wronged. The prince implored and obtained his father's pardon, and the prison doors were opened. But no sooner was this done than the wizard king took the form of some unknown bird, exclaiming as he flew off that he would never forgive either his son or the fairy the cruel wrong they had done him.

Everyone entreated the fairy to settle in the kingdom where she now was, to which she consented. She built herself a magnificent palace, to which she transported her books and fairy secrets, and where she enjoyed the sight of the perfect happiness she had helped to bestow on the entire royal family.

[From *Les Fées Illustrés.*]

The Nixy

THERE WAS ONCE UPON
a time a miller who was very well off. He had as much money
and goods as he knew what to do with. But sorrow comes in
the night, and the miller all of a sudden became so poor that
at last he could hardly call his mill his own. He wandered
about all day in despair and misery, and when he lay down
at night he could get no rest but lay awake for hours sunk in
sorrowful thoughts.

One morning he rose before dawn and went outside, for he
thought his heart would be lighter in the open air. As he
wandered up and down on the banks of the millpond he heard
a rustling in the water, and when he looked closely he saw a
woman rising up from the waves.

He realized at once that this could be none other than the
nixy of the millpond, and in his terror he didn't know if he
should fly away or remain where he was. While he hesitated,
the nixy spoke, called him by his name and asked him why
he was so sad.

When the miller heard how friendly her tone was, he plucked
up heart and told her how rich and prosperous he had been

all his life, when now he didn't know what to do for want and misery.

Then the nixy spoke comforting words to him and promised that she would make him richer and more prosperous than he had ever been in his life before, if he would give her in return the youngest thing in his house.

The miller thought she must mean one of his puppies or kittens, so he promised at once what the nixy asked and returned to his mill full of hope. On the threshold he was greeted with the news that his wife had just given birth to a boy.

The poor miller was horrified by these tidings, and went in with a heavy heart to tell his wife and his relations of the fatal bargain he had just made with the nixy. 'I would gladly give up all the good fortune she promised me,' he said, 'if I could only save my child.' But no one could think of any advice to give him beyond taking care that the child never went near the millpond.

The boy throve and grew big, and in the meantime all prospered with the miller and in a few years he was richer than he had ever been before. But he did not enjoy his good fortune, for he could not forget his compact with the nixy, and he knew that sooner or later she would demand his fulfilment of it. But year after year went by, and the boy grew up and became a great hunter, and the lord of the land took him into his service, for he was smart and bold. In a short time he married a pretty young wife and lived with her in great peace and happiness.

One day when he was out hunting, a hare sprang up at his feet and ran for some way in front of him in the open field. The hunter pursued it hotly for a time and at last shot it dead.

Then he proceeded to skin it, never noticing that he was close to the millpond, which from childhood he had been taught to avoid. He soon finished the skinning and went to the water to wash the blood off his hands. He had hardly dipped them in the pond when the nixy rose up in the water and, seizing him in her wet arms, dragged him down under the waves.

When the hunter did not come home in the evening his wife grew very anxious, and when his game bag was found close to the millpond she guessed at once what had befallen him. She was nearly beside herself with grief, and roamed round and round the pond, calling on her husband without ceasing. At last, worn out with sorrow and fatigue, she fell asleep and dreamed that she was wandering along a flowery meadow, when she came to a hut where she found an old witch, who promised to restore her husband to her.

When she awoke next morning she determined to set out and find the witch; so she wandered on for many a day and at last reached the flowery meadow and the hut where the old witch lived. The poor wife told her all that had happened and how she had been told in a dream of the witch's power to help her.

The witch counselled her to go to the pond the first time there was a full moon and to comb her black hair with a golden comb and then to place the comb on the bank. The hunter's wife gave the witch a handsome present, thanked her heartily and returned home.

Time dragged heavily till the time of the full moon, but it came at last, and as soon as it rose the young wife went to the pond, combed her black hair with a golden comb and, when she had finished, placed the comb on the bank. Then she watched the water impatiently. Soon she heard a rushing sound, and a big wave rose suddenly and swept the comb off the bank, and a moment afterward the head of her husband rose from the pond and gazed sadly at her. But immediately another wave came, and the head sank back into the water without having said a word. The pond lay still and motionless, glittering in the moonshine, and the hunter's wife was not a bit better off than she had been before.

In despair she wandered about for days and nights, and at last, worn out by fatigue, she sank once more into a deep sleep and dreamed exactly the same dream about the old witch. So next morning she went again to the flowery meadow and sought the witch in her hut and told her of her grief. The old woman counselled her to go to the millpond the next full moon and play upon a golden flute and then to lay the flute on the bank.

As soon as the next moon was full the hunter's wife went to the millpond, played on a golden flute and when she had finished placed it on the bank. Then a rushing sound was heard, and a wave swept the flute off the bank, and soon the head of the hunter appeared and rose up higher and higher till he was half out of the water. Then he gazed sadly at his wife and stretched out his arms toward her. But another rushing wave rose and dragged him under once more. The hunter's wife, who had stood on the bank full of joy and hope, sank into despair when she saw her husband snatched away again before her eyes.

But for her comfort she dreamed the same dream a third time and betook herself once more to the old witch's hut in the flowery meadow. This time the old woman told her to go the next full moon to the millpond and to spin there with a golden spinning wheel and then to leave the spinning wheel on the bank.

The hunter's wife did as she was advised, and the first night the moon was full she sat and spun with a golden spinning wheel and then left the wheel on the bank. In a few minutes a rushing sound was heard on the waters, and a wave swept the spinning wheel from the bank. Immediately the head of the hunter rose up from the pond, getting higher and higher each moment, till at length he stepped on to the bank and fell on his wife's neck.

But the waters of the pond rose up suddenly, overflowed the bank where the couple stood and dragged them under the flood. In her despair the young wife called on the old witch to help her, and in a moment the hunter was turned into a frog and his wife into a toad. But they were not able to remain together, for the water tore them apart, and when the flood was over, though both resumed their own shapes again, the hunter and the hunter's wife found themselves each in a strange country, and neither knew what had become of the other.

The hunter determined to become a shepherd, and his wife

became a shepherdess. So they herded their sheep for many years in solitude and sadness.

Now it happened once that the shepherd came to the country where the shepherdess lived. The neighbourhood pleased him, and he saw that the pasture was rich and suitable for his flocks. He brought his sheep there and herded them as before. The shepherd and shepherdess became great friends, but they did not recognize each other in the least.

One evening, when the moon was full, they sat together watching their flocks, and the shepherd played upon his flute. Then the shepherdess thought of that evening when she had sat by the millpond and had played on the golden flute; the recollection was too much for her, and she burst into tears. The shepherd asked her why she was crying and left her no peace till she told him all her story.

Then the scales fell from the shepherd's eyes, and he recognized his wife, and she him. So they returned joyfully to their own home and lived in peace and happiness ever afterward.

[From the German. Kletke.]

The Glass Mountain

ONCE UPON A TIME there was a glass mountain, on the top of which stood a castle made of pure gold, and in front of the castle grew an apple tree on which there were golden apples. Anyone who picked an apple gained admittance into the golden castle, and there in a silver room sat an enchanted princess of surpassing fairness and beauty. She was as rich as she was beautiful, for the cellars of the castle were full of precious stones, and great chests of the finest gold stood round the walls of all the rooms.

Many knights had come from afar to try their luck, but it was in vain they attempted to climb the mountain. In spite of having their horses shod with sharp nails, no one managed to get more than halfway up, and then they all fell back right down to the bottom of the steep slippery hill. Some broke an arm, some a leg, and many a brave man had broken his neck.

The beautiful princess sat at her window and watched the bold knights trying to reach her on their splendid horses. The sight of her always gave men fresh courage, and they flocked from the four quarters of the globe to attempt her rescue. But all in vain, and for seven years the princess had sat waiting for someone to scale the glass mountain.

A heap of corpses both of riders and horses lay round the mountain, and many dying men lay groaning there unable to go any farther with their wounded limbs. The whole neighbourhood had the appearance of a vast churchyard. In three more days the seven years would be at an end, when a knight in golden armour and mounted on a spirited steed was seen making his way toward the fatal hill.

Spurring his horse he made a rush at the mountain, and got up halfway, then he calmly turned his horse's head and came down again without a slip or stumble. The following day he started in the same way; the horse trod on the glass as if it had been level earth and sparks of fire flew from its hoofs. All the other knights gazed in astonishment, for he had almost gained the summit and in another moment he would have reached the apple tree. But of a sudden a huge eagle rose up and spread its mighty wings, hitting as it did so the knight's horse in the eye. The beast shied, opened its wide nostrils and tossed its mane, then rearing high up in the air, its hind feet slipped and it fell with its rider down the steep mountainside. Nothing was left of either of them except their bones, which rattled in the battered and broken golden armour like dry peas in a pod.

And now there was only one more day before the close of the seven years. Then there arrived on the scene a mere schoolboy—a merry, happy-hearted youth, but at the same time strong and well-grown. He saw how many knights had broken their necks in vain, but undaunted he approached the steep mountain on foot and began the ascent.

For long he had heard his parents speak of the beautiful princess in the golden castle at the top of the glass mountain. He listened to all he heard and determined that he too would try his luck. But first he went to the forest and caught a lynx and, cutting off the creature's sharp claws, he fastened them on to his own hands and feet.

Armed with these weapons he boldly started up the glass mountain. The sun was going down, and the youth was not more than halfway up. He could hardly draw breath he was so worn out, and his mouth was parched by thirst. A huge black cloud passed over his head, but in vain did he beg and beseech it to let a drop of water fall on him. He opened his mouth, but the black cloud sailed past and not as much as a drop of dew moistened his dry lips.

His feet were torn and bleeding, and he could only hold on now with his hands. Evening closed in, and he strained his eyes to see if he could behold the top of the mountain. Then he gazed beneath him, and what a sight met his eyes! A yawning abyss, with certain and terrible death at the bottom, reeking with half-decayed bodies of horses and riders! And this had been the end of all the other brave men who like himself had attempted the ascent.

It was almost dark now, and only the stars lit up the glass mountain. The poor boy still clung on as if glued to the glass by his blood-stained hands. He made no struggle to get higher, for all his strength had left him, and seeing no hope he calmly awaited death. Then all of a sudden he fell into a deep sleep, and forgetful of his dangerous position, he slumbered sweetly. But all the same, although he slept, his sharp claws held so firmly in the glass that he was quite sure not to fall.

Now the golden apple tree was guarded by the eagle which had overthrown the golden knight and his horse. Every night it flew round the glass mountain keeping a careful lookout, and no sooner had the moon emerged from the clouds than the bird rose up from the apple tree and, circling round in the air, caught sight of the sleeping youth.

Greedy for carrion, the bird swooped down upon the boy. But he was awake now, and perceiving the eagle, he determined by its help to save himself.

The eagle dug its sharp claws into the tender flesh of the youth, but he bore the pain without a sound and seized the bird's two feet with his hands. The creature in terror lifted him high up into the air and began to circle round the tower of the castle. The youth held on bravely. He saw the glittering palace, which by the pale rays of the moon looked like a dim lamp; and he saw the high windows and round one of them a balcony in which the beautiful princess sat lost in sad thoughts. Then the boy saw that he was close to the apple tree and, drawing a small knife from his belt, he cut off both the eagle's feet. The bird rose up in the air in its agony and vanished into the clouds, and the youth fell on to the broad branches of the apple tree.

Then he drew out the claws of the eagle's feet that had remained in his flesh and put the peel of one of the golden apples on the wound, and in one moment it was healed and well again. He picked several of the beautiful apples and put them in his pocket; then he entered the castle. The door was guarded by a great dragon, but as soon as he threw an apple at it, the beast vanished.

At the same moment a gate opened, and the youth perceived a courtyard full of flowers and beautiful trees, and on a balcony sat the lovely enchanted princess with her retinue.

As soon as she saw the youth, she ran toward him and greeted him as her husband and master. She gave him all her treasures, and the youth became a rich and mighty ruler. But he never returned to earth, for only the mighty eagle, who had been the guardian of the princess and of the castle, could have carried on his wings the enormous treasure down to the world. But as the eagle had lost its feet, it died; and its body was found in a wood on the glass mountain.

ONE DAY when the youth was strolling in the palace garden with the princess, his wife, he looked down over the edge of the glass mountain and saw to his astonishment a great number of people gathered there. He blew his silver whistle, and the swallow who acted as messenger in the golden castle flew past.

'Fly down and ask what the matter is,' he said to the little bird, who sped off like lightning and soon returned saying:

'The blood of the eagle has restored all the people below to

life. All those who have perished on this mountain are awaken-
ing today, as it were from a sleep, and are mounting their
horses, and the whole population are gazing on this unheard-of
wonder with joy and amazement.'

[From the Polish. Kletke.]

The Green Monkey

ANY YEARS AGO
there lived a king, who was twice married. His first wife, a
good and beautiful woman, died at the birth of her little son,
and the king her husband was so overwhelmed with grief at
her loss that his only comfort was in the sight of his heir.

When the time for the young prince's christening came the
king chose as godmother a neighbouring princess, so celebrated
for her wisdom and goodness that she was commonly called
'the Good Queen.' She named the baby Alphege, and from
that moment took him to her heart.

Time wipes away the greatest grief, and after two or three
years the king married again. His second wife was a princess
of undeniable beauty, but by no means of amiable disposition.
In due time a second prince was born, and the queen was devoured with rage at the thought that Prince Alphege came
between her son and the throne. She took care however to
conceal her jealous feelings from the king.

At length she sent a trusty servant to her old and faithful
friend, the Fairy of the Mountain, to beg her to devise some
means by which she might get rid of her stepson. The fairy
replied that, much as she desired to aid the queen in every

way, it was impossible for her to attempt anything against the young prince, for he was under the protection of some greater power than her own.

The Good Queen on her side watched carefully over her godson, although from a distance, her own country being a remote one. But she was well informed of all that went on and knew all about the queen's wicked designs. She therefore sent the prince a large and splendid ruby; he was to wear it night and day as it would protect him from all attacks, but the talisman only retained its power as long as the prince remained within his father's dominions. The wicked queen, knowing this, made every attempt to get the prince out of the country, but her efforts failed, till one day accident did what she was unable to accomplish.

The king had an only sister who was deeply attached to him and who was married to the sovereign of a distant country. She entreated the king to allow the prince to visit her, and after some hesitation, which was ridiculed by his wife, he finally consented.

Prince Alphege was at this time fourteen years old, and the handsomest and most engaging youth imaginable. In his infancy he had been placed in the charge of one of the great ladies of the court who, according to the prevailing custom, acted first as his head nurse and then as his governess. When he outgrew her care her husband was appointed as his tutor and governor and so he had never been separated from this excellent couple, who loved him as tenderly as they did their only daughter Zayda and were warmly loved by him in return.

When the prince set forth on his travels it was but natural this devoted couple should accompany him, and accordingly they started, attended by a numerous retinue. For some time all went well; but soon after passing the frontier they had to cross a desert plain under a burning sun. They were glad to take shelter under a group of trees, and here the prince complained of burning thirst.

A tiny stream ran close by and some water was soon procured, but no sooner had he tasted it than he disappeared in a moment. In vain did his anxious followers seek for him, he was nowhere to be found.

The courtiers were sadly perplexed, but as all their efforts to find the prince were useless they had no choice but to go home, bringing with them the sad news, which so greatly distressed the king that he fell ill and died not long after.

The queen, whose ambition was boundless, was delighted to see the crown on her son's head and to have the power in her own hands. Her hard rule made her very unpopular, and it was commonly believed that she had made away with Prince Alphege. Indeed, had the king her son not been deservedly beloved a revolution would certainly have come.

Meantime the former governess of Prince Alphege, who was now widowed, retired to her own house with her daughter Zayda, who grew up a lovely and most lovable girl, and both continued to mourn the loss of their dear prince.

The young king was devoted to hunting, and often enjoyed his favourite pastime, attended by the noblest youths in his kingdom. One day, after a long morning's chase, he stopped to rest near a brook in the shade of a little wood. While at luncheon he spied a little monkey of the brightest green sitting on a tree and gazing so tenderly at him that he felt quite moved. He forbade his courtiers to frighten him, and the monkey sprang from bough to bough and at length approached the king, who offered him some food. The monkey took it daintily and finally came to the table. The king took him on his knees and, delighted with his capture, brought him home

While at luncheon he spied a little green monkey

with him. He would trust no one else with his care, and the whole court soon talked of nothing but the pretty green monkey.

One morning, as Prince Alphege's governess and her daughter were alone together, the little monkey sprang in through an open window. He had escaped from the palace, and his manners were so gentle and caressing that he had quite won their hearts when the king discovered where he was and sent to fetch him back. But the monkey made such piteous cries when anyone attempted to catch him, that the two ladies begged the king to leave him a little longer with them, to which he consented.

One evening, as they sat by the fountain in the garden, the little monkey kept gazing at Zayda with such sad and loving eyes that she and her mother could not think what to make of it, and they were still more surprised when they saw big tears rolling down his cheeks.

The mother said, 'My dear child, I cannot get the thought out of my mind that the green monkey is our beloved Prince Alphege, transformed in this strange fashion. I know the idea sounds wild, but I cannot get it out of my heart, and it leaves me no peace.'

As she spoke she glanced up. The little monkey's gestures seemed to confirm her words.

The following night she dreamed that she saw the Good Queen, who said, 'Do not weep any longer but follow my directions. Go into your garden and lift up the little marble slab at the foot of the great myrtle tree. You will find beneath it a crystal vase filled with a bright green liquid. Take it and place the thing most in your thoughts in a bath filled with roses and rub it well with the green liquid.'

At these words the sleeper awoke and lost no time in hurry-

ing to the garden, where she found all as the Good Queen
had described. Then she hastened to rouse her daughter and
together they prepared the bath, for they would not let their
women know what they were about. Zayda gathered quantities
of roses, and when all was ready they put the monkey into a
large jasper bath, where the mother rubbed him all over with
the green liquid.

Suddenly the monkey skin dropped off, and there stood
Prince Alphege, the handsomest and most charming of men.
Their joy was beyond words. After a time the ladies begged
the prince to relate his adventures, and he told them of all his
sufferings. His only comfort had been the Good Queen, who
had at length put him in the way of meeting his brother.

Several days were spent in these interesting conversations,
but at length Zayda's mother began to think of the best means
for placing the prince on the throne, which was his by right.

The queen was feeling very anxious. She had felt sure from
the first that her son's pet monkey was no other than Prince
Alphege, and her suspicions were confirmed by the Fairy of
the Mountain. She hastened in tears to the king, her son.

'I am informed,' she cried, 'that some ill-disposed people
have raised up an impostor in the hopes of dethroning you.
You must at once have him put to death.'

The king, who was very brave, assured the queen that he
would soon punish the conspirators. He made careful inquiries
and thought it hardly probable that a quiet widow and a young
girl would be plotting a revolution. One night, without saying
anything to the queen or his ministers, he set out for the palace
where Zayda and her mother lived, attended only by a small
band of followers.

The two ladies were at the moment deep in conversation

with Prince Alphege and, hearing a knocking so late at night, begged him to keep out of sight. What was their surprise when the door was opened to see the king and his suite!

'I know,' said the king, 'that you are plotting against my crown and person, and I have come for an explanation.'

As she was about to answer, Prince Alphege came forward and said, 'It is from me you must ask it, brother.' He spoke with such grace and dignity that everyone gazed at him with mute surprise.

At length the king, recovering from his astonishment exclaimed, 'Yes, you are indeed my brother and, now that I have found you, take the throne to which I have no longer a right.' So saying, he respectfully kissed the prince's hand.

Alphege threw himself into his arms, and the brothers hastened to the royal palace, where in the presence of the entire court he received the crown from his brother's hand. To clear away any possible doubt, he showed the ruby which the Good Queen had given him in his childhood. As they were gazing at it, it suddenly split with a loud noise, and at the same moment the wicked queen expired.

King Alphege lost no time in marrying his dear and lovely Zayda, and his joy was complete when the Good Queen appeared at his wedding. After spending some time with the young couple and bestowing the most costly presents on them, she retired to her own country.

King Alphege insisted on his brother sharing his throne, and they all lived to a good old age, universally beloved and admired.

Fairer-than-a-Fairy

ONCE THERE LIVED A king who had no children for many years after his marriage. At length Heaven granted him a daughter of such remarkable beauty that he could think of no name so appropriate for her as 'Fairer-than-a-Fairy.'

It never occurred to the good-natured monarch that such a name was certain to call down on the child the hatred and jealousy of the fairies, but this was what happened. No sooner had they heard of this presumptuous name than they resolved either to torment the princess cruelly or at least conceal her from the eyes of men.

The eldest of their tribe was to carry out their revenge. This fairy was named Lagree. She was so old she only had one eye and one tooth left. She was so spiteful that she gladly devoted her time to carrying out all the mean or ill-natured tricks of the whole body of fairies.

She found but little difficulty in carrying off Fairer-than-a-Fairy. The poor child, who was only seven years old, nearly died of fear on finding herself in the power of this hideous creature. However, when after an hour's journey underground she found herself in a splendid palace with lovely gardens, she felt a little reassured and was further cheered when she discovered that her pet cat and dog had followed her.

The old fairy led her to a pretty room which she said should be hers, at the same time bidding her never to let the fire go out. She then gave two glass bottles into the princess's charge, desiring her to take the greatest care of them, with the most awful threats in case of disobedience. She vanished, leaving the little girl a good deal relieved at having only two apparently easy tasks set her.

Several years passed. The princess grew accustomed to her lonely life, obeyed the fairy's orders, and by degrees forgot all about the court of the king, her father.

One day, while passing near a fountain in the garden, she noticed that the sun's rays fell on the water in such a manner as to produce a brilliant rainbow. She stood still to admire it, when, to her great surprise, she heard a voice addressing her which seemed to come from the centre of its rays. The voice was that of a young man, and its sweetness of tone and the agreeable things it uttered led her to infer that its owner must be equally charming.

The beautiful rainbow informed Fairer-than-a-Fairy that he was young, the son of a powerful king, and that the Fairy Lagree, who owed his parents a grudge, had deprived him of his natural shape and had imprisoned him in the palace, where he had found his confinement hard to bear. Now, he owned, he no longer sighed for freedom since he had seen and learned to love Fairer-than-a-Fairy. He added many other tender speeches to this declaration, and the princess, to whom such remarks were new, could not help feeling pleased and touched by his attentions.

The prince could only appear or speak under the form of a

To her great surprise she heard a voice addressing her

rainbow, so the sun must shine on water to enable the rays to form themselves.

Fairer-than-a-Fairy lost no moment to meet her prince, and they enjoyed many hours together. One day, however, time passed so quickly that the princess forgot to attend to the fire, and it went out. Lagree, on her return, soon found out and ordered Fairer-than-a-Fairy to start next day at dawn to ask Locrinos for fire to relight the one she had allowed to go out. Now Locrinos was a cruel monster who devoured everyone and he especially enjoyed eating young girls.

The princess obeyed with great sweetness and, without having been able to take leave of the prince, set off to ask Locrinos for the fire. As she was crossing a wood a bird sang to her to pick up a shining pebble which she would find in a fountain close by and to use it when needed. She took the bird's advice, and in due time arrived at the house of Locrinos. Luckily she only found his wife at home, who was much struck by the princess's youth and beauty and sweet gentle manners, and still further impressed by the present of the shining pebble.

She readily let Fairer-than-a-Fairy have the fire, and in return for the stone she gave her another which, she said, might prove useful some day. Then she sent the princess away without doing her any harm.

Lagree was as much surprised as displeased at the happy result of this expedition, and Fairer-than-a-Fairy waited anxiously to tell Prince Rainbow of her adventures. She found, however, that he had already been told about them by a fairy to whom he was related.

The dread of danger to his beloved princess made him devise a better meeting place than the garden fountain. Every morning Fairer-than-a-Fairy placed a large basin full of water on her window sill, and as soon as the sun's rays fell on the water the rainbow appeared as clearly as it had in the fountain. By this means they were able to meet without losing sight of the fire or of the two bottles the old fairy had placed in her care, and for some time they enjoyed every hour of sunshine together.

One day Prince Rainbow heard that he was to be banished from this lovely spot, but he had no idea where he was to go. The poor young couple were in despair, and only parted with the last rays of sunshine, and in hopes of meeting next morning. Alas, next day was dark and gloomy, and it was only late in the afternoon that the sun broke through the clouds for a few minutes.

Fairer-than-a-Fairy eagerly ran to the window, but in her haste she upset the basin and spilled the water with which she had carefully filled it overnight. No other water was at hand except that in the two bottles. It was the only chance of seeing her lover before they were separated, and she did not hesitate to break the bottles and pour their contents into the basin, when the rainbow appeared at once. Their farewells were full of tenderness; the prince made the most ardent and sincere protestations. He would try to deliver his dear Fairer-than-a-Fairy from her captivity, and implored her to consent to their marriage as soon as they should both be free. The princess, on her side, vowed to have no other husband and declared herself willing to brave death itself in order to rejoin him.

They were not allowed much time for their adieus. The rainbow vanished, and the princess, resolved to run all risks, started off at once, taking nothing with her but her dog, her cat, a sprig of myrtle and the stone which the wife of Locrinos had given her.

When Lagree became aware of her prisoner's flight she was furious and set off in pursuit. She overtook her in a cave which the stone had formed to shelter her. The little dog who was watching her mistress promptly flew at Lagree and bit her so severely that she stumbled against a corner of the cave and broke off her only tooth. Before she had recovered from the pain and rage this caused her, the princess had time to escape. Fear gave her strength for some time, but at last she could go no farther and sank down to rest. And as she did so, the sprig of myrtle she carried touched the ground, and immediately a green and shady bower sprang up round her, in which she hoped to sleep in peace.

But Lagree had not given up her pursuit, and arrived just as Fairer-than-a-Fairy had fallen fast asleep. This time she made sure of catching her victim, but the cat spied her out and, springing from one of the boughs of the arbour, she flew at Lagree's face and tore out her only eye, thus delivering the princess forever from her persecutor.

It was with some difficulty that she dragged herself as far as a pretty little green and white house, which stood at no great distance. Here she was received by a beautiful lady dressed in green and white to match the house. She greeted the fainting princess most kindly, gave her an excellent supper, and after a long night's rest in a delightful bed told her that after many troubles she should finally attain her desire. As the green and white lady took leave of the princess she gave her a nut, telling her to open it only in the most urgent need.

After a long and tiring journey Fairer-than-a-Fairy was once more kindly received by a lady exactly like the first one who had helped her. Here again she received a present with the same injunctions, but instead of a nut this lady gave her a golden pomegranate. The mournful princess had to continue her weary way, and after many troubles and hardships she again found rest and shelter in a third house exactly similar to the two others.

These houses belonged to three sisters, all endowed with fairy gifts, and all so alike in mind and person that they wished their houses and garments to be equally alike. Their occupation was helping those in misfortune, and they were as gentle and benevolent as Lagree had been cruel and spiteful.

The third lady comforted the poor traveller, begged her not to lose heart, and assured her that her troubles should be rewarded. She accompanied her advice by the gift of a crystal smelling bottle, with strict orders to open it only in case of urgent need. Fairer-than-a-Fairy thanked her warmly and resumed her way cheered by pleasant thoughts.

After a time her road led through a wood, full of soft airs and sweet odours, and before she had gone a hundred yards she saw a wonderful silver castle suspended by strong silver chains from four of the largest trees. It was so perfectly hung that a gentle breeze rocked it sufficiently to send one pleasantly to sleep.

Fairer-than-a-Fairy felt a strong desire to enter this castle, but besides being hung a little above the ground there seemed to be neither doors nor windows. She had no doubt that the moment had come to use the nut which had been given her. She opened it, and out came a diminutive hall porter at whose belt hung a tiny chain, at the end of which was a golden key half as long as the smallest pin ever seen.

The princess climbed up one of the silver chains, holding in her hand the little porter who opened a secret door with his golden key and let her in. She entered a magnificent room lighted by gold and jewelled stars in the ceiling. In the midst of this room stood a couch, with coverlets of all the colours of the rainbow and suspended by golden cords so that it swayed with the castle in a manner which rocked its occupant delightfully to sleep. On this elegant couch lay Prince Rainbow, sunk in profound slumber, in which he had been held ever since his disappearance.

Fairer-than-a-Fairy, who now saw him for the first time in his real shape, hardly dared to gaze at him, fearing lest his appearance might not be in keeping with the voice and language which had won her heart. At the same time she could not help feeling hurt at the apparent indifference with which she was received.

She related all the dangers and difficulties she had gone through, and though she repeated the story twenty times in a loud clear voice, the prince slept on and took no heed. She then had recourse to the golden pomegranate, and on opening it found that all the seeds were little violins which at once began playing melodiously.

The prince was not completely roused, but he opened his eyes a little and looked all the handsomer.

Impatient at not being recognized, Fairer-than-a-Fairy now drew out her third present, and on opening the crystal scent bottle a little siren flew out, who silenced the violins and then sang close to the prince's ear the story of all his lady had suffered in her search for him. She added some gentle reproaches to her tale, but before she had said much he was wide awake and, transported with joy, threw himself at the princess's feet.

At the same moment the walls of the room opened out, revealing a golden throne covered with jewels. A magnificent court now began to assemble, and at the same time several elegant carriages filled with ladies in magnificent dresses drove up. In the first and most splendid of these carriages sat Prince

Rainbow's mother. She fondly embraced her son, after which she informed him that his father had been dead for some years, that the anger of the fairies was at length appeased and that he might return in peace to reign over his people, who were long-ing for his presence.

The court received the new king with joyful acclamations which would have delighted him at any other time, but all his thoughts were full of Fairer-than-a-Fairy. He was just about to present her to his mother and the court, feeling sure her charms would win all hearts, when the three green and white sisters appeared.

They declared Fairer-than-a-Fairy's royal birth, and the queen taking Prince Rainbow and Fairer-than-a-Fairy in her carriage set off with them for the capital of her kingdom.

Here they were received with tumultuous joy. The wedding was celebrated without delay, and succeeding years diminished neither the virtues, beauty, nor the mutual affection of King Rainbow and his queen, Fairer-than-a-Fairy.

The Three Brothers

THERE WAS ONCE UPON
a time a witch, who in the shape of a hawk would every night
break the windows of a certain village church. In the same
village there lived three brothers, who determined to kill the
mischievous hawk. But in vain did the two eldest mount guard.
As soon as the bird appeared high above their heads, sleep
overpowered them, and they only awoke to hear the windows
crashing in.

Then the youngest brother took his turn at guarding the
windows, and to prevent sleep he placed a lot of thorns under
his chin, so that if he felt drowsy and nodded his head, they
would prick him and keep him awake. The moon was already
risen, and it was as light as day, when suddenly he heard a
fearful noise, and at the same time his eyelids closed, and his
head sank on his shoulders.

But the thorns were so painful that he awoke at once. He
saw the hawk swooping down upon the church, and in a moment he seized his gun and shot at the bird. The hawk fell
heavily upon a big stone, severely wounded. The youth ran to
look at it and saw that a huge abyss had opened below the
stone.

He went at once to fetch his brothers, and with their help dragged pine wood and ropes to the spot. They fastened some of the burning pine wood to the end of the rope and let it slowly down to the bottom. At first it was quite dark, and the flaming torch only lit up gray stone walls. But the youngest brother determined to explore the abyss and, letting himself down by the rope, soon reached the bottom. Here he found a lovely meadow full of green trees and exquisite flowers.

In the middle of the meadow stood a huge stone castle, with its iron gate wide open. Everything in the castle was made of copper. A lovely girl was combing her golden hair; and he noticed that whenever one of her hairs fell on the ground it rang out like pure metal. The youth looked at her more closely and saw that her skin was smooth and fair, her blue eyes bright and sparkling and her hair as golden as the sun. He fell in love with her on the spot and, kneeling at her feet, implored her to become his wife.

The lovely girl accepted him gladly but warned him she could never come up to the world above till the old witch was dead. The only way the witch could be killed was with the sword hanging in the castle; but the sword was so heavy no one could lift it.

Then the youth found a room where everything was made of silver, and here he found another beautiful girl, the sister of his bride. She was combing her silver hair, and every hair that fell on the ground rang out like pure metal. The second girl handed him the sword, but though he tried with all his strength he could not lift it.

At last a third sister came to him and gave him a drop of something to drink, which she said would give him the needful strength. He drank one drop, but still he could not lift the sword; then he drank a second, and the sword began to move;

but only after he had drunk a third drop was he able to swing the sword over his head.

Then he hid himself in the castle and awaited the old witch's arrival. At last, as it was beginning to grow dark, she swooped down upon a big apple tree and, after shaking some golden apples from it, pounced down upon the earth. When her feet touched the ground she turned from a hawk into a woman. This was the moment. The youth swung his mighty sword in the air with all his strength and the witch's head fell off.

Without fear of any further danger, he packed up all the treasures of the castle in a great chest, and gave his brothers a signal to pull them up out of the abyss. First the treasures were attached to the rope and then the three lovely girls. Now everything was up above and only he remained below. As he was a little suspicious of his brothers, he fastened a heavy stone to the rope and let them pull it up. At first they heaved with a will, but when the stone was halfway up they let it drop suddenly, and it fell to the bottom and broke into a hundred pieces.

'So that's what would have happened to my bones had I trusted myself to them,' said the youth sadly. He mourned bitterly, not because of the treasures, but because of the lovely girl with her swanlike neck and golden hair.

For a long time he wandered sadly through the beautiful underworld, and one day he met a magician who asked him the cause of his sorrow. The youth told him all that had befallen him, and the magician said:

'Do not grieve, young man! Guard my children hidden in the golden apple tree, and I will bring you at once up to the earth. It is in vain that I have hidden them under the earth and locked them up in the castle. Now I have hidden them in the apple tree; hide yourself there too, and at midnight you will see my enemy.'

The youth climbed up the tree and picked some of the beautiful golden apples, which he ate for his supper.

At midnight the wind began to rise and a rustling sound was heard at the foot of the tree. The youth looked down and beheld a long thick serpent crawling up the tree. It wound itself round the trunk and gradually came higher and higher. It thrust its huge head, in which the eyes glittered fiercely, among the branches, searching for the nest in which the little children lay. They trembled with terror when they saw the hideous creature and hid themselves beneath the leaves.

Then the youth swung his mighty sword in the air and with one blow cut off the serpent's head. He cut up the rest of the body into bits and strewed them to the four winds. The father of the rescued children was so delighted over the death of his enemy that he told the youth to get on his back, and in this way he carried him up to the world above.

With what joy did he hurry now to his brothers' house! He burst into a room where they were all assembled, but no one knew who he was. Only his bride, who was serving as cook to her sisters, recognized him at once.

His brothers, who had quite believed he was dead, yielded him up his treasures at once and flew into the woods in terror. But the good youth forgave them all they had done and divided his treasures with them. Then he built himself a great castle with golden windows, and there he lived happily with his golden-haired wife till the end of their lives.

[From the Polish. Kletke.]

The Glass Axe

THERE WAS ONCE UPON
a time a king and queen who had everything they could
possibly wish for in this world except a child. At last, after
twelve years, the queen had a son; but she did not live long to
enjoy her happiness, for on the following day she died. But
before her death she called her husband to her, and said,
'Never let the child put his feet on the ground, for if he does,
he will fall into the power of a wicked fairy, who will do him
much harm.' And these were the last words the poor queen
spoke.

The boy throve and grew big, and when he was too heavy
for his nurse to carry, a chair was made for him on little wheels,
in which he could wander through the palace gardens without
help. At other times he was carried about on a litter, and he
was always carefully watched and guarded for fear he should
at any time put his feet to the ground.

But as this sort of life was bad for his health, the doctors
ordered him horse exercise, and he soon became a first-rate
rider and used to go out for long excursions on horseback,
accompanied always by his father's stud groom and a numerous
retinue.

Every day he rode through the neighbouring fields and woods and always returned home in the evening safe and well. In this way many years passed, and the prince grew to manhood, and hardly anyone remembered the queen's warning, though precautions were still taken, more from use and wont than for any other reason.

One day the prince and his suite went out for a ride in a wood where his father sometimes held a hunt. Their way led through a stream whose banks were overgrown with thick brushwood. Just as the horsemen were about to ford the river, a hare, startled by the sound of the horses' hoofs, started up from the grass and ran toward the thicket. The young prince pursued the little creature and had almost overtaken it, when the girth of his saddle suddenly broke in two and he fell heavily to the ground. No sooner had his foot touched the earth than he disappeared before the eyes of the horrified courtiers.

They sought him far and near, but all in vain, and they were forced to recognize the power of the evil fairy, against which the queen had warned them on her death bed. The king gave himself up to an old age of grief and loneliness, cherishing at the same time the hope chance might one day deliver the youth.

Hardly had the prince touched the ground than he felt himself violently seized by an unseen power and hurried away. A whole new world stretched out before him, quite unlike the one he had left. A splendid castle surrounded by a huge lake was the abode of the fairy, and the only approach to it was over a bridge of clouds. On the other side of the lake high mountains rose up, and dark woods stretched along the banks; over all hung a thick mist, and deep silence reigned everywhere.

The fairy made herself visible and, turning to the prince, told him that, unless he obeyed all her commands down to the minutest detail, he would be severely punished. Then she gave him an axe made of glass and bade him cross the bridge of clouds and go into the wood beyond and cut down all the trees there before sunset. At the same time she cautioned him with many angry words against speaking to a brown girl he would meet in the wood.

The prince listened to her words meekly, took up the glass axe, and set out for the forest. At every step he seemed to sink into the clouds, but fear gave wings to his feet, and he crossed in safety and set to work at once.

But no sooner had he struck the first blow than his axe broke into a thousand pieces against the tree. The poor youth was so terrified he did not know what to do. He wandered to and fro in the wood, not knowing where he was going, and at last, worn out by fatigue and misery, he sank on the ground and fell fast asleep.

He did not know how long he had slept when a sudden sound awoke him. Opening his eyes, he saw a brown girl standing beside him. Mindful of the fairy's warning he did not address her, but she greeted him in the most friendly manner and asked him if he were under the power of the wicked fairy. The prince nodded his head in answer.

Then the girl told him that she too was in the power of the fairy and was doomed to wander in her present guise until some youth should bear her in safety to the other side of the river which they saw in the distance, and on the other side of which the fairy's domain and power ended.

The girl's words inspired the prince with confidence and he told her his tale of woe, and ended by asking her advice.

'If you will only promise to try and free me, I will stand by you and will accomplish for you all the tasks which the witch sets you.'

Opening his eyes he saw a brown girl standing beside him

The prince promised joyfully all she asked. Then she handed him a draught to drink and very soon he sank in deep slumber.

His astonishment was great when he awoke to find the glass axe whole and unbroken at his side, and all the trees of the wood lying felled around him!

He made all haste across the bridge of clouds and told the fairy that her commands were obeyed. She was much amazed when she heard that all the wood was cut down and saw the axe unbroken in his hand. She questioned him narrowly if he had seen or spoken to the girl. But the prince said it was hard enough to cut down a wood with a glass axe without looking up from his work for a moment. Seeing she could get nothing more out of him, she gave him a little bread and water, and told him he might sleep.

Morning had hardly dawned when the fairy awoke the prince. Giving him the glass axe again she told him to cut up all the trees he had felled the day before and to put them in bundles ready for firewood. At the same time she warned him once more against speaking to the girl if he met her in the wood.

Although his task was no easier than that of the day before, the youth set out much more cheerfully, because he knew he could count on help. With quicker and lighter step he crossed the bridge of clouds, and hardly had he reached the other side than his friend stood before him and greeted him cheerfully. When she heard what the fairy demanded this time, she answered smilingly, 'Never fear,' and handed him another draught, which very soon caused the prince to sink into a deep sleep.

When he awoke everything was done. All the trees were cut up into firewood and arranged in bundles ready for use. He returned to the castle as quickly as he could. The fairy was even more amazed and asked him again if he had either seen or spoken to the girl. But the prince knew better than to tell her.

On the following day the fairy set him a third task, even harder than the other two. She told him he must build a castle on the other side of the lake, made of nothing but gold, silver and precious stones, and unless he could accomplish this within an hour the most frightful doom awaited him.

The prince heard her words without anxiety, so entirely did he rely on the help of his friend. Full of hope he hurried across the bridge, and recognized at once the spot where the castle was to stand, for spades, hammers, axes, and every other building implement lay scattered on the ground ready for the workman's hand, but of gold, silver and precious stones there was not a sign. Before the prince even had time to feel despondent the girl beckoned to him from behind a rock, where she had hidden herself for fear the fairy should catch sight of her.

But this time the fairy had watched the prince's movements from her window, and she saw him hiding himself behind the rock with the girl. She uttered a piercing shriek so that the mountains re-echoed with the sound of it, and the terrified pair had hardly dared to look out from their hiding place when the enraged woman, with her dress and hair flying in the wind, hurried over the bridge of clouds.

The prince at once gave himself up for lost, but the girl told him to be of good courage and to follow her as quickly as he could. But before they left their shelter she broke off a bit of the rock, spoke some magic words over it, and threw it toward the fairy. In a moment a palace of dazzling splendour rose round her. Its many doors and passages prevented the fairy for some time from finding her way out of it.

In the meantime the girl hurried on with the prince, hastening to reach the river. Once on the other side they would forever be out of the wicked fairy's power. But before they had gone half the way they heard the rustle of her garments.

The prince was terrified. Without giving him time to despair the girl uttered some more magic words. Immediately she herself was changed into a pond, and the prince into a duck swimming on its surface.

When the fairy saw this her rage knew no bounds, and she used all her magic to make the pond disappear. She caused a hill of sand to rise at her feet, meaning it to dry up the water at once. But the sand hill only drove the pond a little farther away, and its waters seemed to increase instead of diminishing. When the old woman saw that her powers of magic were of so little avail, she had recourse to cunning. She threw a lot of gold nuts into the pond, hoping in this way to catch the duck, but all her efforts were fruitless, for the little creature refused to let itself be caught.

Then the wicked old woman, hiding herself behind the rock which had sheltered the fugitives, waited behind it, watching carefully for the moment when the prince and the girl should resume their natural forms to continue their journey.

She had not to wait long, for as soon as the girl thought her safely out of the way, she changed herself and the prince once more into their human shape and set out cheerfully for the river. But they had not gone many steps when the wicked fairy hurried after them, a drawn dagger in her hand, and was close upon them, when suddenly, instead of the prince and the girl, she found herself in front of a great stone tower, at its entrance a huge guard.

Breathless with rage and passion, she tried to plunge her dagger into the guard's heart, but it fell shattered in pieces at her feet. In her desperation she determined to pull down the tower, and thus destroy her two victims forever. She stamped three times on the ground: the earth trembled, and the tower began to shake. As soon as the fairy saw this she retreated to some distance so as not to be hurt by its fall. But once more her scheme was doomed to failure, for hardly had she gone a yard than both tower and guard disappeared, and she found herself in a wood black as night, and full of wolves and bears and other wild animals.

Then her wrath gave place to terror, for she feared every moment to be torn in pieces by the beasts who one and all seemed to defy her power. She thought it wisest to make her way as best she could out of the forest, and then to pursue the fugitives once more and accomplish their destruction either by force or cunning.

In the meantime the prince and the girl had again assumed their natural forms, and were hurrying on as fast as they could to reach the river. But when they arrived they found there was no way in which they could cross it, and the girl's magic art seemed no longer to have any power. Then turning to the prince she said:

'The hour for my deliverance has not yet come, but as you promised to do all you could to free me, you must do exactly as I bid you now. Take this bow and arrow and kill every beast you see with them, and spare no living creature.'

With these words she disappeared, and hardly had she done so than a huge wild boar started out of a thicket and made straight for the prince. But the youth did not lose his presence of mind, and drawing his bow he pierced the beast with his arrow right through the skull. The creature fell heavily to the ground, and out of its side sprang a little hare, which ran like the wind along the river bank. The prince drew his bow once more, and the hare lay dead at his feet. But at the same moment a dove rose up in the air and circled round the prince's head in the most confiding manner. But mindful of the girl's commands, he dared not spare the little creature's life and, taking another arrow from his quiver, laid it as dead as the boar and the hare. When he went to look at the body of the bird he found instead of the dove a round white egg lying on the ground.

While he was gazing on it and wondering what it could mean, he heard the sweeping of wings above him, and looking up he saw a huge vulture with open claws swooping down upon him. In a moment he seized the egg and flung it at the bird with all his might, and lo and behold! Instead of the ugly monster the most beautiful girl he had ever seen stood before the astonished eyes of the prince.

But while all this was going on the wicked old fairy had managed to make her way out of the wood and was now using the last resource in her power to overtake the prince. As soon as she was in the open again she mounted her chariot, which was drawn by a fiery dragon, and flew through the air in it. But just as she reached the river she saw the two she was pursuing in each other's arms, swimming through the water as easily as two fishes.

Quick as lightning, and forgetful of every danger, she flew down upon them. But the waters seized her chariot and bore the wicked old woman down the stream till she was caught in some thorn bushes, where she made a good meal for the little fishes swimming about.

And so at last the prince and his lovely bride were free. They hurried as quickly as they could to the old king, who received them with joy and gladness. On the following day a most gorgeous wedding feast was held, and as far as is known the prince and his bride lived happily forever afterward.

[From the Hungarian. Kletke.]

The White Duck

ONCE UPON A TIME
a great and powerful king married a lovely princess. No couple
were ever so happy; but before their honeymoon was over they
were forced to part, for the king had to go on an expedition
to a far country and leave his young wife alone at home. Bitter
were the tears she shed. Her husband sought in vain to soothe
her with words of comfort and counsel. He warned her, above
all things, never to leave the castle, not to talk to strangers, to
beware of evil counsellors, and especially to be on her guard
against strange women. The queen promised faithfully to obey
her royal lord and master in these matters.

So when the king set out on his expedition she shut herself
up with her ladies in her own apartments and spent her time
in spinning and weaving and in thinking of her royal husband.
Often she was very sad and lonely, and it happened that one
day while she was seated at the window, letting salt tears drop
on her work, an old woman, a kind, homely-looking old body,
stepped up to the window and, leaning upon her crutch,
addressed the queen in friendly, flattering tones, saying:

'Why are you sad and cast down, fair Queen? You should
not mope all day in your rooms, but should come out into

the green garden and hear the birds sing with joy among the trees, see the butterflies fluttering above the flowers, hear the bees and insects hum and watch the sunbeams chase the dew drops through the rose leaves and in the lily cups. All the brightness outside would help to drive away your cares, O Queen.'

For long the queen resisted her coaxing words, remembering the promise she had given the king, her husband. But at last she said to herself, 'After all, what harm would it do?'

For she had no idea that the kind-looking old woman leaning on her crutch was in reality a wicked witch, who envied the queen her good fortune and was determined to ruin her. And so, in all ignorance, the queen followed her out into the garden and listened to her flattering words. Now, in the middle of the garden there was a pond of water, clear as crystal, and the old woman said to the queen:

'The day is so warm, and the sun's rays so scorching that the water in the pond looks cool and inviting. Would you not like to bathe in it, fair Queen?'

'No, I think not,' answered the queen. But the next moment she said, 'Why shouldn't I bathe in that cool, fresh water? No harm could come of it.'

And, so saying, she slipped off her robes and stepped into the water. But scarcely had her tender feet touched the cool ripples when she felt a great shove on her shoulders, and the wicked witch had pushed her into the deep water, exclaiming:

'Swim henceforth, White Duck!'

Then the witch assumed the form of the queen, decked herself out in the royal robes, and sat among the court ladies, awaiting the king's return. Suddenly the tramp of horses' hoofs was heard, and the barking of dogs, and the witch

The witch pushed her, exclaiming, 'Swim henceforth, White Duck!'

hastened forward to meet the royal carriages. Throwing her arms round the king's neck, she kissed him. In his great joy the king did not know that the woman he held in his arms was not his own dear wife but a wicked witch.

In the meantime, outside the palace walls, the poor white duck swam up and down the pond. Near it she laid three eggs, out of which there hatched one morning two little fluffy duck- lings and a little ugly drake. And the white duck brought the little creatures up, and they paddled after her in the pond and caught goldfish and hopped upon the bank and waddled about, ruffling their feathers and saying, 'Quack, quack,' as they strutted about on the green banks of the pond.

But their mother used to warn them not to stray too far, telling them that a wicked witch lived in the castle beyond the garden, adding, 'She has ruined me, and she will do her best to ruin you.'

But the young ones did not listen to their mother, and play- ing about the garden one day they strayed close up to the castle windows. The witch at once recognized them and ground her teeth with anger; but pretending to be very kind, she called them to her, joked with them, and led them into a beautiful room. There she gave them food to eat and showed them a soft cushion on which they might sleep. Then she left them and went down into the palace kitchens, where she told the servants to sharpen the knives, make a great fire ready, and hang a large kettleful of water over it.

In the meantime the two little ducklings had fallen asleep. But the little drake could not sleep, and as he lay wide awake in the night, he heard the witch come to the door and say:

'Little ones, are you asleep?'

And the little drake answered for the other two:

'We cannot sleep, we wake and weep,
Sharp is the knife, to take our life;
The fire is hot, now boils the pot,
And so we wake, and lie and quake.'

'They are not asleep yet,' muttered the witch to herself. And she walked up and down in the passage, and then came back to the door, and said:

'Little ones, are you asleep?'

And again the little drake answered for his sisters:

'We cannot sleep, we wake and weep,
Sharp is the knife, to take our life;
The fire is hot, now boils the pot,
And so we wake, and lie and quake.'

'Just the same answer,' muttered the witch; 'I think I'll go in and see.' So she opened the door gently, and seeing the two little ducklings sound asleep, she there and then killed them all.

The next morning the white duck wandered round the pond in a distracted manner, looking for her little ones. She called and she searched, but could find no trace of them. And in her heart she had a foreboding that evil had befallen them, and she fluttered up out of the water and flew to the palace. And there, laid out on the marble floor of the court, dead and stone cold, were her three children. The white duck threw herself upon them, and, covering up their little bodies with her wings, she cried:

'Quack, quack—my little loves!
Quuck, quack—my turtle doves!
I brought you up with grief and pain,
And now before my eyes you're slain.

I gave you always of the best;
I kept you warm in my soft nest.
I loved and watched you day and night—
You were my joy, my one delight.'

The king heard the sad complaint of the white duck, and called to the witch, 'Wife, what a wonder is this? Listen to that white duck.'

But the witch answered, 'My dear husband, what do you mean? There is nothing wonderful in a duck's quacking. Here, servants! Chase that duck out of the courtyard.'

But though the servants chased and chevied, they could not get rid of the duck; for she circled round and round, and always came back to the spot where her children lay, crying:

'Quack, quack—my little loves!
Quack, quack—my turtle doves!
The wicked witch your lives did take—
The wicked witch, the cunning snake.
First she stole my king away,
Then my children did she slay.
Changed me from a happy wife
To a duck for all my life.
Would I were the queen again;
Would that you had ne'er been slain.'

And as the king heard her words he began to suspect that he had been deceived, and he called out to the servants, 'Catch that duck and bring it here.' But, though they ran to and fro, the duck always fled past them and would not let herself be caught. So the king himself stepped down among them. Instantly the duck fluttered down into his hands, and as he stroked her wings she was changed into a beautiful woman, and he recognized his dear wife.

She told him that a bottle would be found in her nest in the garden, containing some drops from the spring of healing. It was brought to her; and the ducklings and the little drake were sprinkled with the water and three lovely children arose. And the king and queen were overjoyed when they saw their children, and they all lived happily together in the beautiful palace. But the wicked witch was taken by the king's command, and she came to no good end.

A Witch and her Servants

ALONG TIME AGO
there lived a king who had three sons; the eldest was called
Szabo, the second Warza, and the youngest Iwanich. One
beautiful spring morning the king was walking through his
gardens with his three sons, gazing with admiration at the
various fruit trees, some of which were a mass of blossom,
while others were bowed to the ground laden with rich fruit.

During their wanderings they came unperceived on a piece
of waste land where three splendid trees grew. The king looked
on them for a moment and then, shaking his head sadly, passed
on in silence. The sons, who could not understand why he did
this, asked him the reason for his dejection, and the king told
them as follows:

'These three trees, which I cannot see without sorrow, were
planted by me on this spot when I was a youth of twenty. A
celebrated magician, who had given the seed to my father,
promised that they would grow into the three finest trees the
world had ever seen. My father did not live to see his words
come true; but on his deathbed he bade me transplant them
here and look after them with the greatest care, which I accordingly did. At last, after the lapse of five long years, I noticed

172

some blossoms on the branches, and a few days later the most exquisite fruit my eyes had ever seen.

'I gave my head gardener the strictest orders to watch the trees carefully, for the magician had warned that if one unripe fruit were plucked from the tree, all the rest would become rotten at once. When ripe the fruit would become a golden yellow.

'Every day I gazed on the lovely fruit, which became gradually more and more tempting, and it was all I could do not to break the magician's command.

'One night I dreamed that the fruit was perfectly ripe. I ate some of it and it was more delicious than anything I had ever tasted in real life. As soon as I awoke I sent for the gardener and asked him if the fruit on the three trees had not ripened in the night to perfection.

'But instead of replying, the gardener threw himself at my feet and swore that he was innocent. He said that he had watched by the trees all night, but in spite of it and as if by magic, the beautiful trees had been robbed of all their golden fruit.

'Grieved as I was over the theft, I did not punish the gardener, of whose fidelity I was well assured, but I determined to pluck off all the fruit in the following year before it was ripe, as I had not much belief in the magician's warning.

'I carried out my intention and had all the fruit picked off the tree, but when I tasted one of the apples it was bitter and unpleasant, and the next morning the rest of the fruit had all rotted away.

'After this I had the beautiful fruit of these trees carefully guarded by my most faithful servants; but every year, on this very night, the fruit was plucked and stolen by an invisible hand, and next morning not a single apple remained on the trees. For some time past I have given up even having the trees watched.'

When the king had finished his story, Szabo, his eldest son, said to him, 'Forgive me, Father, if I say I think you are mistaken. I am sure there are many men in your kingdom who could protect these trees from the cunning arts of a thieving magician. I myself, who as your eldest son claim the first right to do so, will mount guard over the fruit this very night.'

The king consented, and as soon as evening drew on Szabo climbed up on to one of the trees, determined to protect the fruit even if it cost him his life. So he kept watch half the night; but a little after midnight he was overcome by drowsiness and fell fast asleep. He did not awake till it was bright daylight, and all the fruit on the trees had vanished.

The following year Warza, the second brother, tried his luck, but with the same result. Then it came to the turn of the third and youngest son.

Iwanich was not the least discouraged by the failure of his brothers and, when night came, climbed up the tree as they had done. The moon had risen and with her soft light lit up the whole neighbourhood, so the prince could distinguish the smallest object distinctly.

At midnight a gentle west wind shook the tree, and at the same moment a snow-white swanlike bird sank down gently on his breast. The prince hastily seized the bird's wings in his hands, when, lo! To his astonishment he found he was holding in his arms not a bird but the most beautiful girl he had ever seen.

'You need not fear Militza,' said the beautiful girl, looking at the prince with friendly eyes. 'No evil magician has robbed you of your fruit, but he stole the seed from my mother and thereby caused her death. When she was dying she bade me take the fruit from the trees every year as soon as it was ripe. This I would have done tonight too, if you had not seized me and so broken the spell I was under.'

Iwanich, prepared to meet a terrible magician and not a lovely girl, fell desperately in love with her. They spent the rest of the night in pleasant conversation, and when Militza wished to go away, he begged her not to leave him.

'I would gladly stay with you,' said Militza, 'but a wicked witch once cut off a lock of my hair when I was asleep, which has put me in her power. If morning were to find me here she would do me some harm, and you, too, perhaps.'

Having said these words, she drew a sparkling diamond ring from her finger, which she handed to the prince, saying, 'Keep this ring in memory of Militza and think of her sometimes if you never see her again. But if your love is really true, come and find me in my own kingdom. I may not show you the way there, but this ring will guide you. If you have love and courage enough to undertake this journey, whenever you come to a crossroad always look at this diamond. If it sparkles as brightly as ever go straight on, but if its lustre is dimmed choose another path.'

Then Militza kissed the prince on his forehead, and before he had time to say a word she vanished through the branches of the tree in a little white cloud.

Morning broke, and the prince returned to the palace like one in a dream, without even knowing if the fruit had been taken or not, for his whole mind was absorbed by thoughts of Militza and how he was to find her.

As soon as the head gardener saw the trees laden with ripe fruit he hastened to tell the king the joyful news. The king was beside himself for joy and hurried at once to the garden and made the gardener pick him some of the fruit. He tasted it, and found the apple as luscious as it had been in his dream. He went at once to his son Iwanich, and after embracing him tenderly and heaping praises on him, he asked him how he had succeeded in protecting the fruit from the power of the magician.

Iwanich did not want the real story known, so he muttered some sort of story, and fortunately the king's thoughts were taken up with a celebration.

The whole capital was in a stir, and everyone shared in the king's joy. The prince alone took no part in the festivities. While the king was at a banquet, Iwanich took some purses of gold and, mounting the quickest horse, sped off like the wind.

It was only on the next day that they missed him; the king was distressed at his disappearance and sent search parties all over the kingdom to look for him, but in vain, and after six months they gave him up as dead, and in another six months they had forgotten all about him. But in the meantime the prince, with the help of his ring, had made a successful journey and no evil had befallen him.

At the end of three months he came to a huge forest, which seemed to stretch out indefinitely. The prince was about to enter the wood by a little path he saw, when he heard a voice shouting to him:

'Hold, youth! Whither are you going?'

Iwanich turned round and saw a tall, gaunt-looking man, clad in miserable rags, seated at the foot of an oak tree so much the same colour as himself that it was little wonder the prince had ridden past without noticing him.

'Where else should I be going,' he said, 'than through the wood?'

'Through the wood?' said the old man in amazement. 'It's easily seen that you have heard nothing of this forest, that you rush so blindly to meet your doom. Listen to me before you ride any farther. This wood hides in its depths a countless number of the fiercest tigers, hyenas, wolves, bears and snakes and all sorts of monsters. If I were to cut you and your horse up into tiny morsels and throw them to the beasts, there wouldn't be one bit for each hundred of them. Take my advice, therefore, and if you wish to save your life follow some other path.'

The prince was taken aback by the old man's words, and considered for a minute what he should do. Then looking at his ring and, perceiving that it sparkled as brightly as ever, he called out:

'If this wood held even more terrible things I cannot help myself, for I must go through it.'

He spurred his horse and rode on; but the old beggar screamed so loudly after him that the prince turned round and rode back to the oak tree.

'I am really sorry for you,' said the beggar, 'but if you are determined to brave the dangers of the forest, let me at least give you a piece of advice to help you against these monsters.

'Take this bagful of bread crumbs and this live hare. I will make you a present of them both. But you must leave your horse behind you, for it would stumble over the fallen trees or get entangled in the briers and thorns. When you have gone about a hundred yards into the wood the wild beasts will surround you. Then you must instantly seize your bag and scatter the bread crumbs among them. They will rush to eat them and when you have scattered the last crumb lose no time in throwing the hare to them. As soon as the hare feels itself on the ground it will run away quickly and the wild beasts will turn to pursue it. In this way you will be able to get through the wood unhurt.'

Iwanich thanked the old man, dismounted and, taking the

bag and the hare in his arms, entered the forest. He had hardly
lost sight of his gaunt gray friend when he heard growls and
snarls in the thicket close to him, and before he had time to
think he found himself surrounded by the most dreadful-look-
ing creatures. On one side he saw the glittering eye of a cruel
tiger, on the other the gleaming teeth of a great wolf. Here a
huge bear growled fiercely, and there a horrible snake coiled
itself in the grass at his feet.

But Iwanich did not forget the old man's advice, and quickly
took out as many bread crumbs as he could hold in his hand
at a time. He threw them to the beasts, but soon the bag grew
lighter and lighter, and the prince began to feel frightened.
And now the last crumb was gone, and the hungry beasts
thronged round him, greedy for fresh prey. Then he seized
the hare and threw it to them.

No sooner did the little creature feel itself on the ground
than it laid back its ears and flew through the wood like an
arrow from a bow, closely pursued by the wild beasts. The
prince was left alone. He looked at his ring, and when he saw
that it sparkled as brightly as ever he went straight on through
the forest.

He had not gone very far when he saw a most extraordinary-
looking man coming toward him. He was not more than three
feet high, his legs were quite crooked, and his body was covered
with prickles like a hedgehog. Two lions walked with him,
fastened to his side by the two ends of his long beard. He
stopped the prince and asked him in a harsh voice:

'Are you the man who has just fed my bodyguard?' Iwanich
was so startled that he could hardly reply, but the little man
continued, 'I am most grateful to you for your kindness. What
can I give you as a reward?'

The lions were fastened to him by the ends of his beard

'All I ask is that I be allowed to go through this wood in safety,' replied Iwanich.

'Most certainly,' answered the little man. 'And I will give you one of my lions as a protector. But when you leave this wood and come near a palace which does not belong to my domain, let the lion go so he is not killed by an enemy.'

With these words he loosened the lion from his beard and bade the beast guard the youth carefully. With this new protector Iwanich wandered on through the forest, and though he came upon a great many more wolves, hyenas, leopards and other wild beasts, they always kept at a respectful distance.

Iwanich hurried through the wood as quickly as his legs would carry him, but hour after hour went by and not a trace of green field or human habitation met his eyes. At length, toward evening, the mass of trees grew less and through the interlaced branches a wide plain was visible.

At the exit of the wood the lion stood still and the prince took leave of him, having first thanked him warmly for his kind protection. It had become quite dark, and Iwanich was forced to wait for daylight before continuing his journey. He made himself a bed of grass and leaves, lit a fire of dry branches and slept soundly. Next morning he walked toward a beautiful white palace gleaming in the distance. In about an hour he reached the building and, opening the door, walked in. After wandering through many marble halls, he came to a huge staircase made of porphyry, leading down to a lovely garden.

The prince shouted with joy when he suddenly perceived Militza in a group of girls who were weaving wreaths of flowers with their mistress. As soon as Militza saw the prince she ran to him and embraced him tenderly.

After he had told her all his adventures, they went into the palace, where a sumptuous meal awaited them. Then the princess called her court together and introduced Iwanich to them as her future husband.

The wedding was held soon after with great pomp and magnificence. Three months of great happiness followed, when Militza received one day an invitation to visit her mother's sister. Although the princess was very unhappy at leaving her husband, she did not like to refuse the invitation and, promising to return in seven days at the latest, she took a tender farewell of the prince, saying:

'Before I go I will hand over to you all the keys of the castle. Go everywhere and do anything you like. Only one thing I beg and beseech you. Do not open the little iron door in the north tower, which is closed with seven locks and seven bolts. If you do, we shall both suffer for it.'

Iwanich promised what she asked, and Militza departed, repeating her promise to return in seven days.

When the prince found himself alone he was tormented by curiosity about the room in the tower. For two days he resisted the temptation, but on the third day, taking a torch in his hand, he hurried to the tower, and unfastened one lock after the other of the little iron door until it burst open.

What an unexpected sight met his gaze! The prince perceived a small room black with smoke, lit feebly by a fire from which issued long blue flames. Over the fire hung a huge cauldron full of boiling pitch, and in it, fastened by iron chains, stood a wretched man screaming with agony.

Iwanich was horrified at the sight, and asked the man what terrible crime he had committed to be punished in this dreadful fashion.

'I will tell you everything,' said the man in the cauldron. 'But first relieve my torments a little, I implore you.'

'How can I do that?' asked the prince.

'With a little water,' replied the man; 'only sprinkle a few drops over me and I shall feel better.'

The prince, moved by pity and without thinking what he was doing, ran to the courtyard of the castle and filled a jug with water, which he poured over the man in the cauldron.

In a moment a most fearful crash was heard, as if all the pillars of the palace were giving way, and the palace itself, with towers and doors, windows and the cauldron, whirled round the bewildered prince's head. This continued for a few minutes, and then suddenly everything vanished into thin air, and Iwanich found himself alone upon a desolate heath covered with rocks and stones.

The prince now realized what his heedlessness had done. In his despair he wandered on over the heath, never looking where he put his feet. At last he saw a light in the distance from a miserable-looking little hut.

It belonged to none other than the kind-hearted gaunt gray beggar who had given the prince the bag of bread crumbs and the hare. Without recognizing him, he opened the door when Iwanich knocked and gave him shelter for the night.

On the following morning the prince asked his host if he could get him any work to do, as he was quite unknown in the neighbourhood and had not enough money to take him home.

'My son,' replied the old man, 'all this country round here is uninhabited. I myself have to wander to distant villages for my living, and even then I do not very often find enough to satisfy my hunger. But if you would like to take service with the old witch, Corva, go straight up the little stream, which flows below my hut, for about three hours and you will come to a sandhill on the left-hand side. That is where she lives.'

Iwanich thanked the gaunt gray beggar and went on his way.

After walking for about three hours the prince came upon a dreary-looking gray stone wall. This was the back of the building and did not attract him. But when he came to the front he found it even less inviting, for the old witch had surrounded her dwelling with a fence of spikes, on every one of which was stuck a man's skull. In this horrible enclosure stood a small black house, which had only two barred windows, covered with cobwebs, and a battered iron door.

The prince knocked, and a rasping woman's voice told him to enter. Iwanich opened the door and found himself in a smoke-begrimed kitchen, in the presence of a hideous old woman who was warming her skinny hands at a fire. The prince offered to become her servant, and she told him he seemed to be just the person to suit her.

When Iwanich asked what his work and how much his wages would be, the witch bade him follow her, and led the way through a narrow damp passage into a vault, which served as a stable. Here he perceived two pitch-black horses in a stall.

'You see before you,' said the old woman, 'a mare and her foal. You have nothing to do but lead them out to the fields every day and to see that neither of them runs away from you. If you look after them both for a whole year I will give you anything you like. But if, on the other hand, you let either of the animals escape, your last hour is come, and your head shall be stuck on the last spike of my fence. The other spikes, as you see, are already adorned, and the skulls are all those of different servants I have had who failed to do what I demanded.'

Iwanich, who thought he could not be much worse off than he was already, agreed to the witch's proposal.

At daybreak next morning he drove his horses to the field and brought them back in the evening without their ever having attempted to break away from him. The witch stood at her door, received him kindly, and set a good meal before him.

So it continued for some time, and all went well with the prince. Early every morning he led the horses out to the fields and brought them home safe and sound in the evening.

One day, while he was watching the horses, he came to the banks of a river and saw a big fish, which through some mischance had been cast on the land, struggling hard to get back into the water. Iwanich, who felt sorry for the poor creature, seized it in his arms and flung it into the stream. But no sooner did the fish find itself in the water again than, to the prince's amazement, it swam up to the bank and said:

'My kind benefactor, how can I reward you for your goodness?'

'I desire nothing,' answered the prince. 'I am quite content to have been able to be of some service to you.'

'You must do me the favour,' replied the fish, 'to take a scale from my body, and keep it carefully. If you should ever need my help, throw it into the river, and I will come to your aid at once.'

Iwanich loosened a scale from the body of the grateful fish, put it carefully away, and returned home.

A short time after this, when he was going early one morning to the usual grazing place with his horses, he noticed a flock of birds assembled together, making a great noise and flying wildly backward and forward. Full of curiosity, Iwanich hurried to the spot and saw that a large number of ravens had attacked an eagle, and although the eagle was big and powerful and was making a brave fight at last it was overpowered by numbers.

But the prince was sorry for the poor bird, seized the branch of a tree and hit out at the ravens. Terrified at this unexpected onslaught they flew away.

As soon as the eagle saw itself free from its tormentors it plucked a feather from its wing and, handing it to the prince, said:

'Here, my kind benefactor, take this feather as a proof of my gratitude. Should you ever be in need of my help, blow this feather into the air, and I will help you as much as is in my power.'

Iwanich thanked the bird and, placing the feather beside the scale, drove the horses home.

Another day he had wandered farther than usual, and came close to a farmyard. The place pleased the prince, and as there was plenty of good grass for the horses he determined to spend the day there. Just as he was sitting down under a tree he heard a cry close to him, and saw a fox which had been caught in a trap.

In vain did the poor beast try to free itself. Then the good-natured prince came once more to the rescue and let the fox out of the trap. The fox thanked him heartily, tore two hairs out of his bushy tail, and said:

'Should you ever stand in need of my help, throw these two hairs into the fire, and in a moment I shall be at your side ready to obey you.'

Iwanich put the fox's hairs with the scale and the feather, and as it was getting dark he hastened home with his horses.

In the meantime his service was drawing near to an end, and in three more days the year was up, and he would be able to get his reward and leave the witch.

On the first evening of these last three days, when he came home and was eating his supper, he noticed the old woman stealing into the stables.

The prince followed her to see what she was going to do. He heard the wicked witch tell the horses to wait next morning till Iwanich was asleep, and then to hide themselves in the river. They were to stay there till she told them to return. If they did not the old woman threatened to beat them till they bled. Iwanich went back to his room, determined that he would not fall asleep that day.

On the following morning he led the mare and foal to the fields as usual, but bound a cord round them both which he kept in his hand. But after a few hours, by the magic arts of the old witch, he was overpowered by sleep, and the mare and foal escaped and did as they had been told to do. The prince did not awake till late in the evening and found, to his horror, that the horses had disappeared. Filled with despair, already he saw his head sticking up on the sharp spike beside the others.

Then he suddenly remembered the fish's scale which, with the eagle's feather and the fox's hairs, he always carried about with him. He drew the scale from his pocket and, hurrying to the river, threw it in. In a moment the grateful fish swam toward the bank on which Iwanich was standing, and said:

'What do you command, my friend and benefactor?'

The prince replied, 'I had to look after a mare and foal, and they have hidden themselves in the river. If you wish to save my life drive them back to the land.'

Almost immediately a rushing sound was heard in the waters, waves dashed against the banks, foam was tossed into the air, and the two horses leaped suddenly on to the dry land, trembling and shaking with fear. Iwanich sprang at once on to the mare's back, seized the foal by its bridle, and hastened home in the highest spirits.

Iwanich saw his horses driven by a host of eagles

When the witch saw the prince bringing the horses home she could hardly conceal her wrath, and as soon as she had placed Iwanich's supper before him she stole away again to the stables. The prince followed her and heard her scolding the beasts harshly for not having hidden themselves better. She bade them wait next morning till Iwanich was asleep and then to hide themselves in the clouds and remain there till she called. If they did not do so she would beat them.

Next morning, after Iwanich had led his horses to the fields, he fell once more into a magic sleep. The horses at once hid themselves in the clouds, which hung down from the mountains in soft billowy masses. When the prince awoke and found that both the mare and the foal had again disappeared, he bethought him at once of the eagle, and taking the feather out of his pocket he blew it into the air. In a moment the bird swooped down beside him and asked:

'What do you wish me to do?'

'My mare and foal,' replied the prince, 'have run away from me and have hidden themselves in the clouds. If you wish to save my life, restore both animals to me.'

The bird flew up into the air and disappeared among the clouds. Almost directly Iwanich saw his two horses being driven toward him by a host of eagles of all sizes. He caught the mare and foal and, having thanked the eagle, drove them cheerfully home again.

The old witch was more disgusted than ever when she saw him, and having set his supper before him she stole into the stables, where Iwanich heard her scolding the horses for not having hidden themselves better. Then she bade them hide themselves next morning, as soon as Iwanich was asleep, in the king's hen house, which stood on a lonely part of the heath, and to remain there till she called. If they failed to do as she told them she would certainly beat them this time.

On the following morning the prince drove his horses as usual to the fields. Again he was overpowered by sleep, and the mare and foal ran away and hid themselves in the royal hen house.

When the prince awoke and found the horses gone, he determined to appeal to the fox. So, lighting a fire, he threw the two hairs into it, and in a few moments the fox stood beside him and asked:

'In what way can I serve you?'

'I wish to know,' replied Iwanich, 'where the king's hen house is.'

'Hardly an hour's walk from here,' answered the fox, and offered to show the prince the way.

While they were walking along the fox asked him what he wanted to do at the royal hen house. The prince told him what had befallen him and of the necessity of recovering the mare and foal.

'That is no easy matter,' replied the fox. 'But I have an idea. Stand at the door of the hen house, and wait there for your horses. I will slip in among the hens through a hole in the wall and give them a good chase. The noise they make will arouse the royal henwives, who will come to see what is the matter. When they see the horses they will at once imagine them to be the cause of the disturbance, and will drive them out. Then you must catch the mare and foal.'

All turned out exactly as the sly fox had foreseen. The prince swung himself on the mare, seized the foal by its bridle, and hurried home. While he was riding over the heath in the highest of spirits the mare suddenly said to her rider:

'You are the first person who has ever succeeded in out-witting old Corva, and now you may ask what reward you like for your service. If you promise never to betray me I will give you a piece of advice which you will do well to follow.'

The prince promised never to betray her confidence, and the mare continued:

'Ask nothing else as a reward than my foal, for there is not its like in the world, for it can go from one end of the earth to another in a few minutes. Of course the cunning Corva will do her best to dissuade you from taking the foal and will tell you that it is both idle and sickly, but do not believe her.'

Iwanich longed to possess such an animal and promised to follow the mare's advice.

This time Corva received him in the most friendly manner and set a sumptuous repast before him. As soon as he had finished she asked him what reward he demanded for his year's service.

'Nothing more nor less,' replied the prince, 'than the foal of your mare.'

The witch pretended to be astonished at his request and said that he deserved something better than the foal, for the beast was lazy and nervous, blind in one eye and, in short, quite worthless. But the prince knew what he wanted, and when the old witch saw he had made up his mind to have the foal, she said:

'I am obliged to keep my promise and to give you the foal; and as I know who you are and what you want, I will tell you in what way the animal will be useful to you. The man in the cauldron, whom you set free, is a mighty magician. Through your curiosity and thoughtlessness Militza came into his power, and he has transported her and her castle and belongings into a distant country.

'You are the only person who can kill him, and he fears you so much that he has set spies to watch you. They report your movements to him daily. When you have reached him, beware of speaking a single word to him, or you will fall into the power of his friends. Seize him at once by the beard and dash him to the ground.'

Iwanich thanked the old witch, mounted his foal, put spurs to its sides, and they flew like lightning through the air.

Already it was growing dark, when Iwanich perceived some figures in the distance. The prince saw that it was the magician and his friends who were driving through the air in a carriage drawn by owls. When the magician found himself face to face with Iwanich, without hope of escape, he turned to him with false friendliness and said:

'Thrice my kind benefactor!'

But the prince, without saying a word, seized him at once by his beard and dashed him to the ground. Then Iwanich found himself once more in the palace of his bride, and Militza herself flew into his arms. From this time forward they lived in undisturbed peace and happiness till the end of their lives.

[From the Russian. Kletke.]

The Magic Ring

O NCE UPON A TIME there lived an old couple who had one son called Martin. Now when the old man's time had come, he stretched himself out on his bed and died. Though all his life long he had toiled and moiled, he left his widow and son only about two hundred florins. The old woman determined to put by the money for a rainy day. But alas, the rainy day was close at hand, for their meal was all consumed, and who is prepared to face starvation with two hundred florins? So the old woman counted out a hundred of her florins and, giving them to Martin, told him to lay in a store of meal for a year.

So Martin started off for the town. When he reached the meat market he found the whole place in turmoil, with a great noise of angry voices and barking of dogs. Mixing in the crowd, he noticed a staghound the butchers had tied to a post, and were flogging mercilessly. Overcome with pity, Martin spoke to the butchers, saying:

'Friends, why are you beating the poor dog so cruelly? Stop! Stop!'

'We have every right to beat him,' they replied. 'He has just devoured a newly killed pig.'

'Leave off beating him,' said Martin, 'and sell him to me instead.'

'If you choose to buy him,' answered the butchers derisively. 'But for such a treasure we won't take a penny less than a hundred florins.'

'A hundred!' exclaimed Martin. 'Well, so be it.' Taking the money out of his pocket, he handed it over in exchange for the dog, whose name was Schurka.

When Martin came home, his mother met him, asking, 'Well, what have you bought?'

'Schurka, the dog,' replied Martin.

Whereupon his mother was angry and scolded him roundly. He ought to be ashamed of himself, when there was scarcely a handful of meal in the house, to have spent the money on a useless animal. On the following day she sent him back to the town, saying:

'Here, take our last hundred florins, and buy provisions with them. I have just emptied the last grains of meal out of the chest, and baked a bannock. It won't last over tomorrow.'

Just as Martin was entering the town he met a rough-looking peasant who was dragging a cat after him by a string fastened round the poor beast's neck.

'Stop!' cried Martin. 'Where are you dragging that poor cat?'

'I mean to drown her,' was the answer.

'What harm has the poor beast done?' said Martin.

'She has just killed a goose,' replied the peasant.

'Don't drown her, sell her to me instead,' begged Martin.

'Not for a hundred florins,' was the answer.

'Surely for a hundred florins you'll sell her?' said Martin. 'See, here is the money,' and, so saying, he handed him the hundred florins, which the peasant pocketed, and Martin took the cat, which was called Waska.

When he reached his home his mother greeted him with the question, 'Well, what have you brought back?'

'I have brought this cat, Waska,' answered Martin.

'And what besides?'

'I had no money over to buy anything else,' replied Martin.

'You useless ne'er-do-weel!' exclaimed his mother in a great passion. 'Leave the house and beg your bread of strangers.'

Martin called Schurka and Waska and started off to the nearest village in search of work. On the way he met a rich peasant, who asked him where he was going.

'I want work as a day labourer,' he answered.

'Come along with me, then. But I must tell you I engage my labourers without wages. If you serve me faithfully for a year, I promise you it shall be to your advantage.'

So Martin consented, and for a year he served his master faithfully, not sparing himself in any way. On the day of reckoning the peasant led him into a barn and, pointing to two full sacks, said:

'Take whichever of these you choose.'

Martin examined them and, seeing that one was full of silver and the other of sand, he said to himself, 'There must be some trick about this. I had better take the sand.'

Throwing the sack over his shoulders he started out into the world, in search of work. On and on he walked, and at last he reached a great gloomy wood. In the middle of the wood he came upon a meadow, where a fire was burning. Surrounded by the flames was a lovely damsel, more beautiful than anyone Martin had ever seen. When she saw him she called:

'Martin, if you would win happiness, save my life. Put out the flames with the sand you earned in payment for your faithful service.'

'Truly,' said Martin to himself, 'it would be more sensible

'Martin, if you would win happiness, save my life.'

to save her life with this sand than to drag it about, seeing what a weight it is.'

Forthwith he lowered the sack from his shoulders and emptied its contents on the flames, and instantly the fire was extinguished, but at the same moment, lo and behold! The lovely damsel turned into a serpent and, darting upon him, coiled itself round his neck and whispered in his ear:

'Do not be afraid of me, Martin. I love you and will go with you through the world. But first you must follow me boldly into my father's kingdom, underneath the earth, and remember this—he will offer you gold and silver and dazzling gems, but do not touch them. Ask him, instead, for the ring which he wears on his little finger, for in that ring lies a magic power. You have only to throw it from one hand to the other, and at once twelve young men will appear, who will do your bidding, no matter how difficult, in a single night.'

So they started on their way, and after much wandering they reached a spot where a great rock rose straight up in the middle of the road. The serpent, uncoiling from his neck, touched the damp earth, and resumed the shape of the lovely damsel. Pointing to the rock, she showed him an opening just big enough for a man to wriggle through. They entered a long underground passage, which led out onto a wide field, above which spread a blue sky. In the middle of the field stood a magnificent castle, built out of porphyry, with a roof of gold and with glittering battlements. His beautiful guide told Martin that this was the palace where her father lived and reigned over the underworld.

Together they entered the palace and were received by the king with great kindness. Turning to his daughter, he said:

'My child, I had almost given up hope of ever seeing you again. Where have you been all these years?'

'My father,' she replied, 'I owe my life to this youth, who saved me from a terrible death.'

Upon which the king turned to Martin with a gracious smile, saying, 'I will reward your courage by granting you whatever your heart desires. Take as much gold, silver and precious stones as you choose.'

'I thank you for your gracious offer,' answered Martin, 'but I covet neither gold, silver, nor precious stones. If you will grant me a favour, give me the ring from off the little finger of your royal hand. Every time my eye falls on it I shall think of Your Gracious Majesty, and when I marry I shall present it to my bride.'

So the king took the ring from his finger and gave it to Martin, saying, 'Take it, good youth; but I make one condition—you are never to confide to anyone that this is a magic ring. If you do, you will straightway bring misfortune on yourself.'

Martin took the ring and, having thanked the king, set out on the same road by which he had come into the underworld. When he had regained the upper air he started for his old home and, having found his mother still living in the old house, they settled down together very happily. So uneventful was their life it seemed as if it would go on this way always. But one day it suddenly came into Martin's mind that he would like to get married and, moreover, that he would choose a very grand wife—a king's daughter, in short. But as he did not trust himself as a wooer, he determined to send his old mother on the mission.

'You must go to the king,' he said to her, 'and demand the hand of his lovely daughter for me.'

'What are you thinking of, my son?' answered the old woman aghast. 'Why cannot you marry someone of your own rank? That would be more fitting than to send a poor old woman like me a-wooing to the king's court for the hand of a princess. Why, it is as much as our heads are worth, if I went on such a fool's errand.'

'Never fear, little mother,' answered Martin. 'Trust me. All will be well. But see that you do not come back without an answer of some kind.'

And so, obedient to her son's behest. the old woman hobbled off to the palace and began to mount the flight of steps leading to the royal presence chamber. Rows of courtiers were collected in magnificent attire, who stared and explained that it was strictly forbidden to bother the king. But their stern words made no impression on the old woman, and she resolutely continued to climb the stairs, bent on carrying out her son's orders.

Upon this some of the courtiers seized her by the arms, and held her back by force, at which she made so much noise that the king heard her and ordered her to be brought into his presence. Forthwith she was conducted into the golden presence chamber. Leaning back amongst cushions of royal purple, the king sat, surrounded by his counsellors and courtiers. Curtseying low, the old woman stood silent before him.

'Well, my good dame, what can I do for you?' asked the king.

'I have come,' replied Martin's mother—'and Your Majesty must not be angry with me—I have come a-wooing.'

'Is the woman out of her mind?' said the king, with an angry frown.

But Martin's mother answered boldly, 'You, O King, have a lovely daughter. I have a son—a wooer—as clever a youth and as good a son-in-law as you will find in your whole kingdom. There is nothing he cannot do. Now tell me, O King, plump and plain, will you give your daughter to my son as wife?'

The king listened to the end of the old woman's strange request, but every moment his face grew blacker, and his features sterner. 'Is it worth while that I, the king, should be angry with this poor old woman?' he said to himself.

All the courtiers and counsellors were amazed when they saw the frown on his brow grow smooth and heard the mild but mocking voice answer the old woman, saying:

'If your son is wonderfully clever and if there is nothing in the world he cannot do, let him build a magnificent castle just opposite my palace windows, in four and twenty hours. The palace must be joined to mine by a bridge of pure crystal. On each side of the bridge there must be growing trees, having golden and silver apples, with birds of paradise among the branches. At the right of the bridge there must be a church, with five golden cupolas. In this church your son shall be wedded to my daughter, and we will keep the wedding festivities in the new castle. But if he fails to execute this, my royal command, then I shall order that you and he shall be taken, and dipped first in tar and then in feathers, and executed in the market place.'

A smile played round the king's lips and his courtiers and counsellors shook with laughter when they thought of the old woman's folly, and praised the king's wise device, and said to each other:

'What a joke it will be when we see the pair of them tarred and feathered! The son is just as able to grow a beard on the palm of his hand as to execute such a task in twenty-four hours.'

Now the poor old woman was mortally afraid and, in a trembling voice, she asked, 'Is that really your royal will, O King? Must I take this order to my poor son?'

'Yes, old dame; such is my command. If your son carries out my order, he shall be rewarded with my daughter; but if he fails, away to the tar barrel with you both!'

On her way home the poor old woman shed bitter tears. When she told Martin what the king had said she sobbed:

'Didn't I tell you, my son, that you should marry someone of your own rank? It would have been better for us this day if you had. As I told you, my going to court has been as much as our lives are worth, and now we will both be tarred and feathered in the public market place. It is terrible!'

'Never fear, little mother,' answered Martin. 'Trust me, and you will see all will be well. You may go to sleep with a quiet mind.'

Stepping outside, Martin threw his ring from the palm of one hand into the other. Twelve youths instantly appeared and asked what he wanted them to do. Then he told them the king's commands, and they answered that by next morning all should be accomplished exactly as the king had ordered.

Next morning when the king awoke, and looked out of his window, to his amazement he beheld a magnificent castle, just opposite his own palace, and joined to it by a bridge of pure crystal.

At each side of the bridge trees were growing, from whose branches hung golden and silver apples, among which birds of paradise perched. At the right, gleaming in the sun, were the five golden cupolas of a splendid church, whose bells rang out, as if to summon people from all corners of the earth to behold the wonder. Now, the king remembered his royal oath and had to make the best of a bad business. So he made Martin a duke, gave his daughter a rich dowry, and prepared such a wedding feast that the old people in the country still talk of it.

After the wedding Martin and his royal bride went to dwell

in the magnificent new palace. But though he was as happy as the day was long, and as merry as a grig, the king's daughter fretted all day.

She determined to learn the secret of his power and, with flattering, caressing words, tried to coax him to tell her how he was so clever that there was nothing in the world that he could not do. At first he would tell her nothing; but she gave him a potion to drink, with a sweet, strong taste. And when he had drunk it Martin's lips were unsealed and he told her that his power lay in the magic ring he wore on his finger and told her how to use it. Still speaking, he fell into a deep sleep.

And when she saw that the potion had worked, the princess took the magic ring from his finger and, going into the court-yard, she threw it from one hand to the other. When the twelve youths appeared she commanded them to do away with the castle and the bridge and the church, and put in their stead the humble hut where Martin used to live with his mother, and leave her husband in his old lowly room. They were to bear her away to the utmost ends of the earth where an old king lived who would make her welcome in his palace, and surround her with the state that befitted a royal princess.

'You shall be obeyed,' answered the twelve youths at the same moment. And lo and behold! The following morning, when the king awoke and looked out of his window, to his amazement the palace, bridge, church and trees had all vanished, and there was nothing in their place but a miserable-looking hut.

Immediately the king sent for his son-in-law and com-manded him to explain what had happened. But Martin looked at his royal father-in-law, and answered never a word. Then the king was very angry and, calling a council together, charged Martin with having been guilty of witchcraft and of having deceived the king and having made away with the princess. Martin was condemned to imprisonment in a high stone tower, with neither meat nor drink, till he should die of starvation.

Then his old friends Schurka, the dog, and Waska, the cat, remembered how Martin had once saved them from a cruel death. They took counsel together. Schurka growled and was of the opinion that he would like to tear everyone in pieces; but Waska purred meditatively and scratched the back of her ear with a velvet paw. At the end of a few minutes she had made up her mind and, turning to Schurka, said:

'Let us go together into the town. The moment we meet a baker rush between his legs and upset the tray from off his head. I will lay hold of the rolls and carry them off to our master.'

No sooner said than done. Together the two faithful creatures trotted off into the town. Soon they met a baker bearing a tray on his head and looking round on all sides, while he cried:

'Fresh rolls, sweet cake,
    Fancy bread of every kind.
Come and buy, come and take,
    Sure, you'll find it to your mind.'

At that moment Schurka rushed between his legs—the baker stumbled, the tray was upset and the rolls fell to the ground. While the man angrily pursued Schurka, Waska dragged the rolls out of sight behind a bush. And when a moment later, Schurka joined her they set off full tilt to the stone tower where Martin was a prisoner, taking the rolls with them. Waska climbed up to the grated window and called in an anxious voice:

'Are you alive, master?'

'Scarcely alive—almost starved to death,' answered Martin. 'I little thought it would come to this, that I should die of hunger.'

'Never fear, dear master. Schurka and I will look after you,' said Waska. In another moment she brought him a roll and

then another and another, till she had brought him the whole trayful. Upon which she said, 'Dear master, Schurka and I are going off to a distant kingdom at the utmost ends of the earth to fetch you back your magic ring. You must be careful that the rolls last till our return.'

So Waska took leave of her beloved master and set off with Schurka. On and on they travelled, looking always to right and left for traces of the princess, making inquiries of every cat and dog they met, listening to the talk of every wayfarer they passed. At last they heard that the kingdom at the utmost ends of the earth was not very far off.

Going at once to the palace, they began to make friends with all the dogs and cats in the place and to question them about the princess and the magic ring. But no one could tell them much. Now one day Waska went down to the palace cellar to hunt for mice and rats. Seeing an especially fat, well-fed mouse, she pounced upon it, and was just going to gobble it up, when she was stopped by the pleading tones of the little creature, saying:

'If you will only spare my life I may be of great service to you. I will do everything in my power for you. I am King of the Mice, and if I perish the whole race will die out.'

'So be it,' said Waska. 'I will spare your life, but in return you must do something for me. In this castle there lives a princess, the wicked wife of my dear master. She has stolen away his magic ring. You must get it away from her at whatever cost. Do you hear? Till you have done this I won't take my claws out of your fur.'

'Good!' replied the mouse. 'I will do what you ask.' And, so saying, he summoned all the mice in his kingdom together. A countless number of mice, small and big, brown and gray, assembled and formed a circle round their king, who was a prisoner under Waska's claws. Turning to them he said:

'Dear and faithful subjects, whoever among you will steal the magic ring from the strange princess will release me from a cruel death. I shall honour him above all the other mice in the kingdom.'

Instantly a tiny mouse stepped forward and said, 'I often creep about the princess's bedroom at night, and I have noticed that she has a ring which she treasures. All day she wears it on her finger, and at night she keeps it in her mouth. I will undertake, sire, to steal away the ring for you.'

The tiny mouse tripped away into the bedroom of the princess and waited for nightfall. When the princess had fallen asleep, it crept to her bed and gnawed a hole in the pillow, through which one by one it dragged little down feathers and threw them under the princess's nose. The fluff flew into the princess's nose, and starting up, she sneezed and coughed, and the ring fell out of her mouth onto the coverlet. In a flash the tiny mouse had seized it, and brought it to Waska as a ransom for the King of the Mice.

Thereupon Waska and Schurka started off and travelled night and day till they reached the stone tower where Martin was imprisoned. The cat climbed up to the window, and called out to him:

'Martin, dear master, are you still alive?'

'Ah, Waska, my faithful little cat, is that you?' replied a weak voice. 'I am dying of hunger. For three days I have not tasted food.'

'Be of good heart, dear master,' replied Waska. 'Schurka and I have brought you your ring!'

At these words Martin stroked her fondly, and she rubbed up against him and purred happily while below Schurka bounded in the air and barked joyfully. Then Martin took the ring, and threw it from one hand into the other, and instantly the twelve youths appeared and asked what they were to do.

'Fetch me first something to eat and drink, and after that bring musicians hither, and let us have music all day long.'

Now when the people in the town and palace heard music coming from the tower they were filled with amazement, and came to the king with the news that witchcraft must be going on in Martin's tower, for instead of dying of starvation, he was making merry to the sound of music and to the clatter of plates and glass and knives and forks. The music was so enchantingly sweet that all the passers-by stood still to listen to it. The king sent a messenger to the tower, and he was so astonished that he remained rooted to the spot. Then the king sent his chief counsellors, and they too were transfixed with wonder. Finally the king came himself, and he likewise was spellbound by the beauty of the music.

Then Martin summoned the twelve youths, 'Build up my castle again and join it to the king's palace with a crystal bridge. Do not forget the trees with the golden and silver apples, and the birds of paradise in the branches. Put back the church with the five cupolas, and let the bells ring out, summoning the people from the four corners of the kingdom. One thing more: bring back my faithless wife.'

And it was all done as he commanded and, leaving the tower, he took the king, his father-in-law, by the arm and led him into the new palace, where the princess sat in fear and trembling, awaiting her death. Martin spoke to the king, saying:

'King and royal father, I have suffered much at the hands of your daughter. What punishment shall be dealt to her?'

Then the mild king answered, 'Beloved prince and son-in-law, if you love me, let your anger be turned to grace. Forgive my daughter and restore her to your heart and favour.'

Martin's heart was softened and he forgave his wife, and they lived happily together ever after. And his old mother came and lived with him, and he never parted with Schurka and Waska. And it need not be said that he never again parted with the ring.

The Flower Queen's Daughter

A YOUNG PRINCE
was riding one day through a meadow that stretched for miles
in front of him when he came to a deep open ditch. He was
turning aside to avoid it, when he heard the sound of someone
crying. He dismounted from his horse and to his astonishment
found an old woman, who begged him to help her. The prince
bent down and lifted her out of the ditch, asking at the same
time how she came there.

'My son,' answered the old woman, 'I am very poor. Soon
after midnight I set out for the neighbouring town to sell my
eggs in the market on the following morning. But I lost my
way in the dark and fell into this deep ditch, where I might
have remained forever but for your kindness.'

Then the prince said to her, 'You can hardly walk. I will put
you on my horse and lead you home. Where do you live?'

'At the edge of the forest in the little hut you see in the
distance,' replied the old woman.

The prince lifted her on to his horse, and soon they reached her hut, where the old woman got down, and turning to the prince said, 'Just wait a moment, and I will give you something. Would you like to have the most beautiful woman in the world for your wife?'

'Most certainly I would,' replied the prince.

'The most beautiful woman in the whole world, the daughter of the Queen of the Flowers, has been captured by a dragon. If you wish to marry her, you must first set her free, and this I will help you to do. I will give you this little bell. If you ring it once, the King of the Eagles will appear; if you ring it twice, the King of the Foxes will come to you; and if you ring it three times, you will see the King of the Fishes by your side. These will help you if you are in any difficulty. Now farewell, and Heaven prosper your undertaking.'

She handed him the little bell, and then disappeared, hut and all, as though the earth had swallowed her up. Then it dawned on the prince that he had been speaking to a good fairy. Putting the little bell carefully in his pocket he rode home and told his father that he meant to set the daughter of the Flower Queen free and intended setting out on the following day into the wide world in search of the maid.

So the prince mounted his fine horse and left his home. He had roamed round the world for a whole year and he and his horse had suffered much from want and misery, but still he had come on no trace of the princess. At last one day he came to a hut, in front of which sat a very old man. The prince asked him:

'Do you not know where the dragon lives who keeps the daughter of the Flower Queen prisoner?'

'No, I do not,' answered the old man. 'But if you go straight along this road for a year, you will reach a hut where my father lives, and possibly he may be able to tell you.'

The prince thanked him and continued his journey for a

whole year along the same road. At the end of it he came to
the little hut, where he found a very old man. He asked him
the same question, and the old man answered:

'No, I do not know where the dragon lives. But go straight
along this road for a year, and you will come to a hut in which
my father lives. I know he can tell you.'

And so the prince wandered on for another year, always on
the same road, and at last he found the third old man. He put
the same question to him as he had put to his son and grand-
son; but this time the old man answered:

'The dragon lives up there on the mountain and he has just
begun his year of sleep. For one whole year he is always awake,
and the next he sleeps. But if you wish to see the Flower
Queen's daughter go up the second mountain: the dragon's old
mother lives there and she has a ball every night, to which the
Flower Queen's daughter goes regularly.'

So the prince went up the second mountain, where he found
a castle all made of gold with diamond windows. He was just
going to walk in, when seven dragons rushed on him and
asked him what he wanted.

The prince replied, 'I have heard so much of the beauty and
kindness of the dragon's mother that I would like to enter
her service.'

This pleased the dragons, and the eldest said, 'Well, you may
come with me, and I will take you to the mother dragon.'

They entered the castle and walked through twelve splendid
halls, all made of gold and diamonds. In the twelfth room
they found the mother dragon seated on a diamond throne.
She was the ugliest woman under the sun, and added to it all
she had three heads. Her appearance was a great shock to the
prince, and so was her voice, which was like the croaking of
many ravens. She asked him:

'Why have you come here?'

The prince answered at once, 'I have heard much of your beauty and kindness. I would very much like to enter your service.'

'Very well,' said the mother dragon. 'But first you must lead my mare out to the meadow and look after her for three days. If you don't bring her home safely every evening, we will eat you up.'

The prince led the mare out to the meadow. But no sooner had they reached the grass than she vanished. The prince sought for her in vain; at last in despair he sat down on a stone and contemplated his sad fate. As he sat lost in thought, he noticed an eagle flying over his head. Then he suddenly bethought him of his little bell, and taking it out of his pocket he rang it once. In a moment he heard a rustling sound in the air beside him, and the King of the Eagles sank at his feet.

'I know what you want of me,' the bird said. 'You are looking for the mother dragon's mare which is galloping about among the clouds. I will catch the mare and bring her to you.'

And with these words the King of the Eagles flew away. Toward evening the prince heard a mighty rushing sound in the air, and looking up he saw thousands of eagles driving the mare before them. They sank to the ground at his feet and gave the mare over to him. Then the prince rode home to the old mother dragon, who was full of wonder when she saw him, and said:

'You have succeeded today in looking after my mare, and as a reward you shall come to my ball tonight.' She gave him a cloak made of copper and led him to a big room where several young dragons were dancing together. Here, too, was the Flower Queen's beautiful daughter. Her dress was woven of lovely flowers and her complexion was like lilies and roses. As the prince was dancing with her he whispered in her ear:

They flew like the wind

'I have come to set you free!'

Then the beautiful girl said to him, 'If you succeed in bringing the mare back safely the third day, ask the mother dragon to give you a foal of the mare as a reward.'

The ball came to an end at midnight, and early next morning the prince again led the mother dragon's mare into the meadow. Again she vanished before his eyes. Then he took out his little bell and rang it twice. In a moment the King of the Foxes stood before him and said:

'I know what you want. The mare which has hidden herself in a hill.'

With these words the King of the Foxes disappeared. In the evening many thousands of foxes brought the mare to the prince. He rode home to the mother dragon, from whom he received this time a cloak made of silver, and again she led him to the ballroom.

The Flower Queen's daughter was delighted to see him and when they were dancing together she whispered in his ear, 'If you succeed again tomorrow, wait for me with the foal in the meadow. After the ball we will fly away together.'

On the third day the prince led the mare to the meadow again, but once more she vanished before his eyes. Then the prince took out his little bell and rang it three times. In a moment the King of the Fishes appeared, and said to him:

'I know quite well what you want me to do, and I will summon all the fishes of the sea together, and tell them to bring you back the mare, which is hiding in a river.'

Toward evening the mare was returned to him, and when he led her home the mother dragon said to him, 'You are a brave youth, and I will make you my body servant. But what shall I give you as a reward?'

The prince begged for a foal of the mare, which the mother

THE FLOWER QUEEN'S DAUGHTER   213

dragon at once gave him, and also a cloak made of gold, for she had fallen in love with him.

So in the evening he appeared at the ball in his golden cloak; but before it was over he slipped away and went straight to the stables, where he mounted his foal and rode out into the meadow to wait for the Flower Queen's daughter. Toward midnight the beautiful girl came. Placing her in front of him on his horse, they flew like the wind till they reached the Flower Queen's dwelling.

But the dragons had noticed their flight and woke their brother out of his year's sleep. He flew into a terrible rage and determined to lay siege to the Flower Queen's palace. The queen caused a forest of flowers as high as the sky to grow up round her dwelling, through which no one could force a way.

When the Flower Queen heard that her daughter wanted to marry the prince, she said to him, 'I give my consent to your marriage gladly, but my daughter can only stay with you in summer. In winter, when everything is dead and the ground is covered with snow, she must come and live with me in my palace underground.'

The prince consented and led his beautiful bride home, where the wedding was held with great pomp and magnificence. The young couple lived happily together till winter came, when the Flower Queen's daughter went home to her mother. In summer she returned to her husband, their life of joy and happiness began again and lasted till the approach of winter. This coming and going continued all her life long, and in spite of it they lived happily together.

[From the *Bukowinaer*. Von Wliolocki.]

The Flying Ship

ONCE UPON A TIME
there lived an old couple who had three sons; the two elder were
clever, but the third was a dunce. The clever sons were very
fond of their mother, gave her good clothes and always spoke
pleasantly to her; but the youngest was always getting in her
way, and she had no patience with him. Now, one day, the
king issued a decree, offering his daughter in marriage to
whosoever built a ship that could fly.

Immediately the two elder brothers determined to try their
luck, and asked their parents' blessing. So the old mother
smartened up their clothes and gave them a store of provisions
for their journey, not forgetting to add a bottle of brandy.
When they had gone the poor simpleton began to tease his
mother to smarten him up and let him start off.

'What would become of you?' she answered. 'Why, you
would be eaten up by the wolves.'

But the foolish youth kept repeating, 'I will go, I will go,
I will go!'

Seeing that she could do nothing with him, the mother gave
him a crust of bread and a bottle of water and took no further
heed of him. So the simpleton set off on his way. When he had

gone a short distance he met a little old manikin. They greeted
one another, and the manikin asked him where he was going.

'I am off to the king's court,' he answered. 'He has promised
to give his daughter to anyone who can make a flying ship.'

'And can you make such a ship?'

'Not I.'

'Then why in the world are you going?'

'Can't tell,' replied the simpleton.

'Well, if that is the case,' said the manikin, 'sit down beside
me. We can rest for a little and have something to eat. Give
me what you have in your satchel.'

Now the poor simpleton was ashamed to show what was
in it. However, he thought it best not to make a fuss, so he
opened the satchel. He could scarcely believe his own eyes,
when instead of the hard crust, he saw two beautiful fresh
rolls and some cold meat. He shared them with the manikin,
who licked his lips and said:

'Now, go into that wood and stop in front of the first tree,
bow three times, and then strike the tree with your axe, fall
on your knees on the ground, with your face on the earth and
remain there till you are raised up. You will then find a ship
at your side, step into it and fly to the king's palace. If you
meet anyone on the way, take him with you.'

The simpleton thanked the manikin kindly, bade him farewell and went into the wood. When he reached the first tree
he did everything just as he had been told and, with his face
to the earth, fell asleep. After a little time he awoke and,
rubbing his eyes, saw a ship at his side. At once he got into it,
and in another minute the ship was flying through the air.

The simpleton cast his eyes down to the earth and saw a man
beneath him on the road, kneeling with his ear to the damp
ground.

'Hallo!' he called out. 'What are you doing down there?'

'I am listening to what is going on in the world,' replied the man.

'Come with me in my ship,' said the simpleton.

The man was only too glad to get in beside him. The ship flew and flew and flew through the air, till again the simpleton saw a man on the road below. He was hopping on one leg, while his other leg was tied up behind his ear. So he hailed him, calling out:

'Hallo! What are you doing, hopping on one leg?'

'I can't help it,' replied the man. 'I walk so fast that unless I tied up one leg I should be at the end of the earth in a bound.'

'Come with us on my ship,' he answered, and the man joined them. And the ship flew on and on and on till suddenly the simpleton, looking down on the road below, beheld a man aiming with a gun into the distance.

'Hallo!' he shouted to him. 'What are you aiming at? As far as eye can see, there is no bird in sight.'

'What would be the good of my taking a near shot?' replied the man. 'I can hit beast or bird at a hundred miles' distance. That is the kind of shot I enjoy.'

'Come into the ship with us,' answered the simpleton. The man was only too glad to join them, and the ship flew on, farther and farther, till again the simpleton saw a man on the road below, carrying on his back a basketful of bread. And he waved to him, calling out:

'Hallo! Where are you going?'

'To fetch bread for my breakfast.'

'Bread? Why, you have a whole basketload of it on your back.'

'That's nothing,' answered the man; 'I should finish that in one mouthful.'

'Come along with us in my ship, then.'

And so the glutton joined the party. And the ship mounted again into the air, and flew up and onward, till the simpleton saw a man walking by the shore of a great lake, evidently looking for something.

'Hallo!' he cried to him. 'What are you seeking?'

'I want water to drink, I'm so thirsty,' replied the man.

'Well, there's a whole lake in front of you. Why don't you drink some of that?'

'Do you call that enough?' answered the other. 'Why, I should drink it up in one gulp.'

'Well, come with us in the ship.'

The mighty drinker was added to the company and the ship flew farther, and even farther, till again the simpleton looked out. This time he saw a man dragging a bundle of wood, walking through the forest beneath them.

'Hallo!' he shouted to him. 'Why are you carrying wood through a forest?'

'This is not common wood,' answered the other.

'What sort of wood is it, then?' asked the simpleton.

'If you throw it upon the ground,' said the man, 'it will be changed into an army of soldiers.'

'Come into the ship with us, then.'

And so he too joined them. Away the ship flew, on and on and on, and once more the simpleton looked out. This time he saw a man carrying straw upon his back.

'Hallo! Where are you carrying that straw?'

'To the village,' said the man.

'Do you mean to say there is no straw in the village?'

'Ah, but this is quite peculiar straw. If you strew it about even in the hottest summer the air at once becomes cold. Snow falls, and the people freeze.'

Then the simpleton asked him also to join them.

At last the ship with its strange crew arrived at the king's court. The king was having his dinner, but he sent at once to find out what the huge, strange new bird could be that had come flying through the air. A courtier told him it was a flying ship, manned by a few peasants.

The king remembered his royal oath, but he made up his mind that he would never consent to let the princess marry a poor peasant. So he thought and thought, and then said to himself:

'I will give him some impossible tasks to perform. That will be the best way of getting rid of him.'

And he there and then determined to despatch one of his courtiers to the simpleton with the command to fetch the king the healing water from the world's end before he finished his dinner. But while the king was still instructing the courtier exactly what he was to say, the man with the miraculous power of hearing, had overheard the king's words, and hastily reported them to the poor simpleton.

'Alas, alas!' he cried. 'What am I to do now? It would take me a year, possibly my whole life, to find the water.'

'Never fear,' said his fleet-footed comrade, 'I will fetch what the king wants.'

At that moment the courtier arrived, bearing the king's command.

'Tell his majesty,' said the simpleton, 'that his orders will be obeyed.' Forthwith the swift runner unbound the foot that was tied up behind his ear and started off. In less than no time he had reached the world's end and drawn the healing water from the well.

'Dear me,' he said to himself, 'that's rather tiring! I'll just rest for a few minutes. It will be some time yet before the king

The marksman seized his gun, took aim, and fired

eats his dessert.' So he threw himself down on the grass. As the sun was dazzling, he closed his eyes, and in a few seconds he had fallen sound asleep.

In the meantime all the ship's crew were anxiously awaiting him. The king's dinner would soon be finished and their comrade had not yet returned. So the man with the marvellous hearing put his ear to the ground.

'That's a nice sort of fellow!' he suddenly exclaimed. 'He's lying on the ground, snoring hard!'

At this the marksman seized his gun, took aim, and fired in the direction of the world's end to awaken the sleeper. A moment later the swift runner reappeared and, stepping on board the ship, handed the healing water to the simpleton, while the king was still sitting at table.

What was to be done now? The king thought of a still more impossible task. He told another courtier to go to the simpleton with the command that he and his comrades were instantly to eat up twelve oxen and twelve tons of bread. Once more the sharp-eared comrade overheard the king's words to the courtier, and reported them to the simpleton.

'Alas, alas!' he sighed. 'What in the world shall I do? Why, it would take us a year, possibly our whole lives, to eat up twelve oxen and twelve tons of bread.'

'Never fear,' said the glutton. 'It will scarcely be enough for me, I'm so hungry.'

So when the courtier arrived with the royal message he was told to take back word that the king's orders should be obeyed. Then twelve roasted oxen and twelve tons of bread were brought alongside the ship, and at one sitting the glutton devoured all.

'I call that a small meal,' he said. 'I wish they'd brought me some more.'

Next, the king ordered that forty casks of wine, containing forty gallons each, were to be drunk up on the spot by the simpleton and his party. When these words were overheard by the sharp-eared comrade and repeated to the simpleton, he was in despair.

'Alas, alas!' he exclaimed. 'What is to be done? It would take us a year, possibly our whole lives, to drink so much.'

'Never fear,' said his thirsty comrade. 'I'll drink it all at a gulp, see if I don't.' And sure enough, when the forty casks of wine were empty he remarked:

'Why, I'm still thirsty! I should have been glad of two more casks.'

Then the king took counsel with himself and sent an order to the simpleton that he was to have a bath at the royal palace, and after that the betrothal should take place. Now the bath room was built of iron, and the king gave orders that it was to be heated to such a pitch that it would suffocate the simpleton. But, fortunately, his comrade with the straw entered behind him, and when the door was shut upon them he scattered the straw about, and suddenly the red-hot walls cooled and it became so cold that the simpleton could scarcely bear to take a bath, and all the water in the room froze. So the simpleton climbed up on the stove and, wrapping himself up in the bath blankets, lay there the whole night. In the morning, when they opened the door, there he lay sound and safe, singing cheerfully to himself.

Now when this strange tale was told to the king he became quite sad, not knowing what he should do to get rid of so undesirable a son-in-law. Suddenly a brilliant idea occurred to him.

'Tell the rascal to raise me an army, now at this instant!'

16

The quick-eared comrade had overheard the king's command and repeated it to the simpleton.

'Alas, alas!' he groaned. 'Now I am quite done for.'

'Not at all,' replied the one who had dragged the bundle of wood through the forest. 'Have you forgotten me?'

In the meantime the courtier, who had run all the way from the palace, reached the ship panting and breathless, and delivered the king's message.

'Good!' remarked the simpleton. 'I will raise an army for the king. But if, after that, the king refuses to accept me as his son-in-law, I will wage war against him, and carry the princess off by force.'

During the night the simpleton and his comrade went together into a big field, taking the bundle of wood with them, which the man spread out in all directions. In a moment a mighty army stood upon the spot, regiment on regiment of foot and horse soldiers; the bugles sounded and the drums beat, the chargers neighed, and their riders put their lances in rest, and the soldiers presented arms.

In the morning when the king awoke he was startled by these warlike sounds, the bugles and the drums, and the clatter of the horses, and the shouts of the soldiers. Stepping to the window, he saw the lances gleam in the sunlight and the armour and weapons glitter. And the proud monarch said to himself, 'I am powerless in comparison with this man.'

So he sent him royal robes and costly jewels and commanded him to come to the palace to be married to the princess. His son-in-law put on the royal robes, and he looked so grand and stately that it was impossible to recognize the poor simpleton, so changed was he. The princess fell in love with him as soon as ever she saw him.

Never before had so grand a wedding been seen, and there was so much food and wine that even the glutton and the thirsty comrade had enough to eat and drink.

[From the Russian.]

The Story of King Frost

THERE WAS ONCE UPON a time a peasant woman who had a daughter and a stepdaughter. The daughter had her own way in everything, and whatever she did was right in her mother's eyes; but the poor stepdaughter had a hard time. Let her do what she would, she was always blamed and got small thanks for all the trouble she took. Nothing was right, everything wrong. Yet, if the truth were known, the girl was worth her weight in gold she was so unselfish and good-hearted. Her stepmother was determined to get rid of the girl by fair means or foul, and kept saying to her father:

'Send her away, old man; send her away—anywhere so that my eyes will not be plagued any longer by the sight of her, or my ears tormented by the sound of her voice. Send her out into the fields, and let the cutting frost do for her.'

In vain did the poor old father weep and implore her pity. She was firm, and he dared not gainsay her. So he placed his daughter in a sledge, without even a horse cloth to keep her warm. He drove her out where the trees were thick and dark. He kissed her and left her, driving home as fast as he could.

Deserted by her father, the poor girl sat down under a fir tree at the edge of the forest and began to weep silently. Sud-

denly she heard a faint sound. It was King Frost springing
from tree to tree and cracking his fingers as he went. At length
he reached the fir tree beneath which she was sitting, and with
a crisp crackling sound he alighted beside her and looked at
her lovely face.

'Well, maiden,' he snapped out, 'do you know who I am?
I am King Frost, king of the red noses.'

'All hail to you, great King!' answered the girl, in a gentle
voice. 'Have you come to take me?'

'Are you warm, maiden?' he replied.

'Quite warm, King Frost,' she answered, though she shiv-
ered as she spoke.

Then King Frost bent over the girl and the crackling sound
grew louder. The air seemed full of knives and darts. Again
he asked:

'Maiden, are you warm? Are you warm, beautiful girl?'

And though her breath was almost frozen on her lips, she
whispered gently, 'Quite warm, King Frost.'

Then King Frost gnashed his teeth and cracked his fingers,
his eyes sparkled, and the crackling, crisp sound was louder
than ever, and for the last time he asked her:

'Maiden, are you still warm? Are you still warm, little love?'

The poor girl was so stiff and numb that she could just gasp, 'Still warm, O King!'

Now her gentle, courteous words and her uncomplaining ways touched King Frost and he had pity on her. He wrapped her up in furs and covered her with blankets, and he fetched a great box, in which were beautiful jewels and a rich robe embroidered in gold and silver. She put it on, and looked more lovely than ever, and King Frost stepped with her into his sledge, drawn by six white horses.

In the meantime the wicked stepmother was preparing pancakes. She said to her husband, 'Old man, you had better go out into the fields and see what has happened to your daughter.' Just as the old man was leaving the house, the little dog under the table began to bark, saying:

> 'Your daughter shall live to be your delight;
> Her daughter shall die this very night.'

'Hold your tongue, you foolish beast!' scolded the woman. 'There's a pancake for you, but you must say:

> "Her daughter shall have much silver and gold;
> His daughter is frozen quite stiff and cold."

But the dog ate up the pancake and barked, saying:

> 'His daughter shall wear a crown on her head;
> Her daughter shall die unwooed, unwed.'

Then the old woman tried to coax the dog with more pancakes but he barked on, always repeating the same words. Suddenly the door creaked and flew open, and a great heavy chest was pushed in. Behind it came the stepdaughter, radiant and beautiful, in a dress all glittering with silver and gold. For a moment the stepmother's eyes were dazzled. Then she called to her husband:

'Old man, yoke the horses at once into the sledge, and take my daughter to the same field and leave her on the same spot exactly.' And so the old man took the girl and left her beneath the same tree where he had parted from his daughter. In a few minutes King Frost came past, and looking at the girl, he said:

'Are you warm, maiden?'

'What a blind fool you must be to ask such a question!' she answered angrily. 'Can't you see that my hands and feet are nearly frozen?'

Then King Frost sprang to and fro in front of her, getting only rude, rough words in reply to his questions till at last he cracked his fingers, gnashed his teeth, and froze her to death.

But in the hut her mother was waiting for her return, and as she grew impatient she said to her husband:

'Get out the horses, old man, to go and fetch her home. But see that you are careful not to upset the sledge and lose the chest.'

But the dog beneath the table began to bark, saying:

> *'Your daughter is frozen quite stiff and cold,*
> *And shall never have a chest full of gold.'*

'Don't tell such wicked lies!' scolded the woman.
But the dog went on:

> *'His daughter shall marry a mighty king.*
> *A mighty king, a mighty king.'*

At that moment the door flew open, and she rushed out to meet her daughter, and as she took her frozen body in her arms she too was chilled to death.

[From the Russian.]

The Death of the Sun-Hero

M ANY, MANY THOU-
sands of years ago there lived a mighty king whom Heaven had
blessed with a clever and beautiful son. When he was only ten
years old the boy was more clever than all the king's counsellors,
and when he was twenty he was thought the greatest hero in the
whole kingdom. His father always had him clothed in golden
garments which shone and sparkled like the sun; and his
mother gave him a white horse, which never slept and which
flew like the wind. All the people in the land loved him dearly,
and called him the Sun-Hero, for they did not think his like
existed under the sun.

Now it happened one night that both his parents had the
same extraordinary dream. They dreamed that a girl all dressed
in red had come to them and said, 'If you wish that your son
might really become the Sun-Hero in deed and not only in
name, let him go out into the world and search for the Tree
of the Sun, and when he has found it, let him pluck a golden
apple from it and bring it home.'

When the king and queen had each related their dreams to
the other, they were much amazed that they should both have
dreamed exactly the same thing about their son, and the king

said to his wife, 'This is clearly a sign from Heaven.' Then he at once bade his son set forth in search of the Tree of the Sun, from which he was to pluck a golden apple. The prince was delighted and set out on his travels that very day.

For a long time he wandered all through the world, and it was not till the ninety-ninth day that he found an old man who was able to tell him where the Tree of the Sun grew. He followed his directions and rode on his way. After another ninety-nine days he arrived at a golden castle, which stood in the middle of a vast wilderness. He knocked at the door, which was opened noiselessly and by invisible hands.

Finding no one about, the prince rode on and came to a great meadow, where the Tree of the Sun grew. When he reached it he put out his hand to pick a golden apple. But all of a sudden the tree grew higher so he could not reach its fruit. Then he heard someone behind him laughing. Turning round, he saw a girl in red walking toward him.

'Do you really imagine, brave son of the earth, that you can pluck an apple so easily from the Tree of the Sun?' she said. 'Before you can do that, you have a difficult task before you. You must guard the tree for nine days and nine nights from the ravages of two wild black wolves. Do you think you can undertake this?'

'Yes,' answered the Sun-Hero, 'I will guard the Tree of the Sun nine days and nine nights.'

Then the girl continued, 'Remember though, if you do not succeed, the Sun will kill you. Now begin your watch.'

With these words the Red Girl went back into the golden castle. She had hardly left him when the two black wolves appeared. The Sun-Hero beat them off with his sword, and they retired, only to reappear in a very short time. The Sun-Hero chased them away once more, but he had hardly sat down to rest when they came again. This went on for seven days and nights, when the white horse, who had never done such a thing before, turned to the Sun-Hero and said:

'Listen to what I am going to say. A fairy gave me to your mother that I might be of service to you. Let me tell you, if you go to sleep and let the wolves harm the tree, the Sun will surely kill you. The fairy put everyone in the world under a spell, to prevent their obeying the Sun's command to take your life. But all the same, she forgot one person, who will certainly kill you if you fall asleep and let the wolves damage the tree. So watch and keep the wolves away.'

Then the Sun-Hero strove with all his might and kept the black wolves at bay and conquered his desire to sleep. But on the eighth night his strength failed him, and he fell fast asleep. When he awoke a woman in black stood beside him, who said:

'You have fulfilled your task very badly, for you have let the two black wolves damage the Tree of the Sun. I am the mother of the Sun, and I command you to ride away from here at once. I pronounce sentence of death upon you, for you proudly let yourself be called the Sun-Hero without having done anything to deserve the name.'

The youth mounted his horse sadly and rode home. The people thronged round him on his return, anxious to hear his adventures, but he told them nothing. Only to his mother did he confide what had befallen him. But the old queen laughed, and said to her son:

'Don't worry, my child; you see the fairy has protected you so far, and the Sun has found no one to kill you. So cheer up and be happy.'

After a time the prince forgot all about his adventure, and married a beautiful princess, with whom he lived very happily.

But one day, when he was out hunting, he felt very thirsty, and coming to a stream he stooped down to drink from it. This caused his death, for a crab came swimming up, and with its claws tore out his tongue. He was carried home, and as he lay on his deathbed the black woman appeared and said:

'So the Sun has, after all, found someone who was not under the fairy's spell. A similar fate will overtake everyone who wrongfully assumes a title to which he has no right.'

[From the *Bukowinaer Tales and Legends*. Von Wliolocki.]

The Witch

ONCE UPON A TIME there was a peasant whose wife died, leaving him with two children—twins—a boy and a girl. For some years the poor man lived on alone with the children, caring for them as best he could. But everything in the house seemed to go wrong without a woman to look after it, and at last he made up his mind to marry again, feeling that a wife would take care of his motherless children.

So he married, but peace and order did not come to the household. For the stepmother was very cruel to the twins and half-starved them. All day she thought of nothing but how she could get rid of them; and at last she determined to send them out into the great gloomy wood where a wicked witch lived. And so one morning she spoke to them, saying:

'You have been such good children that I am going to send you to visit my granny, who lives in a little house in the wood. You will have to wait upon her and serve her, but you will be well rewarded, for she will surely give you the best of everything.'

So the children left the house together; and the little sister, who was very wise for her years, said to the brother:

'We will first go and see our own dear grandmother and tell her where our stepmother is sending us.'

And when the grandmother heard where they were going, she cried, 'You poor motherless children! Your stepmother is not sending you to her granny, but to a wicked witch who lives in that great gloomy wood. Now listen to me, children. You must be civil and kind to everyone. Never say a cross word and never touch a crumb belonging to anyone else. Who knows if, after all, help may not be sent to you?'

She gave her grandchildren a bottle of milk, a piece of ham and a loaf of bread, and they set out for the great gloomy wood. There they saw in the thickest of the trees, a queer little hut. When they looked into it, there lay the witch, with her head on the threshold of the door, with one foot in one corner and the other in the other corner, and her knees cocked up, almost touching the ceiling.

'Who's there?' she snarled in an awful voice, when she saw the children.

And they answered civilly, though they were so terrified they hid behind one another. 'Good morning, granny; our stepmother has sent us to wait upon you, and serve you.'

'See that you do it well, then,' growled the witch. 'If I am pleased with you, I'll reward you. If I am not, I'll put you in a pan and fry you in the oven—that's what I'll do with you, my pretty dears! You have been gently reared, but you'll find my work hard enough. See if you don't.'

And, so saying, she set the girl down to spin yarn, and she gave the boy a sieve in which to carry water from the well, and she herself went out into the wood. Now, as the girl was sitting at her distaff, weeping bitterly because she could not spin, she heard the sound of hundreds of little feet. From every hole and corner in the hut mice came pattering along the floor, squeaking and saying:

'Little girl, why are your eyes so red?
If you want help, then give us some bread.'

The girl gave them the bread her grandmother had given her. Then the mice told her that the witch had a cat, and the cat was very fond of ham. If she would give the cat her ham, it would show her the way out of the wood. In the meantime they would spin the yarn for her. So the girl set out to look for the cat, and, as she was hunting about, she met her brother. He could not carry water from the well in a sieve; it came pouring out as fast as he put it in. As she was trying to comfort him they heard a rustling of wings, and a flight of wrens alighted on the ground beside them. And the wrens said:

> *'Give us some crumbs, then you need not grieve.*
> *For you'll find that water will stay in the sieve.'*

Then the twins crumbled the bread on the ground, and the wrens pecked it and chirruped and chirped. And when they had eaten the last crumb they told the boy to fill up the holes of the sieve with clay and then draw water from the well. So he did what they said and carried the sieve full of water into the hut without spilling a drop. When they entered the hut the cat was curled up on the floor. So they stroked her, and fed her with ham, and said to her:

'Pussy, gray pussy, tell us how we are to get away from the witch.'

The cat thanked them for the ham and gave them a pocket handkerchief and a comb, and told them that when the witch pursued them, as she certainly would, all they had to do was to throw the handkerchief on the ground and run as fast as they could. As soon as the handkerchief touched the ground a deep, broad river would spring up. If the witch managed to get across it, they must throw the comb behind them and run for their lives. Where the comb fell a dense forest would start up, which would delay the witch so long that they would be able to get safely away.

The cat had scarcely finished speaking when the witch returned to see if the children had fulfilled their tasks.

'Well, you have done well enough for today,' she grumbled, 'but tomorrow you'll have something more difficult to do, and if you don't do it well, you pampered brats, straight into the oven you go.'

The poor children lay down to sleep on a heap of straw in the corner of the hut, but they dared not close their eyes and scarcely ventured to breathe. In the morning the witch gave the girl two pieces of linen to weave before night, and the boy a pile of wood to cut into chips. Then she left them to their tasks and went out into the wood.

As soon as she was out of sight the children took the comb and the handkerchief and, hand in hand, they started and ran and ran and ran. First they met the watchdog, who was going to leap on them, but they threw the remains of their bread to him, and he ate, and wagged his tail. They were hindered by the birch trees, whose branches almost put out their eyes. But the little sister tied the twigs together with a piece of ribbon, and after running through the wood, they came out on to the open fields.

In the meantime the cat was busy weaving the linen and tangling the threads as it wove. The witch returned to see how the children were getting on, and she crept up to the window, and whispered:

'Are you weaving, my little dear?'

'Yes, granny, I am weaving,' answered the cat.

Then the witch saw that the children had escaped her. She was furious and, hitting the cat with a porringer, she said:

'Why did you let the children leave the hut? Why did you not scratch out their eyes?'

But the cat curled up its tail and put its back up, and answered, 'I have served you all these years and you never even threw me a bone, but the dear children gave me their one piece of ham.'

Then the witch was furious with the watchdog and with the birch trees, because they let the children pass. But the dog answered:

17

'I have served you all these years and you never gave me so much as a hard crust, but the dear children gave me their own bread.'

And the birch rustled its leaves, and said, 'I have served you longer than I can say, and you never tied even a bit of twine round my branches. The dear children bound them up with their brightest ribbon.'

So the witch saw there was no help to be had from her old servants, and the best thing she could do was to mount on her broom and set off in pursuit of the children. As the children ran they heard the sound of the broom sweeping the ground close behind them, so they threw the handkerchief down, and in a moment a deep, broad river flowed there.

When the witch came to the river it took her a long time to find a place she could ford on her broomstick. But at last she got across, and continued the chase faster than before.

As the children ran they heard a sound, and the little sister put her ear to the ground and heard the broom sweeping the earth close behind them again. Quick as thought, she threw the comb down on the ground, and in an instant a dense forest sprang up, in which the roots and branches were so closely intertwined, that it was impossible to force a way through. So when the witch came up to the forest on her broom she found there was nothing for it but to turn round and go back to her hut.

But the twins ran straight on till they reached their own home. Then they told their father all that they had suffered, and he was so angry that he drove their stepmother out of the house and never let her return. But he and the children lived happily together. He took care of them himself and never let a stranger come near them.

[From the Russian.]

The Hazelnut Child

THERE WAS ONCE UPON
a time a couple who had no children, and they prayed every
day for a child, though it were no bigger than a hazelnut. At
last their prayer was heard and they had a child exactly the
size of a hazelnut, who never grew an inch. The parents were
devoted to the little creature and nursed and tended it carefully.
Their tiny son was as clever as could be, and so sensible that
all the neighbours marvelled over the wise things he said and did.

When the hazelnut child was fifteen years old, he was sitting
one day in an eggshell on the table beside his mother. She
turned to him, and said:

'You are now fifteen years old. What do you intend to be?'

'A messenger,' answered the hazelnut child.

Then his mother burst out laughing, and said, 'What an idea!
Why, your little feet would take an hour to go the distance an
ordinary person could do in a minute!'

But the hazelnut child replied, 'Nevertheless I mean to
be a messenger. Just send me with a message and you'll see
that I shall be back in next to no time.'

So his mother said, 'Very well, go to your aunt in the neighbouring village, and fetch me a comb.'

The hazelnut child jumped quickly out of the eggshell and ran out into the street. Here he found a man on horseback who was just setting out for the neighbouring village. He crept up the horse's leg, sat down under the saddle, and then began to pinch the horse. The horse plunged and reared and then set off at a hard gallop, in spite of its rider's efforts to stop it. When they reached the village, the hazelnut child left off pinching the horse, and the poor tired creature pursued its way at a snail's pace. The hazelnut child took advantage of this and crept down the horse's leg. Then he ran to his aunt and asked her for a comb. On the way home he met another rider and did the return journey in exactly the same way.

When he handed his mother the comb she was amazed, and asked him, 'But how did you manage to get back so quickly?'

'Ah, Mother,' he replied, 'you see I was quite right.'

His father too possessed a horse which he often used to take out into the fields to graze. One day he took the hazelnut child with him. At midday the father turned to his small son and said:

'Stay here and look after the horse. I must go home and give your mother a message, but I shall be back soon.'

When his father had gone, a robber passed by and saw the horse grazing without anyone watching it, for of course he could not see the hazelnut child hidden in the grass. So he mounted the horse and rode away. But the hazelnut child climbed up the horse's tail and talked to it so it paid no attention to the robber but galloped straight home. The father was astonished when he saw a stranger riding his horse, but the hazelnut child climbed down quickly and told him all that had happened, and his father had the robber arrested.

One autumn when the hazelnut child was twenty years old he

said to his parents, 'Farewell, my dear Father and Mother. I am going out into the world, and as soon as I have become rich I will return home to you.'

The parents laughed at the little man's words, but did not believe him for a moment. In the evening the hazelnut child crept on to the roof, where some storks had built their nest. The storks were fast asleep and he climbed on to the back of the father stork and bound himself by a silk cord to one of its wings. Then he crept among its soft down feathers and fell asleep.

Next morning the storks flew toward the south, for winter was approaching. The hazelnut child flew through the air on the stork's back. In this way he reached the country of the black people where the storks took up their abode.

When the people saw the hazelnut child they were much astonished, and took him with the stork to the king of the country. The king was delighted with the little creature and kept him always beside him and soon grew so fond of him that he gave him a diamond four times as big as himself.

The hazelnut child fastened the diamond firmly under his stork's neck with a ribbon. When he saw the storks were getting ready for their northern flight he mounted the bird and away they went, getting nearer home every minute. At length the hazelnut child came to his native village. He undid the ribbon from the stork's neck and the diamond fell to the ground. He covered it first with sand and stones and then ran to get his parents, so that they might carry the treasure home. He himself was not able to lift the great diamond.

So the hazelnut child and his parents lived together in happiness and prosperity.

[From the *Bukowinaer*. Von Wliolocki.]

Prince Ring

ONCE UPON A TIME
there was a king and his queen who had one daughter, called
Ingiborg, and one son, whose name was Ring. He was less
fond of adventures than men were in those days and was not
famous for strength or feats of arms.

One fine winter day, when he was twelve years old, Ring
rode into the forest with his men. They went on a long way,
until they caught sight of a hind with a gold ring on its horns.
The prince was eager to catch it, so they gave chase and rode
on until all the horses foundered beneath them. At last the
prince's horse gave way too, and then there came over them a
darkness so black that they could no longer see the hind. By
this time they were far away from any house and thought it
was high time to be making their way home again, but they
found they were lost now. At first they all kept together, but
soon each began to think that he knew the right way; so they
all went in different directions.

The prince, lost like the rest, wandered on until he came to
a little clearing in the forest not far from the sea, where he
saw a woman sitting on a chair with a big barrel beside her.
The prince saluted her politely and she received him graciously.

He looked down into the barrel and saw lying at the bottom an unusually beautiful gold ring, which pleased him so much he could not take his eyes off it. The woman saw this, and said he might have it if he would take the trouble to get it. The prince thanked her and said it was at least worth trying.

He thought he would easily reach the ring, but the more he stretched down the deeper grew the barrel. As he was bending down the woman suddenly pushed him in head first, saying that now he could take up his quarters there. Then she fixed the top on the barrel and threw it out into the sea.

The prince felt the barrel floating out from the land and tossing about on the waves. How many days he spent thus he could not tell, but at last he felt the barrel knocking against rocks. He was a little cheered, thinking it was probably land and not merely a reef in the sea. Being something of a swimmer, he kicked the bottom out of the barrel and swam to shore. Overhead there were high cliffs. It was difficult to get up these but at last he did. Having reached the top, he looked round about him and saw that he was on an island, which was covered with a forest of apple trees and altogether pleasant as far as the land was concerned.

After he had been there several days, he heard a great noise in the forest, which made him so afraid that he ran to hide among the trees. Then he saw a giant approaching, dragging a sledge loaded with wood and making straight for him. When the giant came across him, he stood still and looked at the prince for a little. Then he took him up in his arms and carried him home to his house and was exceedingly kind to him. He gave him to his wife, saying he had found the child in the wood, and she could have it to help her in the house. The old woman was greatly pleased and began to fondle the prince with the utmost delight. He stayed with them and was willing and obedient in everything, while they grew kinder to him every day.

One day the giant took him round and showed him all his rooms except the parlour. This made the prince curious. So later, when the giant had gone into the forest, the prince managed to get the door open halfway. Then he saw that some living creature moved inside and ran along the floor toward him and said something, which so frightened him that he sprang back from the door and shut it again. As soon as his fright passed off he tried it again, for he thought it would be interesting to hear what the creature said. But everything happened just as before. He was angry with himself and, summoning up his courage, tried it a third time and opened the door of the room and stood firm. Then he saw that it was a big dog, which spoke to him and said:

'Choose me, Prince Ring.'

The prince went away rather afraid, thinking it was no great treasure after all. But all the same what it had said to him stayed in his mind.

One day the giant said he would now take him over to the mainland for he himself had no long time to live. He also thanked the prince for his good service and told him to choose of his possessions whatever he wanted. Ring thanked him heartily, and said there was no need, for his services were of little worth. But if he did wish to give him anything he would choose what was in the parlour. The giant was taken by surprise, and said:

'There, you chose the old woman's right hand. But I must not break my word.'

Upon this he went to get the dog, which came running with signs of great delight. But the prince was so much afraid of it it was all he could do to keep from showing his alarm.

He told his wife he had found the child in the wood

After this the giant accompanied him down to the sea, where he saw a stone boat, just big enough to hold the two of them and the dog. On reaching the mainland the giant took a friendly farewell of Ring and told him he might take possession of all that was in the island after he and his wife died, which would happen within two weeks. The prince thanked him for all his kindnesses, and the giant returned home. Ring was afraid to speak to the dog. After they had walked on in silence for a time the dog said:

'You don't seem to have much curiosity, you have never asked my name.'

The prince then forced himself to ask, 'What is your name?'

'You had best just call me Snati,' said the dog. 'Now we are coming to a king's seat, and you must ask the king to keep us all winter, and to give you a little room for us.'

The prince was now less afraid of the dog. They came to the king and asked him to keep them all winter, to which he agreed. When the king's men saw the dog they began to laugh at it and tease it. But when the prince advised them not to do it, they replied that they didn't care a bit what he thought.

The king had a counsellor called Red, who became very jealous when he saw how much the king esteemed Ring. One day he asked him why he had so good an opinion of this stranger, who had not yet shown himself superior in anything. The king replied that it was only a short time since he had come. Red asked him to send them both to cut down wood next morning, and see which of them could do most work.

Snati heard of this and advised Ring to ask for two axes, so that he might have one in reserve if the first one broke. Next morning the king asked Ring and Red to go and cut down trees for him, and both agreed. Ring got the two axes,

and each went his own way. When the prince had got out in
the wood Snati took one of the axes and began to hew along
with him. In the evening the king came to look over their
day's work and found that Ring's wood heap was more than
twice as big.

'I suspected,' said the king, 'that Ring was not quite useless.
Never have I seen such a day's work.'

Ring was now in far greater esteem with the king than
before, and Red was all the more discontented. One day he
came to the king and said, 'If Ring is such a mighty man, I
think you might ask him to kill the wild oxen in the wood
here, flay them the same day, and bring you the horns and
hides in the evening.'

'Don't you think that a desperate errand?' asked the king.
'They are so dangerous and no one has ever yet ventured to go
against them.'

Red answered that Ring had only one life to lose and it would
be interesting to see how brave he was. Reluctantly the king
allowed himself to be won over by Red's persistency. He asked
Ring to go and kill the oxen that were in the wood and bring
their horns and hides to him in the evening. Not knowing how
dangerous the oxen were, Ring was quite ready and went off
at once, to the great delight of Red.

As soon as Ring came in sight of the oxen they ran bellowing
to meet him. One of them was tremendously big, the other
rather less. Ring grew terribly afraid.

'How do you like them?' asked Snati.

'Not at all,' said the prince.

'We can do nothing else than attack them, if it is to go well.
You will go against the little one, and I shall take the other.'

With this Snati leaped at the big one, and was not long in

bringing him down. Meanwhile the prince went against the other. The ox nearly had him under, but Snati was not slow in helping his master kill it.

Each of them then began to flay his own ox, but Ring was only half through by the time Snati had finished his. In the evening, after they had finished this task, Snati told him to lay the horns and hides on his back until they reached the palace gate. The prince agreed, and laid everything on the dog except the skin of the smaller ox, which he staggered along with himself. At the palace gate he left everything lying, went before the king and asked him to come with him, and there handed over to him the hides and horns of the oxen. The king was greatly surprised at his valour and said he knew no one like him and thanked him heartily for what he had done.

After this the king set Ring next to himself, and all esteemed him highly. One day Red came to the king and said he had something to say to him.

'What is that?' said the king.

Red said that he had just remembered the gold cloak, gold chessboard, and bright gold piece that the king had lost about a year before.

'Don't remind me of them!' said the king.

Red, however, went on to say that since Ring was such a mighty man the king might ask him to search for these treasures and come back with them before Christmas. In return the king should promise him his daughter.

The king replied he thought it altogether unbecoming to propose such a thing to Ring, seeing that he could not tell him where the things were. Red pretended not to hear the king's excuses and went on talking about it until the king gave in to him. One day, a month or so before Christmas, the king spoke to Ring, saying that he wished to ask a great favour of him.

'What is that?' said Ring.

'Find for me my gold cloak, my gold chessboard, and my bright gold piece that were stolen from me about a year ago. If you can bring them to me before Christmas I will give you my daughter in marriage.'

'Where am I to look for them, then?' asked Ring.

'That you must find out for yourself,' said the king. 'I don't know.'

Ring was silent, for he saw he was in a great difficulty but, on the other hand, he thought it excellent to have a chance of winning the king's daughter. Snati said he would have to act upon his advice, otherwise he would get into great difficulties. The prince assented to this with many words of gratitude for all the dog had already done, and prepared for the journey.

After he had taken leave of the king Snati said to him, 'Now you must first of all gather as much salt as ever you can.'

The prince did so and gathered so much salt he could hardly carry it, but Snati said, 'Throw it on my back.' And the dog then ran on before the prince, until they came to the foot of a steep cliff.

'We must go up here,' said Snati.

'I don't think that will be child's play,' said the prince.

'Hold fast by my tail,' said Snati. And in this way he pulled Ring up on the lowest shelf of the rock. The prince began to feel giddy, but up went Snati on to the second shelf. Ring was nearly swooning by this time, but Snati made a third effort and reached the top of the cliff, where the prince fell down in a faint. After a little, however, he recovered again, and they went a short distance along a level plain, until they came to a cave. This was on Christmas Eve. They went up above the cave, and found a window in it, through which they looked. Four trolls lay asleep beside the fire, over which a large porridge pot was hanging.

'Now you must empty all the salt into the porridge pot,' said Snati.

Ring did so and soon the trolls awoke. The old hag, who was the most frightful of them all, went first to taste the porridge.

'How comes this?' she said. 'The porridge is salt! I got the milk by witchcraft yesterday out of four kingdoms, and now it is salt!'

All the others then came to taste the porridge, and thought it nice, but after they had finished it the old hag grew so thirsty she could stand it no longer and asked her daughter to bring her some water from the river that ran near by.

'I won't go,' said she, 'without your bright gold piece.'

'Though I should die you shall not have that,' said the hag.

'Die then,' said the girl.

'Well, then, take it,' said the old hag, 'be off with you and make haste with the water.'

The girl took the gold and ran out with it, and it was so bright that it shone all over the plain. As soon as she came to the river she lay down to take a drink of the water, but meanwhile Ring and Snati thrust her into the river.

The old hag longed for the water, and said the girl must be running about with the gold piece all over the plain. She asked her son to get her a drop of water.

'I won't go,' said he, 'unless I get the gold cloak.'

'Though I should die you shall not have that,' said the hag.

'Die, then,' said the son.

'Well, then, take it,' said the old hag, 'and be off with you, but make haste with the water.'

He put on the cloak, and it shone so brightly that he could see the path with it. On reaching the river he went to take a drink like his sister, but at that moment Ring and Snati sprang upon him, took the cloak from him, and threw him into the river.

The old hag could stand the thirst no longer, and asked her husband to go for a drink for her.

'I won't go,' said the old troll, 'unless you lend me the gold chessboard.'

'Though I should die you shall not have that,' said the hag.

'I think you may just as well do that,' said he, 'since you won't grant me such a little favour.'

'Take it, then,' said the old hag.

The old troll now went out with the gold chessboard and down to the river. Ring and Snati came upon him, took the chessboard from him, and threw him into the river. When they got back again to the window they saw the old hag moving toward the door.

'Now we must go in at once,' said Snati, 'and try to master her, for if once she gets out we shall have no chance with her. She is the worst witch that ever lived and no iron can cut her.'

In they went then, and no sooner did the hag see them than she said, 'So you have come, Prince Ring. You must have seen to my husband and children.'

Snati saw that she was about to attack them and sprang at her while Ring poured the boiling porridge over her without stopping, and in this way they at last overcame her. Then they explored the cave, where they found plenty of gold and treasures. The most valuable of these they carried as far as the cliff and left them. Then they hastened home to the king with his three treasures, arriving late on Christmas night.

The king was beside himself with joy and betrothed his daughter to Ring. The festivities were to last all through Christmastide. Ring thanked the king courteously for this and all his other kindnesses, and as soon as he had finished eating and drinking in the hall went off to sleep in his own room. Snati, however, asked permission to sleep in the prince's bed for that night, while the prince should sleep where the dog usually lay. Ring said he was welcome to do so and that he deserved more from him than that. So Snati went up into the prince's bed, but after a time he came back, and told Ring he could go there himself now, but to take care not to meddle with anything that was in the bed.

Now the story comes back to Red, who came into the hall

and showed the king his right arm wanting the hand, and said that now he could see what kind of a man his intended son-in-law was, for he had done this to him without any cause whatever. The king became very angry and said he would soon find out the truth about it. So the king sent for Ring and asked him for what reason he had done this. Snati, however, had just told Ring what had happened during the night, and in reply he asked the king to go with him and he would show him something. The king went with him to his sleeping room, and saw lying on the bed a man's hand holding a sword.

'This hand,' said Ring, 'came over the partition during the night and was about to run me through in my bed, if I had not defended myself.'

The king answered that in that case he could not blame him for protecting his own life, and that Red was well worthy of death. Then Ring married the king's daughter.

That night Snati asked Ring to allow him to lie at their feet, and this Ring allowed him to do. During the night he heard a howling and outcry beside them, struck a light in a hurry and saw an ugly dog's skin lying near him, and a beautiful prince on the bed. Ring instantly took the skin and burned it, and then shook the prince, who was lying unconscious, until he woke up.

The bridegroom then asked his name. He replied he was called Ring, and was a king's son. In his youth he had lost his mother, and his father had then married a witch, who had laid a spell on him. He should turn into a dog, and never be released from the spell unless a prince of the same name allowed him to sleep at his feet the night of his marriage. He added further, 'As soon as she knew you were my namesake she tried to get you destroyed so you might not free me from the spell. She was the hind you and your companions chased;

she was the woman you found with the barrel, and the old hag that we killed in the cave.'

After the feasting was over the two namesakes, along with other men, went to the cliff and brought all the treasure to the palace. Then they went to the island and removed all that was valuable. Ring gave his sister Ingiborg in marriage to his brave namesake and his father's kingdom to look after. He himself stayed with his father-in-law the king and had half the kingdom while he lived and the whole of it after his death.

[From the Icelandic.]

The Blue Mountains

THERE WAS ONCE A
Scotsman and an Englishman and an Irishman serving in the
army together, who took it into their heads to run away. The
chance came and they took it. They went for two days through
a great forest, without food or drink and without coming
across a single house, and every night they had to climb up
into the trees through fear of the wild beasts in the wood.
One morning the Scotsman saw from the top of his tree a great
castle far away. He said to himself that he would certainly die
if he stayed in the forest with nothing to eat but the roots of
grass, which would not keep him alive very long.

He set off for the castle, without so much as telling his
companions what he had seen. He travelled most of the day,
so it was quite late when he reached the castle. To his great
disappointment he found nothing but closed doors and no
smoke rising from the chimneys. He thought there was nothing
for it but to die after all and had lain down beside the wall,
when he heard a window opened high above him. At this he
saw the most beautiful woman he had ever set eyes on.

'Oh, it is Fortune that has sent you to me,' he said. 'I am
dying for want of food and drink.'

'Come inside, then,' she said. 'There is plenty of both here.'

Accordingly she opened a large room for him, where he saw a number of men lying asleep. She then set food before him and after that showed him to the room where the others were. He lay down on one of the beds and fell sound asleep.

Meanwhile the Englishman climbed the very same tree and as soon as the dawn showed him the four quarters of heaven, what did he see but the castle too! Off he went without saying a word to the Irishman, and everything happened to him just as it had to the Scotsman.

The poor Irishman was now left all alone, so he stayed where he was, very sad and miserable. When night came he climbed up into the same tree as the Englishman had the night before. As soon as day came he also saw the castle and set out toward it. But when he reached it he could see no signs of fire or a living being about it. Before long, however, he heard the window open above his head and looked up. When he beheld the beautiful woman he asked if she would give him food and drink. She answered kindly and heartily that she would, if he would only come inside, and she set before him food and drink he had never seen the like of before. In the room there was a bed, with diamond rings hanging at every loop of the curtains, and everything that was in the room besides astonished him so much that he actually forgot he was hungry. When she asked him what he wanted he replied he would neither eat nor drink until he knew who she was, where she came from, and who had put her there.

'I shall tell you that,' said she. 'I am an enchanted princess. My father has promised the man who releases me from the spell the third of his kingdom while he is alive, and the whole of it after he is dead, and he may marry me as well. If ever I saw a man to do this, you are the one. I have been here for sixteen years now, and no one has asked me who I was, except yourself. Every other man lies asleep in the big room down there.'

'Tell me, then,' said the Irishman, 'what is the spell that has been laid on you and how you can be freed from it.'

'There is a little room there,' said the princess, 'and if I could get a man to stay in it from ten o'clock till midnight for three nights on end I should be freed from the spell.'

'I am the man for you, then,' said he. 'I will do it.'

Thereupon she brought him a pipe and tobacco, and he went into the room. Before long he heard a hammering and knocking on the outside of the door and was told to open it.

'I won't,' he said.

The next moment the door came flying open, and those outside along with it. They knocked him down and kicked him and knelt on his body till it came midnight. But as soon as the cock crew they all disappeared. The Irishman was little more than alive by this time. As soon as day dawned the princess came and found him lying full length on the floor, unable to speak a word. She took a bottle, rubbed him from head to foot with something from it, and thereupon he was as sound as ever. But after that night he was very unwilling to try a second time. The princess, however, entreated him to stay, saying that the next night would not be so bad, and in the end he gave in and stayed.

When it was near midnight he heard them ordering him to open the door, and there were three of them for every one there had been the previous evening. He did not make the slightest movement to go out to them or to open the door, but before long they broke it open and were in on top of him. They laid hold of him, and kept throwing him between them up to the ceiling, or jumping on him, until the cock crew, when they all disappeared. When day came the princess went to the room to see if he was still alive and taking the bottle put it to his nostrils, which soon brought him to himself. The first thing he said was that he was a fool to go on getting himself killed and was determined to be off and stay there no longer.

The princess entreated him to stay, reminding him that only another night would free her from the spell. 'Besides,' she said, 'if there is a single spark of life in you when the day comes, that stuff in the bottle will make you as sound as ever you were.'

With all this the Irishman decided to stay, but that night there were three at him for every one the two nights before, and it looked very unlikely that he would be alive in the morning. When morning dawned, and the princess came to see if he was still alive, she found him lying on the floor as if dead.

She put her hand on his pulse and found a faint movement. Accordingly she poured what was in the bottle on him, and before long he rose up on his feet, and was as well as ever he was. So that was finished and the princess was freed from the spell.

The princess then told the Irishman that she must go away for the present, but would return for him in a few days in a carriage drawn by four gray horses. 'I have paid dear for you the last three nights,' he said, 'if I have to part with you now.' But in the twinkling of an eye she had disappeared. He did not know what to do with himself when he saw she was gone, but she had given him a little rod, with which he could, when he pleased, waken the men who had been sleeping there, some of them for sixteen years.

Being thus left alone, he went in and stretched himself on three chairs that were in the room. Then what does he see coming in at the door but a little fair-haired lad!

'Where did you come from, my lad?' said the Irishman.

'I came to make ready your food for you,' said he.

'Who told you to do that?' said the Irishman.

'My mistress,' answered the lad; 'the princess who was under the spell and is now free.'

By this the Irishman knew she had sent the lad to wait on him. The lad also told him that his mistress wished him to be ready next morning at nine o'clock, when she would come for him with the carriage as she had promised. He was greatly pleased at this, and next morning, when the time was drawing near, went out into the garden. But the little fair-haired lad took a big pin out of his pocket, and stuck in into the back of the Irishman's coat without his noticing it, whereupon he fell sound asleep.

Before long the princess came with the carriage and four horses, and asked the lad whether his master was awake. He said that he wasn't. 'It is bad for him,' said she, 'when the night is not long enough for him to sleep. Tell him if he doesn't meet me tomorrow it is not likely he will ever see me again all his life.'

As soon as she was gone the fair-haired lad took the pin out of his master's coat, who instantly awoke. The first word he said to the lad was, 'Have you seen her?'

'Yes,' said he, 'and she bade me tell you that if you don't meet her at nine o'clock tomorrow you will never see her again.'

He was very sorry when he heard this, and could not understand why sleep should have fallen upon him just when she was coming. He decided, however, to go early to bed that night, in order to rise in time next morning. When it was again near nine o'clock he went out to the garden to wait till she came, and the fair-haired lad along with him. But as soon as the lad got the chance he stuck the pin into his master's coat again and he fell asleep as before.

Precisely at nine o'clock came the princess in the carriage with four horses, and asked the lad if his master was awake, but he said, 'No, he is asleep, just as he was the day before.'

'Dear, dear!' said the princess. 'I am sorry for him. Tell him he will never see me here again. Give him this sword in my name and my blessing along with it.'

As soon as she had gone the lad took the pin out of his master's coat. He awoke instantly, and the first word he said was, 'Have you seen her?' The lad said he had, and here was the sword she had left for him. The Irishman was ready to kill the lad out of sheer vexation, but when he glanced over his shoulder not a trace of the fair-haired lad was left.

Being thus left alone, he thought of going into the room where all the men were lying asleep, and there he found his two comrades. Then he remembered that the princess had told him he had only to touch them with the rod and they would all awake. The first he touched were his own comrades. They started to their feet at once, and he gave them as much silver and gold as they could carry when they went away. There was plenty to do before he had wakened all the others, for the two doors of the castle were crowded with them all the day long.

The loss of the princess, however, rankled in his mind day and night, till finally he thought he would go about the world to see if he could find anyone to give him news of her. So he took the best horse in the stable and laid hold of the sword she had given him by the hands of the fair-haired lad. On drawing it from its sheath he noticed some writing on one side of the blade. He read, *You will find me in the Blue Mountains.* This made him take heart again, and he set out, thinking he would go on in hope of meeting someone who could tell him where the Blue Mountains were. After he had gone a long way he saw at last a light and made straight for it. It came from a little house and the man inside asked what brought him there and where he was going.

'I have lived here,' said he, 'for three hundred years, and all that time I have not seen a single human being but yourself.'

'I have been going about for the last three years,' said the Irishman, 'to see if I could find anyone who can tell me where the Blue Mountains are.'

'Come in,' said the old man, 'and stay with me the night. I have a book which contains the history of the world. If there is such a place as the Blue Mountains we shall find it out.'

The Irishman stayed all night and as soon as morning came rose to go. The old man said he had not gone to sleep at all for going through the book, but there was not a word about the Blue Mountains in it. 'But I'll tell you what,' he said, 'I have a brother who lives nine hundred miles from here, and he is sure to know if anyone in this world does.' The Irishman answered that he could never go these nine hundred miles, for his horse was giving in already. 'That doesn't matter,' said the old man; 'I can do better than that. I have only to blow my whistle and you will be at my brother's house before nightfall.'

So he blew the whistle, and the Irishman did not know where he was until he found himself at the other old man's door. It was three hundred years since this brother had seen anyone, and he too asked him where he was going.

'I am going to see if I can find anyone to tell me where the Blue Mountains are,' he said.

'If you will stay with me tonight,' said the old man, 'I have a book of the history of the world. I shall know where they are before daylight, if there is such a place at all.'

He stayed there all night, but there was not a word in the

book about the Blue Mountains. Seeing that he was cast down, the old man told him he had a brother nine hundred miles away. 'He might know and I will enable you,' he said, 'to reach there before night.'

So he blew his whistle, and the Irishman landed at the brother's house before nightfall. This old man said he had not seen a single man for three hundred years, and was very much surprised to see one now.

'Where are you going?' he said.

'To the Blue Mountains,' said the Irishman.

'The Blue Mountains?'

'Yes,' said the Irishman.

'I never heard the name before, but I am master of all the birds in the world, and have only to blow my whistle and every one will come to me. If there is any way of finding the Blue Mountains that is it.'

So he blew his whistle and all the birds of the world began to gather. The old man questioned them but not one of them had come from the Blue Mountains. However, he missed a big eagle and wondered why she had not come. Soon afterward he saw something darkening the sky, coming nearer and growing bigger, and what was this after all but the eagle? When she arrived the old man scolded her, and asked what had kept her so long behind.

'I couldn't help it,' she said. 'I had more than twenty times farther to come than any bird here today.'

'Where have you come from, then?' said the old man.

'From the Blue Mountains,' said she.

'Indeed!' said the old man. 'And what are they doing there?'

'They are making ready this very day,' said the eagle, 'for the marriage of the daughter of the King of the Blue Mountains. For three years now she has refused to marry anyone

He blew his whistle and all the birds of the world arrived

who wooed, until she should give up all hope of the coming of the man who released her from the spell. Now she can wait no longer, for three years is the time she agreed upon with her father.'

The Irishman knew that it was for himself she had been waiting so long, but he had no hope of reaching the Blue Mountains. The old man noticed how sad he grew and asked the eagle if she would carry this man on her back to the Blue Mountains.

'I must have threescore cattle killed,' said she, 'and cut up into quarters, and every time I look over my shoulder he must throw one of them into my mouth.'

As soon as the Irishman and the old man heard her demand they went out hunting, and before evening they had killed threescore cattle. They quartered them, as the eagle told them, and then the old man asked her to lie down, till they could get it all heaped up on her back. First of all, though, they had to get a ladder of fourteen steps, to enable them to get on to the eagle's back, and there they piled up the meat as well as they could. Then the old man told the Irishman to mount and to remember to throw a quarter of beef to her every time she looked round. He went up, and the old man gave the eagle the word to be off. So it was arranged and every time she turned her head the Irishman threw a quarter of beef into her mouth.

As they came near the borders of the kingdom of the Blue Mountains, however, the beef was gone. At this she turned a complete somersault, and threw the Irishman off into the sea, where he fell into the bay right in front of the king's palace. Fortunately the points of his toes just touched the bottom, and he managed to get ashore.

When he went up into the town all the streets were gleaming with light, and the wedding of the princess was just about to begin. He went into the first house he came to, which happened to be the royal henwife's. He asked the old woman what was causing all the noise and light in the town.

'The princess,' said she, 'is going to be married tonight against her will, for she has been expecting every day that the man who freed her from the spell would come.'

'There is a guinea for you,' said he; 'go and bring her here.'

The old woman soon returned with the princess. She and the Irishman recognized each other with great joy and they were married. The great wedding feast lasted for a year and a day.

The Cinderbox

A SOLDIER CAME

marching along the high road—left, right! Left, right! He had
his knapsack on his back and a sword by his side, for he had
been to the wars and was now returning home. An old witch
met him on the road. She was very ugly to look at, for her
underlip hung down to her breast.

'Good evening, soldier!' she said. 'What a fine sword and
knapsack you have! You are something like a soldier! You
ought to have as much money as you would like to carry!'

'Thank you, old witch,' said the soldier.

'Do you see that great tree?' said the witch, pointing to a
tree beside them. 'It is hollow within. You must climb up to
the top, and then you will see a hole through which you can
let yourself down into the tree. I will tie a rope round your
waist so I may pull you up again when you call.'

'What shall I do down there?' asked the soldier.

'Get money!' answered the witch. 'Listen! When you reach
the bottom of the tree you will find yourself in a large hall.
It is light, for there are more than three hundred lamps burning.
Then you will see three doors, which you can open—the keys
are in the locks. If you go into the first room, you will see a

266

great chest in the middle of the floor with a dog sitting upon it; he has eyes as large as saucers, but you needn't trouble about him. I will give you my blue-checked apron, which you must spread out on the floor. Then go back quickly and fetch the dog and set him upon it. Open the chest and take as much money as you like. It is copper there. If you would rather have silver, you must go into the next room, where there is a dog with eyes as large as millwheels. But don't take any notice of him. Just set him upon my apron and help yourself to the money. If you prefer gold, you can get that too, as much as you can carry, if you go into the third room. But the dog that guards the chest there has eyes as large as the Round Tower at Copenhagen! He is a savage dog, I can tell you. But you needn't be afraid of him either. Put him on my apron and he won't touch you, and you can take out of the chest as much gold as you like!'

'Come, this is not bad!' said the soldier. 'But what am I to give you, old witch, for surely you are not doing this for nothing?'

'Yes, I am!' replied the witch. 'Not a single farthing will I take! For me you shall bring nothing but an old tinderbox which my grandmother forgot last time she was down there.'

'Well, tie the rope round my waist!' said the soldier.

'Here it is,' said the witch, 'and here is my blue-checked apron.'

Then the soldier climbed up the tree, let himself down through the hole, and found himself standing, as the witch had said, in the large hall, where more than three hundred lamps were burning.

Well, he opened the first door. There sat the dog with eyes as big as saucers glaring at him.

'You are a fine fellow!' said the soldier and, putting him on the witch's apron, took as much copper as his pockets could hold. Then he shut the chest, put the dog on it again, and went into the second room. Sure enough there sat the dog with eyes as large as millwheels.

'You had better not look at me so hard!' said the soldier. 'Your eyes will come out of their sockets!'

Then he set the dog on the apron. When he saw all the silver in the chest, he threw away the copper he had taken and filled his pockets and knapsack with nothing but silver.

Then he went into the third room. Horrors! The dog had two eyes, each as large as the Round Tower at Copenhagen, spinning round in his head like wheels.

'Good evening!' said the soldier and saluted, for he had never seen a dog like this before. But when he had examined him more closely, he thought, Now then, I've had enough of this, and put him down on the floor and opened the chest. What a heap of gold there was! With all that he could buy up the whole town, and all the sugar pigs, all the tin soldiers, whips and rocking horses in the whole world. Now he threw away all the silver with which he had filled his pockets and knapsack, and filled them with gold instead—yes, all his pockets, his knapsack, cap and boots even, so that he could hardly walk. Now he was rich indeed. He put the dog back upon the chest, shut the door, and then called up through the tree:

'Now pull me up again, old witch!'

'Have you the tinderbox also?' asked the witch.

'Botheration!' said the soldier. 'I had clean forgotten it!' And he went back and fetched it.

The witch pulled him up, and there he stood again on the highroad, with pockets, knapsack, cap and boots filled with gold.

'What do you want to do with the tinderbox?' asked the soldier.

'That doesn't matter to you,' replied the witch. 'You have your money, give me my tinderbox.'

'We'll see!' said the soldier. 'Tell me at once what you want to do with it, or I will draw my sword and cut off your head!'

'No!' screamed the witch.

The soldier immediately cut off her head. That was the end of her! But he tied up all his gold in her apron, slung it like a bundle over his shoulder, put the tinderbox in his pocket and set out toward the town.

It was a splendid town! He turned into the finest inn, ordered the best chamber and his favourite dinner. Now he had so much money he was really rich.

It certainly occurred to the servant who had to clean his boots that they were astonishingly old boots for such a rich lord. But that was because he had not yet bought new ones. Next day he appeared in respectable boots and fine clothes. Now, instead of a soldier he had become a noble lord, and people told him about all the grand doings of the town and the king, and what a beautiful princess his daughter was.

'How can one see her?' asked the soldier.

'She is never to be seen at all!' they told him. 'She lives in a great copper castle, surrounded by many walls and towers! No one except the king may go in or out, for it is prophesied that she will marry a common soldier, and the king cannot submit to that.'

I should very much like to see her, thought the soldier; but he could not get permission.

Now he lived very gaily, went to the theatre, drove in the king's garden and gave the poor a great deal of money, which was very nice of him. He had experienced in former times how hard it is not to have a farthing in the world. Now he was rich, wore fine clothes, and made many friends, who all said that he was an excellent man, a real nobleman. The soldier liked that. But as he was always spending money and never made any more, at last the day came when he had nothing left but two shillings, and he had to leave the beautiful rooms in which he had been living and go into a little attic under the roof, clean his own boots and mend them with a darning needle. None of his friends came to visit him there, for there were too many stairs to climb.

It was a dark evening and he could not even buy a light. But all at once it flashed across him that there was a little end of tinder in the tinderbox, which he had taken from the hollow tree. He found the box with the tinder in it; but just as he was kindling a light and had struck a spark out of the tinderbox, the door burst open, and the dog with eyes as large as saucers, which he had seen down in the tree, stood before him and said:

'What does my lord command?'

'What's the meaning of this?' exclaimed the soldier. 'This is a pretty kind of tinderbox, if I can get whatever I want like this. Get me money!' he cried to the dog, and presto! He was off and back again, holding a great purse full of money in his mouth.

Now the soldier knew what a capital tinderbox this was. If he rubbed once, the dog that sat on the chest of copper appeared. If he rubbed twice, there came the dog that watched over the silver chest. If he rubbed three times, the one that guarded the gold appeared. Now, the soldier went down again to his beautiful rooms and appeared once more in splendid clothes. All his friends immediately recognized him again and paid him great court.

One night he thought, It is very strange that no one can see

There came the dog with eyes as large as saucers

the princess. They all say she is very pretty, but what's the use of that if she has to sit forever in the great copper castle with all the towers? Can I not manage to see her somehow? Where is my tinderbox? He struck a spark, and presto! There came the dog with eyes as large as saucers.

'It is the middle of the night, I know,' said the soldier, 'but I should very much like to see the princess for a moment.'

The dog was already outside the door, and before the soldier could look round, in he came with the princess. She was lying asleep on the dog's back, and was so beautiful that anyone could see she was a real princess. The soldier really could not refrain from kissing her—he was such a thorough soldier. Then the dog ran back with the princess. But when it was morning, and the king and queen were drinking tea, the princess said she had had such a strange dream about a dog and a soldier. She had ridden on the dog's back, and the soldier had kissed her.

'That is certainly a fine story,' said the queen. But the next night one of the ladies-in-waiting was sent to watch at the princess's bed, to see if it was only a dream, or if it had actually happened.

The soldier had an overpowering longing to see the princess again, and so the dog came in the middle of the night and fetched her, running as fast as he could. But the lady-in-waiting followed them. When she saw them disappear into a large house, she thought, Now I know where it is. She made a great cross on the door with a piece of chalk. Then she went home and lay down, and the dog came back also, with the princess. But when he saw that a cross had been made on the door of the house where the soldier lived, he took a piece of chalk also and made crosses on all the doors in the town. That was very clever, for now the lady-in-waiting could not find the right house, as there were crosses on all the doors.

Early next morning the king, queen, ladies-in-waiting and officers came out to see where the princess had been.

'There it is!' said the king, when he saw the first door with a cross on it.

'No, there it is, my dear!' said the queen, when she likewise saw a door with a cross.

'But here is one, and there is another!' they all exclaimed. Wherever they looked there was a cross on the door. Then they realized that the sign would not help them at all.

But the queen was a clever woman, who could do a great deal more than just drive in a coach. She took her great golden scissors, cut up a piece of silk and made a pretty little bag of it. This she filled with the finest buckwheat grains and tied it round the princess's neck. This done, she cut a little hole in the bag so the grains would strew the whole road wherever the princess went.

In the night the dog came again, took the princess on his back and ran with her to the soldier, who was very much in love with her and would have liked to be a prince so that he might have her for his wife.

The dog did not notice how the grains were strewn right from the castle to the soldier's window, where he ran up the wall with the princess.

In the morning the king and the queen saw plainly where their daughter had been and they took the soldier and put him into prison.

There he sat. Oh, how dark and dull it was there! And they told him, 'Tomorrow you are to be hanged.' Hearing that did not exactly cheer him, and he had left his tinderbox in the inn.

Next morning he could see through the iron grating in front of his little window how the people were hurrying out of the town to see him hanged. He heard the drums and saw the soldiers marching. All the people were running to and fro. Just below his window was a shoemaker's apprentice, with leather apron and shoes. He was skipping along so merrily that one of his shoes flew off and fell against the wall, just where the soldier was sitting peeping through the iron grating.

'Oh, shoemaker's boy, you needn't be in such a hurry!' said the soldier to him. 'There's nothing going on till I arrive. But if you will run back to the house where I lived, and fetch me my tinderbox, I will give you four shillings. But you must put your best foot foremost.'

The shoemaker's boy was very willing to earn four shillings and fetched the tinderbox and gave it to the soldier.

Outside the town a great scaffold had been erected, and all round were standing the soldiers and hundreds of thousands of people. The king and queen were sitting on a magnificent throne opposite the judges and the whole council.

The soldier was already standing on the top of the ladder. But when they wanted to put the rope round his neck, he said that the fulfilment of one innocent request was always granted to a poor criminal before he underwent his punishment. He would so much like to smoke a small pipe of tobacco. It would be his last pipe in this world.

The king could not refuse him this, and so he took out his tinderbox and rubbed it once, twice, and three times. And lo, and behold! There stood all three dogs—the one with eyes as large as saucers, the second with eyes as large as millwheels, and the third with eyes each as large as the Round Tower of Copenhagen.

'Help me now, so that I may not be hanged!' cried the

soldier. And thereupon the dogs fell upon the judges and the whole council, seized some by the legs, others by the nose, and threw them high into the air.

'I won't stand this!' said the king. But the largest dog seized him too, and the queen as well, and threw them up after the others. This frightened the soldiers, and all the people cried, 'Good soldier, you shall be our king, and marry the beautiful princess!'

Then they put the soldier into the king's coach, and the three dogs danced in front, crying 'Hurrah!' And the boys whistled and the soldiers presented arms.

The princess came out of the copper castle and became queen and that pleased her very much. The wedding festivities lasted for eight days, and the dogs sat at table and made eyes at everyone.

The Witch in the Stone Boat

THERE WAS ONCE A KING
and a queen, and they had a son called Sigurd, who was very
strong and active and good-looking. When the king came to
be bowed down with the weight of years he spoke to his son
and said that he would like to see him married before he died.
Sigurd was not averse to this and asked his father where he
thought it best to look for a wife. The king answered that in
a certain country there was a king who had a beautiful
daughter, and he thought it would be most desirable if Sigurd
could get her. So Sigurd prepared for the journey and went
where his father had directed him.

He came to the king and asked for his daughter's hand,
which was readily granted him, but only on the condition that
he should remain there, for the king himself was not strong
and not very able to govern his kingdom. Sigurd accepted this
condition, but added he would have to go home again to his
own country when he heard news of his father's death. After
that Sigurd married the princess, and helped his father-in-law
to govern the kingdom. He and the princess loved each other

276

THE WITCH IN THE STONE BOAT 277

dearly and a son came to them, who was two years old when word was brought to Sigurd that his father was dead. Sigurd went on board ship to go home with his wife and child.

They had sailed for several days, when the breeze suddenly fell, and there came a dead calm. Sigurd and his queen were on deck one day, when most of the others on the ship had fallen asleep. There they sat and talked for a while and their little son was with them. After a time Sigurd became so heavy with sleep that he could no longer keep awake. He went below and lay down, leaving the queen alone on the deck, playing with her son.

A good while after Sigurd had gone below, the queen saw something black on the sea, which seemed to be coming nearer. As it approached she could make out a boat and the figure of someone rowing it. At last the boat came alongside the ship, and now the queen saw that it was of stone, out of which there came up on board a fearfully ugly witch. The queen was more frightened than words can describe and could neither speak a word nor move to awaken the king or the sailors. The witch came right up to the queen, took the child from her and laid it on the deck. Then she stripped the queen of all her fine clothes, which she put on herself. Last of all she put the queen into the boat, and said:

'This spell I lay upon you, slacken not your course until you come to my brother in the underworld.'

The queen sat stunned and motionless, but the boat at once shot away from the ship with her, and before long she was out of sight.

When the boat could no longer be seen the child began to cry, and though the witch tried to quiet it she could not. She went below to where the king was sleeping, with the child on her arm, and awakened him, scolding him for leaving them alone on deck, while he and all the crew were asleep. It was great carelessness, she said, to leave no one to watch the ship with her.

Sigurd was greatly surprised to hear his queen scold him, for she had never said an angry word to him before. However, he thought it was quite excusable in this case and tried to quiet the child but it was no use. Then he wakened the sailors and bade them hoist the sails, for a breeze had sprung up and was blowing straight toward the harbour.

They soon reached the land which Sigurd was to rule. All the people were sorrowful for the old king's death, but they were glad Sigurd was back and made him king over them.

The king's son, however, hardly ever stopped crying from the time he had been taken from his mother on the deck of the ship, although he had always been such a good child before. At last the king had to get a nurse for him—one of the maids of the court. As soon as the child was put in her charge he stopped crying and behaved as well as before.

After the sea voyage it seemed to the king that the queen had altered very much in many ways, and not for the better. He thought her much more haughty and stubborn and difficult than she used to be. Others noticed as well as the king. In the court there were two young men, one eighteen years old, the other nineteen, who were very fond of playing chess. Often they sat long playing at it. Their room was next the queen's, and often during the day they heard her talking.

One day they put their ears close to a crack in the wall between the rooms and heard the queen say quite plainly, 'When I yawn a little then I am a nice little maiden. When I yawn halfway then I am half a troll and, when I yawn fully, then I am a troll altogether.'

As she said this she yawned tremendously and in a moment

The beautiful woman took the child from the nurse

had become a fearfully ugly troll. Then there came up through the floor a three-headed giant with a trough full of meat, who saluted her as his sister and set down the trough before her. She began to eat greedily and never stopped till she had emptied it. The young men saw all this going on, but did not hear the two of them say anything to each other. They were astonished though at how greedily the queen devoured the meat and how much she ate of it and were no longer surprised that she took so little when she sat at table with the king. As soon as she had finished it the giant disappeared with the trough by the same way as he had come, and the queen resumed her human shape.

One evening, after the king's son had been put in charge of the nurse, she was holding the child. Suddenly several planks sprang up in the floor of the room, and out at the opening came a beautiful woman dressed in white, with an iron belt round her waist, fastened with an iron chain that went down into the ground. The woman came up to the nurse, took the child from her and pressed it to her breast. Then she gave it back to the nurse and returned by the same way she had come, and the floor closed over her again. Although the woman had not spoken a single word to her, the nurse was very frightened. She told no one about it.

Next evening the same thing happened again, just as before, but as the woman was going away she said in a sad tone, 'Two are gone, and one only is left,' and then disappeared as before. The nurse was still more frightened when she heard the woman say this and thought that perhaps some danger was hanging over the child. The most mysterious thing was the woman saying, 'And only one is left.' But the nurse guessed this must mean that only one day was left, since she had come for two days already.

At last the nurse made up her mind to go to the king, and she told him the whole story and asked him to be present in person next day when the woman usually came. The king promised to do so and came to the nurse's room a little before the time and sat down on a chair with his drawn sword in his hand. Soon after the planks in the floor sprang up as before. The woman came up, dressed in white, with the iron belt and chain. The king saw at once that it was his own queen and immediately hewed asunder the iron chain that was fastened to the belt. This was followed by such noises and crashings down in the earth that all the king's palace shook. No one expected anything else than to see every bit of it shaken to pieces. At last, however, the noises and shaking stopped, and they began to come to themselves again.

The king and queen embraced each other, and she told him the whole story—how the witch came to the ship when they were all asleep and sent her off in the boat. After she had gone so far that she could not see the ship, she sailed on through darkness until she landed beside a three-headed giant. The giant wished her to marry him, but she refused, whereupon he shut her up by herself and told her she would never get free until she consented. After a time she began to plan how to escape, and at last told him she would consent if he would allow her to visit her son on earth three days on end. This he agreed to, but put on her this iron belt and chain, the other end of which he fastened round his own waist, and the great noises that were heard when the king cut the chain must have been caused by the giant's falling down the underground passage when the chain gave way so suddenly.

The king now understood how the queen for some time past had been so ill-tempered. The two young men also now told what they had heard and seen in the queen's room and that was enough to get rid of her. Before this they had been afraid to say anything about it.

The real queen was now restored to all her dignity and was beloved by all. The nurse was married to a nobleman, and the king and queen gave her splendid presents.

[From the Icelandic.]

Thumbelina

THERE WAS ONCE A
woman who wanted to have a tiny, little child, but she did not
know where to get one. So one day she went to an old witch
and said to her:

'I should so much like to have a tiny, little child. Can you
tell me where I can get one?'

'Oh, we have one just ready!' said the witch. 'Here is a
barleycorn for you. It's not the kind the farmer sows in his
field or feeds the cocks and hens with, I can tell you. Put it in
a flowerpot and then you will see something happen.'

'Oh, thank you,' said the woman and gave the witch a
shilling, for that was what it cost. Then she went home and
planted the barleycorn. Immediately there grew out of it a
large and beautiful flower, which looked like a tulip, but the
petals were tightly closed as if it were still only a bud.

'What a beautiful flower!' exclaimed the woman, and she
kissed the red and yellow petals. As she kissed them the flower
burst open. It was a real tulip, such as one can see any day, but
in the middle of the blossom, on the soft velvety petals, sat
a tiny girl, trim and pretty. She was scarcely half a thumb in
height so they called her Thumbelina.

An elegant polished walnut shell served Thumbelina as a cradle, the blue petals of a violet were her mattress and a rose leaf her coverlid. There she lay at night, but in the daytime she used to play about on the table. Here the woman had put a bowl, surrounded by a ring of flowers, with their stalks in water, in the middle of which floated a great tulip petal, and in this Thumbelina sat and sailed from one side of the bowl to the other, rowing herself with two white horsehairs for oars It was such a pretty sight! She could sing, too, with a voice more soft and sweet than had ever been heard before.

One night, when she was lying in her pretty bed, an old toad crept in through a broken pane in the window. She was very ugly and clumsy, and she hopped on to the table where Thumbelina lay asleep under the red rose leaf.

'This would make a beautiful wife for my son,' said the toad, taking up the walnut shell, with Thumbelina inside, and hopped with it through the window into the garden.

There flowed a great wide stream, with slippery and marshy banks; here the toad lived with her son. Ugh, how ugly and clammy he was, just like his mother! 'Croak, croak, croak!' was all he could say when he saw the pretty little girl in the walnut shell.

'Don't talk so loud, or you'll wake her,' said the old toad. 'She might escape us even now. She is as light as a feather. We will put her at once on a broad water-lily leaf in the stream. That will be quite an island for her; she is so small and light. She can't run away from us there, while we are preparing the guest chamber under the marsh where she shall live.'

Outside in the brook grew many water lilies, with broad green leaves, which looked as if they were swimming about on the water. The leaf farthest away was the largest, and to this the old toad swam with Thumbelina in her walnut shell.

The tiny Thumbelina woke up very early in the morning, and when she saw where she was she began to cry bitterly. On every side of the great green leaf was water and she could not get to the land.

The old toad was down under the marsh, decorating her room with rushes and yellow marigold leaves, to make it very grand for her new daughter-in-law. Then she swam out with her ugly son to the leaf where Thumbelina lay. She wanted to fetch the pretty cradle to put it into her room before Thumbelina herself came there. The old toad bowed low in the water before her, and said:

'Here is my son. You shall marry him and live in great magnificence down under the marsh.'

'Croak, croak, croak!' was all the son could say. Then they took the neat little cradle and swam away with it. Thumbelina sat alone on the great green leaf and wept, for she did not want to live with the toad or marry her ugly son. The little fishes swimming about under the water had seen the toad quite plainly and heard what she had said. They put up their heads to see the little girl, and thought her so pretty they were very sorry she should go down with the ugly toad to live. No, that must not happen. They assembled in the water round the green stalk which supported the leaf on which she was sitting and nibbled the stem in two. Away floated the leaf down the stream, bearing Thumbelina far beyond the reach of the toad.

On she sailed past several towns, and the little birds sitting in the bushes saw her and sang, 'What a pretty little girl!' The leaf floated farther and farther away. Thus Thumbelina left her native land.

A beautiful little white butterfly fluttered above her and at last settled on the leaf. Thumbelina pleased him and she, too, was delighted. Now the toads could not reach her, and it was so beautiful where she was travelling. The sun shone on the water and made it sparkle like the brightest silver. She took off her sash and tied one end round the butterfly. The other end she fastened to the leaf so that it glided along with her faster than ever.

A great cockchafer came flying past. He caught sight of Thumbelina and in a moment had put his legs round her slender waist and had flown off with her to a tree. The green leaf floated away down the stream and the butterfly with it, for he was fastened to the leaf and could not get loose. How terrified poor little Thumbelina was when the cockchafer flew off with her to the tree! And she was especially distressed for the beautiful white butterfly because she had tied him fast. If he could not get away he might starve to death. But the cockchafer did not trouble himself about that. He sat down with her on a large green leaf, gave her honey out of the flowers to eat and told her she was very pretty, although she wasn't in the least like a cockchafer. Later on, all the other cockchafers who lived in the same tree came to pay calls. They examined Thumbelina closely, and remarked, 'Why, she has only two legs! How very miserable!'

'She has no feelers!' cried another.

'How ugly she is!' said all the lady chafers—and yet Thumbelina was really very pretty.

The cockchafer who had stolen her knew this very well. But when he heard all the ladies saying she was ugly, he began to think so too and would not keep her. She might go wherever she liked. So he flew down from the tree with her and put her on a daisy. There she sat and wept, because she was so ugly the cockchafer would have nothing to do with her. Yet she was the most beautiful creature imaginable, so soft and delicate, like the loveliest rose leaf.

As she sailed the little birds sang, 'What a pretty little girl!'

The whole summer poor little Thumbelina lived alone in the great wood. She plaited a bed for herself of blades of grass and hung it up under a clover leaf so she was protected from the rain. She gathered honey from the flowers for food and drank the dew on the leaves every morning. Thus the summer and autumn passed, but then came winter—the long, cold winter. All the birds who had sung so sweetly about her had flown away. The trees shed their leaves, the flowers died. The great clover leaf under which she had lived curled up and nothing remained but the withered stalk. She was terribly cold, for her clothes were ragged and she herself was so small and thin. Poor little Thumbelina would surely be frozen to death. It began to snow, and every snow flake that fell on her was like a whole shovelful, for she was only an inch high. She wrapped herself up in a dead leaf, but it was torn in the middle and gave her no warmth. She was trembling with cold.

Just outside the wood where she was now living lay a great cornfield. The corn had been gone a long time. Only the dry, bare stubble was left standing in the frozen ground. This made a forest for her to wander about in. All at once she came across the door of a field mouse, who had a little hole under a cornstalk. There the mouse lived warm and snug, with a storeroom full of corn, a splendid kitchen and dining room. Poor little Thumbelina went up to the door and begged for a little piece of barley, for she had not had anything to eat for two days.

'Poor little creature!' said the field mouse, for she was a kind-hearted old thing. 'Come into my warm room and have some dinner with me.' As Thumbelina pleased her, she said, 'As far as I am concerned you may spend the winter with me. You must keep my room clean and tidy and tell me stories, for I like that very much.'

And Thumbelina did all that the kind old field mouse asked and did it remarkably well too.

'Now I am expecting a visitor,' said the field mouse. 'My neighbour comes to call on me once a week. He is in better circumstances than I am, has great big rooms, and wears a fine black-velvet coat. If you could only marry him, you would be well provided for. But he is blind. You must tell him all the prettiest stories you know.'

But Thumbelina did not trouble her head about him, for he was only a mole. He came and paid them a visit in his black-velvet coat.

'He is so rich and accomplished,' the field mouse told her. 'His house is twenty times larger than mine. He possesses great knowledge, but he cannot bear the sun and the beautiful flowers, and speaks slightingly of them, for he has never seen them.'

Thumbelina had to sing to him, so she sang 'Ladybird, ladybird, fly away home!' and other songs so prettily that the mole fell in love with her. He did not say anything. He was a very cautious man. A short time before he had dug a long passage through the ground from his own house to that of his neighbour. In this he gave the field mouse and Thumbelina permission to walk as often as they liked. But he begged them not to be afraid of the dead bird that lay in the passage. It was a real bird with beak and feathers and must have died a long time ago and now lay buried just where he had made his tunnel.

The mole took a piece of rotten wood in his mouth, for that glows like fire in the dark, and went in front, lighting them through the long dark passage. When they came to the place where the dead bird lay, the mole put his broad nose against the ceiling and pushed a hole through so the daylight could shine down. In the middle of the path lay a dead swallow, his pretty wings pressed close to his sides, his claws and head drawn under his feathers; the poor bird had evidently died of cold. Thumbelina was very sorry, for she was fond of all little birds. They had sung and twittered so beautifully to her all through the summer. But the mole kicked him with his bandy legs and said:

'Now he can't sing any more! It must be very miserable to be a little bird! I'm thankful that none of my little children are. Birds always starve in winter.'

'Yes, you speak like a sensible man,' said the field mouse. 'What has a bird, in spite of all his singing, in the wintertime? He must starve and freeze, and that must be very unpleasant for him, I must say!'

Thumbelina did not say anything. When the other two had passed on she bent down to the bird, brushed aside the feathers from his head, and kissed his closed eyes gently. 'Perhaps he sang to me in the summer,' she said. 'How much pleasure he did give me, dear little bird!'

The mole closed up the hole again which let in the light and then escorted the ladies home. But Thumbelina could not sleep that night. She got out of bed and plaited a big blanket of straw and carried it off and spread it over the dead bird. She piled upon it thistledown as soft as cotton wool, which she had found in the field-mouse's room, so that the poor little thing should lie warmly buried.

'Farewell, pretty little bird!' she said. 'Farewell, and thank you for your beautiful songs in the summer, when the trees were green and the sun shone down warmly on us!' Then she laid her head against the bird's heart. But the bird was not dead. He had been frozen, but now that she had warmed him, he was coming to life again.

In autumn the swallows fly away to foreign lands. But there are some who are late in starting and then they get so cold that they drop down as if dead and the snow comes and covers them over.

Thumbelina trembled, she was so frightened. The bird was very large in comparison with herself—only an inch high. But she took courage, piled up the down more closely over the poor swallow, fetched her own coverlid and laid it over his head.

Next night she crept out again to him. There he was alive, but very weak. He could only open his eyes for a moment and look at Thumbelina, who was standing in front of him with a piece of rotten wood in her hand, for she had no other lantern.

'Thank you, pretty little child!' said the swallow to her. 'I am so beautifully warm! Soon I shall regain my strength, and then I shall be able to fly out again into the warm sunshine.'

'Oh,' she said, 'it is very cold outside. It is snowing and freezing! Stay in your warm bed. I will take care of you!'

Then she brought him water in a petal, which he drank. He told her how he had torn one of his wings on a bramble so he could not keep up with the other swallows, who had flown far away to warmer lands. So at last he had dropped down exhausted, and then he could remember no more. The whole winter he remained down there, and Thumbelina looked after him and nursed him tenderly. Neither the mole nor the field mouse learned anything of this, for they could not bear the poor swallow.

When the spring came, and the sun warmed the earth again, the swallow said farewell to Thumbelina, who opened for him the hole in the roof the mole had made. The sun shone brightly down upon her and the swallow asked her if she would go with him. She could sit upon his back. Thumbelina wanted very much to fly far away into the green wood, but she knew that the old field mouse would be sad if she ran away. 'No, I mustn't come!' she said.

'Farewell, dear good little girl!' said the swallow, and flew off into the sunshine. Thumbelina gazed after him with tears in her eyes, for she was very fond of the swallow.

'Tweet, tweet!' sang the bird, and flew into the green wood. Thumbelina was very unhappy. She was not allowed to go out into the warm sunshine. The corn which had been sowed in the field over the field-mouse's home grew up high into the air and made a thick forest for the poor little girl, who was only an inch high.

'Now you are to be a bride, Thumbelina,' said the field mouse, 'for our neighbour has proposed for you. What a piece of fortune for a poor child like you! Now you must set to work at your linen for your dowry, for nothing must be lacking if you are to become the wife of our neighbour, the mole!'

Thumbelina had to spin all day long, and every evening the mole visited her and told her that when the summer was over the sun would not shine so hot. Now it was burning the earth as hard as a stone. Yes, when the summer had passed, they would have the wedding.

But she was not at all pleased about it, for she did not like the stupid mole. Every morning when the sun was rising, and every evening when it was setting, she would steal out of the house door, and when the breeze parted the ears of corn so that she could see the blue sky through them, she thought how bright and beautiful it must be outside and longed to see her dear swallow again. But he never came. No doubt he had flown far away into the great green wood.

By the autumn Thumbelina had finished the dowry.

'In four weeks you will be married,' said the field mouse.

'Don't be obstinate, or I shall bite you with my sharp white teeth! You will get a fine husband. The king himself has not such a velvet coat. His storeroom and cellar are full, and you should be thankful for that.'

Well, the wedding day arrived. The mole had come to fetch Thumbelina to live with him deep down under the ground, never to come out into the warm sun again, for that was what he didn't like. The poor little girl was very sad, for now she must say good-bye to the beautiful sun.

'Farewell, bright sun!' she cried, stretching out her arms toward it and taking another step outside the house. Now the corn had been reaped, and only the dry stubble was left standing. 'Farewell, farewell!' she said, and put her arms round a little red flower that grew here. 'Give my love to the dear swallow when you see him!'

'Tweet, tweet!' sounded in her ear all at once. She looked up. There was the swallow flying past! As soon as he saw Thumbelina, he was very glad. She told him how unwilling she was to marry the ugly mole, as then she had to live underground where the sun never shone, and she could not help bursting into tears.

'The cold winter is coming now,' said the swallow. 'I must fly away to warmer lands. Will you come with me? You can sit on my back, and we will fly far away from the ugly mole and his dark house, over the mountains to the warm countries. There the sun shines more brightly than here. There it is always summer and there are always beautiful flowers. Do come with me, dear little Thumbelina, who saved my life when I lay frozen in the dark tunnel!'

'Yes, I will go with you,' said Thumbelina, and climbed on the swallow's back, with her feet on one of his outstretched wings. Up into the air he flew, over woods and seas, over the great mountains where the snow is always lying. If she was cold she crept under his warm feathers, only keeping her little head out to admire all the beautiful things in the world beneath. At last they came to warm lands. There the sun was brighter, the sky seemed twice as high, and in the hedges hung the finest green and purple grapes. In the woods grew oranges and lemons. The air was scented with myrtle and mint and on the roads were pretty little children running about and playing with great gorgeous butterflies. But the swallow flew on farther, and it became more and more beautiful. Under the most splendid green trees beside a blue lake stood a glittering white-marble castle. Vines hung about the high pillars; there were many swallows' nests, and in one of these lived the swallow who was carrying Thumbelina.

'Here is my house!' said he. 'But it won't do for you to live with me. I am not tidy enough to please you. Find a home for yourself in one of the lovely flowers that grow down there. Now I will set you down and you can do whatever you like.'

'That will be splendid!' said she, clapping her little hands.

There lay a great white-marble column which had fallen to the ground and broken into three pieces, but between these grew the most beautiful white flowers. The swallow flew down with Thumbelina and set her upon one of the broad leaves. There, to her astonishment, she found a tiny little man sitting in the middle of the flower, as white and transparent as if he were made of glass. He had the prettiest golden crown on his head and the most beautiful wings on his shoulders. He himself was no bigger than Thumbelina. He was the spirit of the flower. In each blossom there dwelt a tiny man or woman. But this one was king over the others.

'How handsome he is!' whispered Thumbelina to the swallow.

The little king was very much frightened by the swallow, for in comparison with one as tiny as himself he seemed a giant. But when he saw Thumbelina, he was delighted, for she was the most beautiful girl he had ever seen. So he took his golden crown off his head and put it on hers, asking her her name and if she would be his wife, and then she would be queen of all the flowers. Yes, he was a different kind of husband from the son of the toad and the mole with the black-velvet coat. So she said yes to the king. And out of each flower came a lady and gentleman, each so tiny and pretty that it was a pleasure to see them. Each brought Thumbelina a present, but the best of all was a beautiful pair of wings which they fastened on her back, and now she too could fly from flower to flower. They all wished her joy, and the swallow sat above in his nest and sang the wedding march as well as he could. But he was sad, because he was very fond of Thumbelina and did not want to be separated from her.

'You shall not be called Thumbelina!' said the spirit of the flower. 'That is an ugly name, and you are much too pretty for that. We will call you May Blossom.'

'Farewell, farewell!' said the little swallow with a heavy heart and flew away to farther lands, far, far away, right back to Denmark. There he had a little nest above a window, where his wife lived, who can tell fairy stories. 'Tweet, tweet!' he sang to her. And that is the way we learned the whole story.

The Nightingale

IN CHINA, THE EMPEROR is Chinese, and all his courtiers are also Chinese. It all happened many years ago, but the story is worth telling again, before it is forgotten.

The emperor's palace was the most splendid in the world, all made of priceless porcelain, but so brittle and delicate one had to take great care in touching it.

In the garden were the most beautiful flowers, and on the loveliest of them were tied silver bells, which tinkled so that if you passed you could not help looking at the flowers. Everything was admirably arranged with a view to effect, and the garden was so large that even the gardener himself did not know where it ended.

Beyond it was a stately forest with great trees and deep lakes. The forest sloped down to the sea, which was a clear blue. Large ships could sail in under the boughs of the trees, where lived a nightingale.

She sang so beautifully that even the poor fisherman, who had so much to do, stopped to listen when he came at night to cast his nets. 'How beautiful it is!' he said. But he had to attend to his work and forgot about the bird. But when she sang the next night and the fisherman came, he said again, 'How beautiful it is!'

From all the countries round travellers came to the emperor's town and were astonished at the palace and the garden. But when they heard the nightingale they all said, 'This is the finest of all!'

The travellers told all about it when they returned home, and learned scholars wrote many books about the town, the palace and the garden. But they did not forget the nightingale. She was praised above everything else, and all the poets composed splendid verses about the nightingale in the forest by the deep sea.

The books were sent throughout the world, and some of them reached the emperor. He sat in his golden chair and read and read. He nodded his head now and then, for he liked the brilliant accounts of the town, the palace and the garden. 'But the nightingale is better than all,' they said.

'What!' said the emperor. 'I don't know anything about the nightingale. Is there such a bird in my empire, and in my own garden? I have never heard of her. Fancy reading about her for the first time in a book!'

And he called his first lord to him. He was so proud that if anyone of lower rank than his own ventured to speak to him or ask him anything, he would say nothing but 'P!' and that does not mean anything.

'Here is a most remarkable bird which is called a night-ingale,' said the emperor. 'They say she is the most glorious thing in my kingdom. Why has no one ever said anything to me about her?'

'I have never before heard the nightingale mentioned,' said the first lord. 'I will look and find her too!'

But where was she to be found? The first lord ran upstairs

and downstairs, through the halls and corridors; but no one
he met had ever heard of the nightingale. So the first lord ran
again to the emperor and told him that it must all be an
invention on the part of those who had written the books.

'Your Imperial Majesty cannot really believe all that is
written. There are some inventions called the black art.'

'But the book in which I read this,' said the emperor, 'was
sent me by his great majesty the Emperor of Japan; so it cannot be untrue, and I will hear the nightingale. She must be
here this evening! She has my gracious permission to appear,
and if she does not, the whole court shall be trampled under
foot after supper!'

'Tsing pe!' said the first lord; and he ran upstairs and downstairs, through the halls and corridors, and half the court ran
with him, for they did not want to be trampled under foot.

Everyone was asking about the wonderful nightingale, of
which all the world knew except those at court.

At last they met a poor little girl in the kitchen, who said,
'Oh, I know the nightingale well. How she sings! Every evening I carry the scraps over from the court table to my poor
sick mother. When I am going home at night, tired and weary,
I stop to rest for a little while in the wood, then I hear the
nightingale singing. It brings tears to my eyes, and I feel as
if my mother were kissing me.'

'Little kitchenmaid,' said the first lord, 'I will give you a
place in the palace kitchen, and you shall have leave to see the
emperor at dinner, if you will lead us to the nightingale, for
she is invited to court this evening.'

So they all went into the forest where the nightingale was
wont to sing, and half the court went too. When they were on
the way they heard a cow mooing.

'Oh,' said the courtiers, 'now we have found her. What a

wonderful power for such a small creature! I am sure we have never heard her before.'

'No, that is a cow mooing,' said the little kitchenmaid. 'We are still a long way off.'

Then the frogs began to croak in the marsh.

'Splendid,' said the court chaplain. 'Now we hear the nightingale; it sounds like little church bells.'

'No, no, those are frogs,' said the little kitchenmaid. 'But I think we shall soon hear her now!'

Then the nightingale began to sing.

'There she is!' cried the girl. 'Listen! She is sitting there.' And she pointed to a little gray bird up in the branches.

'Is it possible?' said the first lord. 'I should never have thought it. How ordinary she looks. She must have lost her colour, seeing so many distinguished men round her.'

'Little Nightingale,' called out the kitchenmaid, 'our gracious emperor wants you to sing for him.'

'With the greatest of pleasure,' said the nightingale, and she sang so gloriously that it was a pleasure to hear her.

'It sounds like glass bells,' said the first lord. 'Look how her little throat throbs! It is strange we have never heard her before. She will be a great success at court.'

'Shall I sing once more for the emperor?' asked the nightingale, thinking that he was present.

'My esteemed little Nightingale,' said the first lord, 'I have the great pleasure to invite you to court this evening, where his gracious imperial highness will be enchanted with your charming song!'

'My song sounds best in the green woods,' said the nightingale; but she went gladly with them when she heard that the emperor wished it.

At the palace everything was splendidly prepared. The porcelain walls and floors glittered in the light of many thousands of golden lamps; gorgeous flowers with tinkling bells were placed in the corridors. There was such a hurrying and a draught that all the bells jingled so one could scarcely hear oneself speak.

In the centre of the great hall, where the emperor sat on his throne, a golden perch had been placed for the nightingale. The whole court was there, and the little kitchenmaid was allowed to stand behind the door, now that she was court cook. Everyone was dressed in his best, and everyone was looking toward the little gray bird to whom the emperor nodded kindly.

The nightingale sang so gloriously that tears came into the emperor's eyes and rolled down his cheeks. Then the nightingale sang even more beautifully, straight to all hearts. The emperor was so delighted that he said she should wear his gold slipper round her neck. But the nightingale thanked him and said she had reward enough already.

'I have seen tears in the emperor's eyes; that is a great reward. An emperor's tears have such power.' Then she sang again with her entrancingly sweet voice.

'That is the most charming coquetry I have ever heard,' said all the ladies round, and they all held water in their mouths that they might make a jug-jugging sound whenever anyone spoke to them. Then they thought themselves nightingales. The lackeys and chambermaids announced they also were pleased, which means a great deal, for they are the most difficult of all to satisfy. In short, the nightingale was a real success.

She had to stay at court now; she had her own cage, with permission to walk out twice in the day and once at night. She was given twelve servants, each of whom held a silken string which was fastened round her leg. There was little pleasure in flying about like this.

The whole town was talking about the wonderful bird, and, when two people met, one would say 'Nightin,' and the other 'Gale,' and then they would sigh and understand each other. Yes, and eleven grocers' children were called after the nightingale, but not one of them could sing a note.

One day the emperor received a large parcel, on which was written *The Nightingale.*

'Here is another new book about our famous bird, I am sure,' said the emperor.

It was not a book, however, but a little mechanical toy, which lay in a box—an artificial nightingale, very like the real one, but covered all over with diamonds, rubies and sapphires. When it was wound up, it could sing one of the songs the real bird sang, and its tail moved up and down, glittering with

There was little pleasure in flying about like this

silver and gold. Round its neck was a little collar on which was written, *The Nightingale of the Emperor of Japan is nothing compared to that of the Emperor of China.*

'Wonderful!' everyone said, and the man who had brought the artificial bird received the title of 'Bringer of the Imperial First Nightingale.'

'Now they must sing together. What a duet we shall have!' And so they sang together, but their voices did not blend, for the real nightingale sang in her way and the other bird sang waltzes.

'It is not its fault!' said the music master. 'It keeps very good time and is quite after my style!'

Then the artificial bird had to sing alone. It gave just as much pleasure as the real one, and some said it was much prettier to look at, for it sparkled like bracelets and necklaces. Three-and-thirty times it sang the same piece without being tired. The courtiers wanted to hear it again, but the emperor thought that the living nightingale should sing now—but where was she? No one had noticed that she had flown out of the open window, away to her green woods.

'What shall we do?' said the emperor.

And all the court scolded and said that the nightingale was very ungrateful. 'But we still have the better bird!' they said. Then the artificial one had to sing again, and that was the thirty-fourth time they had heard the same piece, but they did not yet know it by heart; it was much too difficult. The music master praised the bird and assured them it was better than a real nightingale, not only because of its beautiful diamond-studded plumage, but because of its mechanical interior as well.

'For see, my Lords and Ladies and Your Imperial Majesty, with the real nightingale one can never tell which song will come out, but all is known about the artificial bird! You can explain its mechanism and show people where the waltzes lie, and how one follows the other!'

'That is just what I think!' said everyone, and the music master received permission to show the bird to the people the next Sunday. They should hear it sing, commanded the emperor. And they heard it and were as pleased as if they had had too much tea, after the Chinese fashion. They all said 'Oh!' and held up their forefingers and nodded time.

But the poor fisherman, who had heard the real nightingale, said, 'This one sings well enough, but there is something wanting. I don't know what.'

The real nightingale was banished from the kingdom.

The artificial bird was put on a silken cushion by the emperor's bed; all the presents which it received of gold and precious stones lay round it. It was given the title of Imperial Night Singer, First from the Left. The emperor considered that side the more distinguished, for even an emperor's heart is on the left.

And the music master wrote twenty-five volumes about the artificial bird, all learned, lengthy, and full of the hardest Chinese words—yet all said they had read and understood it, for once they had been very stupid about a book and had been trampled under foot in consequence.

So a whole year passed. The emperor, the court, and all the other Chinese knew every note of the artificial bird's song by heart, and they liked it all the better for that. They could even sing with it, and they did so. The street boys sang 'Tra-la-la-la-la,' and the emperor sang too sometimes. It was indeed delightful.

But one evening, when the artificial bird was singing its best, and the emperor lay in bed listening to it, something in the bird cracked. Something snapped! Whir-r-r! All the wheels ran down and then the music ceased. The emperor sprang up and had his physician summoned, but what could he do? Then the clockmaker came, and, after a great deal of talking and examining, he put the bird in order as well as he could, but he said it must seldom be used as the works were nearly worn out and it was impossible to put in new ones.

Here was a calamity! Only once a year was the artificial bird allowed to sing, and even that was almost too much for it, but then the music master made a little speech full of hard words, saying that it was just as good as before, and so, of course, it was just as good as before. Five years passed, and then a great sorrow came to the nation, for the Chinese were fond of their emperor; and now he was ill, and it was said, not likely to live. Already a new emperor had been chosen, and the people stood in the street and asked the first lord how the old emperor was.

'P,' said he, and shook his head.

Cold and pale lay the emperor in his great splendid bed; all the courtiers believed him dead, and one after the other left him to pay their respects to the new emperor. Everywhere in the halls and corridors cloth was laid down so no footstep could be heard, and everything was still—very, very still—and nothing came to break the silence.

The emperor longed for something to relieve the monotony of this deathlike stillness. If only someone would speak to him. If only someone would sing to him. Music would carry his thoughts away and break the spell lying on him. The moon shone in at the open window, but that, too, was silent, quite silent.

'Music! Music!' cried the emperor. 'Little bright golden bird, sing! Do sing! I gave you gold and jewels; I hung my gold slipper round your neck with my own hand. Sing! Do sing!'

But the bird was silent, there was no one to wind it up and so it could not sing. And all was silent, terribly still!

All at once there came in at the window the most glorious burst of song. It was the little living nightingale, who was sitting outside on a bough. She had heard of the need of her emperor and had come to sing to him of comfort and hope. As she sang, the blood flowed quicker and quicker in the emperor's weak body, and life began to return.

'Thank you, thank you,' said the emperor, 'you divine little bird. I know you. I banished you from my kingdom, and yet you have given me life again. How can I reward you?'

'You have done that already,' said the nightingale. 'I brought tears to your eyes the first time I sang; I shall never forget that. They are jewels that rejoice a singer's heart. But now sleep and grow strong again. I will sing you a lullaby.'

And the emperor fell into a deep, calm sleep as she sang.

The sun was shining through the window when he awoke, strong and well. None of his servants had come back yet, for they all thought he was dead. But the nightingale still sang to him.

'You must stay with me always,' said the emperor. 'You shall sing only when you like, and I will break the artificial bird into a thousand pieces.'

'Don't do that,' said the nightingale. 'It did all it could. Keep it as you have done. I cannot build my nest in the palace and live here, but let me come whenever I like. In the evening I will sit on the bough outside the window and sing you something to make you feel happy and grateful. I will sing of joy and of sorrow; I will sing of the evil and the good which lies hidden from you. The little singing bird flies all around, to the poor fisherman's hut or the farmer's cottage, to all those who are far away from you and your court. I love your heart more than your crown, though that has about it a brightness as of something holy. Now I will sing to you again, but you must promise me one thing—'

'Anything you ask,' said the emperor, standing up in his imperial robes, which he had put on himself, and fastening on his sword richly embossed with gold.

'One thing only I beg of you! Do not tell anyone you have a little bird who tells you everything; it will be much better not to have it known.'

Then the nightingale flew away.

The servants came in to attend their dead emperor, and the emperor said:

'Good morning!'

[Hans Christian Andersen.]

Hermod and Hadvor

ONCE UPON A TIME
there were a king and a queen who had an only daughter,
called Hadvor, who was fair and beautiful, and being an only
child was heir to the kingdom. The king and queen had also
a foster son, named Hermod, who was just about the same age
as Hadvor. He was good-looking as well as clever at most
things. Hermod and Hadvor often played together while they
were children and liked each other so much that, while they
were still young, they secretly plighted their troth to each
other.

As time went on the queen fell sick and, suspecting that it
was her last illness, sent for the king to come to her. She told
him that she wished to ask one thing of him. If he married
another wife he should promise to take no other than the
Queen of Hetland the Good. The king gave the promise, and
thereafter the queen died.

Time passed, and the king, growing tired of living alone,
fitted out his ship and sailed out to sea. As he sailed there came
so thick a mist he altogether lost his bearings but after long
trouble found land. There he laid his ship to and went on
shore alone. After walking for some time he came to a forest,

into which he went a little way and stopped. Then he heard sweet music from a harp and followed the sound until he came to a clearing. There he saw three women, one of whom sat on a golden chair and was beautifully and grandly dressed. She held a harp in her hands and was very sorrowful. The second was also finely dressed, but younger in appearance and she also sat on a chair, but it was not so grand as the first one's. The third stood behind them, and was very pretty to look at. She had a green cloak over her other clothes and it was easy to see that she was maid to the other two.

After the king had looked at them for a little he went forward and saluted them. The one who sat on the golden chair asked him who he was and where he was going. He told her all the story—how he was a king, and had lost his queen, and was now on his way to Hetland the Good, to ask the queen of that country in marriage. She answered that fortune had contrived this wonderfully. Pirates had plundered Hetland and killed the king, and she had fled from the land in terror and had come hither after great trouble, and she was the very person he was looking for and the others were her daughter and maid. The king immediately asked her hand; she gladly received his proposal and accepted him at once. Thereafter they all set out and made their way to the ship; and after that nothing is told of their voyage until the king reached his own country. He made a great feast and celebrated his marriage as soon as they were back in his country.

Hermod and Hadvor took but little notice of the queen and her daughter. But, on the other hand, Hadvor and the new queen's maid, Olof, were very friendly, and Olof came often to visit Hadvor in her castle. Before long the king went out to war and no sooner was he away than the queen came to talk with Hermod and said he was to marry her daughter. Hermod

She was beautifully dressed and held a harp

told her straight and plain he would not. The queen grew terribly angry and said in that case neither should he have Hadvor, for she would now lay this spell on him: he should go to a desert island and there be a lion by day and a man by night, and thinking always of Hadvor would cause him all the more sorrow. From this spell he should never be freed until Hadvor burned the lion's skin and that would not happen very soon.

As soon as the queen had finished her speech Hermod replied that he also laid a spell on her. As soon as he was freed from her enchantments she should become a rat and her daughter a mouse and fight with each other in the hall until he killed them with his sword.

After this Hermod disappeared, and no one knew what had become of him. The queen caused search to be made for him, but he could nowhere be found. One time, when Olof was in the castle beside Hadvor, she asked the princess if she knew where Hermod had gone. At this Hadvor became very sad and said she did not.

'I shall tell you then,' said Olof, 'for I know all about it. Hermod has disappeared through the wicked devices of the queen. She is a witch and so is her daughter, though they have put on these beautiful forms. Because Hermod would not fall in with the queen's plans and marry her daughter, she has laid a spell on him. He is a lion by day and a man by night, and can never be freed until you burn the lion's skin.

'Besides,' said Olof, 'she has looked out a match for you. She has a brother in the underworld, a three-headed giant, whom she means to turn into a beautiful prince and marry him to you. This is no new thing for the queen. She took me away from my parents' house and compelled me to serve her.

But she has never done me any harm, for the green cloak I wear protects me against all mischief.'

Hadvor now became still sadder at the thought of the marriage destined for her and entreated Olof to think of some plan to save her.

'I think,' said Olof, 'that your wooer will come up through the floor of the castle and so you must be prepared. When you hear the noise of his coming, and the floor begins to open, have at hand blazing pitch and pour it into the opening. That will prove too much for him.'

About this time the king came home from his expedition and thought it a great blow that no one knew what had become of Hermod. The queen consoled him as best she could, and after a time the king thought less about his disappearance.

Hadvor remained in her castle, and made the preparations as Olof had said. One night, not long after, a loud noise and rumbling was heard under the castle. Hadvor at once guessed what it was and told her maids to be ready to help her. The noise and thundering grew louder and louder until the floor began to open. Hadvor made them take the cauldron of pitch and pour plenty of it into the opening. With that the noises grew fainter and fainter, till at last they ceased altogether.

Next morning the queen rose early and went out to the palace gate. There she found her brother, the giant, lying dead. She went up to him and said:

'I pronounce this spell, that you become a beautiful prince and that Hadvor shall be unable to say anything against the charges I shall bring against her.'

The body of the dead giant now became that of a beautiful prince, and the queen went in again.

'I don't think,' said she to the king, 'that your daughter is as good as she is said to be. My brother came and asked her hand, and she has had him put to death. I have just found his dead body lying at the palace gate.'

The king went along with the queen to see the body, and thought it all very strange. So beautiful a youth, he said, would have been a worthy match for Hadvor and he would have readily agreed to their marriage. The queen asked leave to decide what Hadvor's punishment should be, which the king was very willing to allow, to escape from punishing his own daughter. The queen's decision was that the king should make a big grave mound for her brother and put Hadvor into it beside him.

Olof knew all the plans of the queen and told the princess what had been done, whereupon Hadvor earnestly entreated her to tell her what to do.

'First and foremost,' said Olof, 'you must get a wide cloak to wear over your other clothes, when you are put into the mound. The giant's ghost will walk after you are both left there. He will have two dogs with him. He will ask you to cut pieces out of his legs to give to the dogs, but you must promise nothing unless he will tell you where Hermod has gone and how to find him. He will let you stand on his shoulders, to get out of the mound. But he means to cheat you and will catch you by the cloak to pull you back again. You must take care to have the cloak loose on your shoulders so he will only get hold of that.'

Everything happened just as Olof had said. The prince became a giant again and asked Hadvor to cut the pieces out of his legs for the dogs. But she refused until he told her that Hermod was in a desert island, which she could not reach unless she took his shoes. With these shoes she could travel both on land and sea. This Hadvor now did and the giant then let her climb on his shoulders to get out of the mound. As she sprang out he caught hold of her cloak, but she had taken care to let it lie loose on her shoulders and so escaped.

She now made her way down to the sea which was nearest the island where Hermod was. This strait she easily crossed, for the shoes kept her up. On reaching the island she found a sandy beach all along by the sea and high cliffs above. Nor could she see any way to climb these and so, being both sad at heart and tired with the long journey, she lay down and fell asleep.

As she slept she dreamed that a tall woman came to her and said, 'I know that you are Princess Hadvor and are searching for Hermod. He is on this island. It will be hard for you to reach him if you have no one to help you, for you cannot climb the cliffs by your own strength. I have therefore let down a rope by which you will be able to climb up. As the island is large and you might not find Hermod's dwelling-place, I lay down this clew beside you. You need only hold the end of the thread, and the clew will run on before and show you the way. I also lay this belt beside you, put it on when you awaken. It will keep you from growing faint with hunger.'

The woman now disappeared, and Hadvor woke and saw that all her dream had been true. The rope hung down from the cliff, and the clew and belt lay beside her. The belt she put on, the rope enabled her to climb up the cliff and the clew led her on till she came to the mouth of a cave. She went into the cave and saw there a low couch. She crept under it and lay down.

When evening came she heard a noise outside. The lion had come to the mouth of the cave and shook itself there, after which she heard a man coming toward the couch. She was sure this was Hermod, because she heard him speaking to himself about his own condition and calling to mind Hadvor and other things in the old days. Hadvor made no sign, but waited till he had fallen asleep and then crept out and burned the lion's skin, which he had left outside. Then she went back into the cave and wakened Hermod, and they had a most joyful meeting.

In the morning they talked over their plans and were most at a loss to know how to get out of the island. Hadvor told Hermod her dream and said she suspected there was someone in the island who would be able to help them. Hermod said he knew of a witch there, who was very ready to help anyone, and that the only plan was to go to her. So they went to the witch's cave and found her there with her fifteen young sons and asked her to help them get to the mainland.

'There are other things easier than that,' said she, 'for the giant that was buried will be waiting for you. He has turned himself into a whale. I shall lend you a boat, however, and if you meet the whale and think your lives are in danger, then you can name me by name.'

They thanked her greatly for her help and advice and set out from the island. On the way they saw a huge whale coming toward them, with great splashing and dashing of waves. They were sure of what it was and thought they had as good reason now as ever to call on the witch and so they did. The next minute they saw coming after them another huge whale, followed by fifteen smaller ones. All of these swam past the boat and went on to meet the whale. There was a fierce battle and the sea became so stormy that it was not easy to keep the boat from being filled by the waves. After this fight had gone on for some time, they saw that the sea was dyed with blood. The big whale and the fifteen smaller ones disappeared, and they got to land safe and sound.

Strange things had happened in the meantime in the king's hall. The queen and her daughter had disappeared, but a rat and a mouse were always fighting with each other there. Many people had tried to drive them away, but no one could manage it. Some time went on, while the king was almost beside himself with sorrow and care for the loss of his queen and because these monsters destroyed all mirth in the hall.

One evening, however, while they all sat dull and down-hearted, in came Hermod with a sword by his side and saluted the king, who received him with the greatest joy, as if he had come back from the dead. Before Hermod sat down he went to where the rat and the mouse were fighting and cut them in two with his sword. All were astonished then to see two witches lying dead on the floor of the hall.

Hermod now told the whole story to the king, who was glad to be rid of such vile creatures. Next he asked for the hand of Hadvor, which the king readily gave him and, being now an old man, gave the kingdom to him as well, and so Hermod became king.

Olof married a good-looking nobleman, and that is the end of the story.

[From the Icelandic.]

The Steadfast Tin Soldier

THERE WERE ONCE UPON
a time five-and-twenty tin soldiers—all brothers, as they were
made out of the same old tin spoon. Their uniform was red
and blue, and they shouldered their guns and looked straight
in front of them. The first words that they heard in this world,
when the lid of the box in which they lay was taken off, were,
'Hurrah, tin soldiers!' This was shouted by a little boy, clapping
his hands. They had been given to him because it was his
birthday and now he began setting them out on the table. Each
soldier was exactly like the other in shape, except one, who
had been made last when the tin had run short. There he stood
as firmly on his one leg as the others did on two and he is the
one who became famous.

There were many other playthings on the table. But the
nicest of all was a pretty little castle made of cardboard, with
windows through which one could see into the rooms. In front
of the castle stood some little trees surrounding a tiny mirror
which looked like a lake. Wax swans were floating about, re-
flecting themselves in it. That was all very pretty, but the most
beautiful of all was a little lady, who stood in the open doorway. She was cut out of paper, but she had on a dress of the

finest muslin, with a scarf of narrow blue ribbon round her
shoulders, fastened in the middle with a glittering rose made
of gold paper, which was as large as her head. The lady was
stretching out both her arms, for she was a dancer, and lifting
one leg so high in the air that the tin soldier couldn't see it
and thought that she, too, had only one leg.

That's the wife for me! he thought; but she is so grand and
lives in a castle, while I have only a box with four-and-twenty
others. This is no place for her! But I must make her acquain-
tance. Then he stretched himself out behind a snuffbox that
lay on the table. From there he could watch the dainty lady,
who continued to stand on one leg without losing her balance.

When night came all the other tin soldiers went into their box and the people of the house went to bed. Then the toys began to play at visiting, dancing and fighting. The tin soldiers rattled in their box, for they wanted to be out too, but they could not raise the lid. The nutcrackers played at leapfrog and the slate pencil ran about the slate. There was so much noise that the canary woke up and began to talk to them—in poetry too! The only two who did not stir from their places were the tin soldier and the little dancer. She remained on tiptoe, with both arms outstretched. He stood steadfastly on his one leg, never moving his eyes from her face.

The clock struck twelve, and crack! Off flew the lid of the snuffbox. But there was no snuff inside, only a little black imp—that was the beauty of it.

'Hullo, tin soldier!' said the imp. 'Don't look at things that aren't intended for the likes of you!'

But the tin soldier took no notice and seemed not to hear.

'Very well, wait till tomorrow!' said the imp.

When it was morning, and the children were up, the tin soldier was put in the window. Whether it was the wind or the little black imp, I don't know, but all at once the window flew open and out fell the little tin soldier, head over heels, from the third-story window! That was a terrible fall, I can tell you! He landed on his head with his leg in the air, his gun being wedged between two paving stones.

The nursery maid and the little boy came down at once to look for him but, though they were so near him they almost trod on him, they did not notice. If the tin soldier had only called out, 'Here I am!' they must have found him. He did not think it fitting for him to cry out, because he had on his uniform.

Soon it began to drizzle. Then the drops came faster and

there was a regular downpour. When it was over, two little
street boys came along.

'Just look!' cried one. 'Here is a tin soldier! He shall sail up
and down in a boat!'

So they made a little boat out of newspaper, put the tin
soldier in it and made him sail up and down the gutter. Both
the boys ran along beside him, clapping their hands. What

great waves there were in the gutter and what a swift current!
The paper boat tossed up and down and in the middle of the
stream it went so fast that the tin soldier trembled. He remained steadfast, showed no emotion, but looked straight in
front of him, shouldering his gun. All at once the boat passed
under a long tunnel that was as dark as his box had been.

'Where can I be now?' he wondered. 'Oh, dear! This is the
black imp's fault! Ah, if only the little lady were sitting beside
me in the boat, it might be twice as dark for all I should care!'

Suddenly there came along a great water rat that lived in
the tunnel.

'Have you a passport?' asked the rat. 'Out with your passport!'

But the tin soldier was silent and grasped his gun more

firmly. The boat sped on and the rat behind it. Ugh! How he showed his teeth, as he cried to the chips of wood and straw:
'Hold him, hold him! He has not paid the toll! He has not shown his passport!'

But the current became swifter and stronger. The tin soldier could already see daylight when the tunnel ended. In his ears there sounded a roaring enough to frighten any brave man. Only think! At the end of the tunnel the gutter discharged itself into a great canal. That would be just as dangerous for him as it would be for us to go down a waterfall.

Now he was so near to it that he could not hold on any longer. On went the boat, the poor tin soldier keeping himself as stiff as he could. No one should say of him afterwards that he had flinched. The boat whirled three, four times round and became filled to the brim with water. It began to sink! The tin soldier was standing up to his neck in water. Deeper and deeper sank the boat. Softer and softer grew the paper. Now the water was over his head. He was thinking of the pretty little dancer, whose face he should never see again and there sounded in his ears, over and over again:

> Forward, forward, soldier bold,
> Death's before thee, grim and cold!

The paper came in two, and the soldier fell—but at that moment he was swallowed by a great fish! Oh, how dark it was inside, even darker than in the tunnel and it was really very close quarters! But there the steadfast little tin soldier lay full length, shouldering his gun.

Up and down swam the fish, then it made the most dreadful contortions and became suddenly quite still. It was as if a flash of lightning had passed through it; the daylight streamed in and a voice exclaimed, 'Why, here is the little tin soldier!' The fish had been caught, taken to market, sold and brought into the kitchen, where the cook had cut it open with a great knife. She took up the soldier between her finger and thumb and carried him into the room, where everyone wanted to see the hero who had been found inside a fish. The tin soldier was not at all proud. They put him on the table and —what strange things do happen in this world! The tin soldier was in the same room in which he had been before! He saw the same children and the same toys on the table. There was the same grand castle with the pretty little dancer. She was still standing on one leg with the other high in the air. She too was steadfast. That touched the tin soldier. He was nearly ready to shed tin tears. But that would not have been fitting for a soldier. He looked at her, but she said nothing.

All at once one of the little boys took up the tin soldier, and threw him into the stove, giving no reason. Doubtless the little black imp in the snuffbox was at the bottom of this too.

There the tin soldier lay and felt a heat that was truly terrible. Whether he was suffering from actual fire or from the ardour of his passion he did not know. All his colour had disappeared. Whether this had happened on his travels or whether it was the result of trouble, who can say? He looked at the little lady, she looked at him and he felt that he was melting. He remained steadfast with his gun at his shoulder.

Suddenly a door opened, the draught caught up the little dancer and off she flew like a sylph to the tin soldier in the stove, burst into flames—and that was end of her! Then the tin soldier melted down into a little lump, and next morning when the maid was taking out the ashes, she found him in the shape of a heart. There was nothing left of the little dancer but her gilt rose, burned as black as a cinder.

[Hans Christian Andersen.]

Blockhead Hans

FAR AWAY IN THE
country lay an old manor house where lived an old squire
who had two sons. They thought themselves so clever, that if
they had known only half of what they did know, it would
have been quite enough. They both wanted to marry the king's
daughter, for she had proclaimed that she would have for her
husband the man who knew best how to choose his words.

Both prepared for the wooing a whole week, which was the
longest time allowed them. But, after all, it was quite long
enough, for they both had preparatory knowledge and everyone knows how useful that is. One knew the whole Latin
dictionary and also three years' issue of the daily paper of the
town by heart, so he could repeat it all backward or forward
as you pleased. The other had worked at the laws of corporation and knew by heart what every member of the corporation
ought to know, so he thought he could quite well speak on
state matters and give his opinion. He understood, besides this,
how to embroider braces with roses and other flowers and
scrolls, for he was very ready with his fingers.

'I shall win the king's daughter!' they both cried.

Their father gave each of them a fine horse. The one who knew the dictionary and the daily paper by heart had a black horse. The other who was so clever at corporation law had a milk-white one. Then they oiled the corners of their mouths so they might be able to speak more fluently. All the servants stood in the courtyard and saw them mount their steeds. Here by chance came the third brother. The squire had three sons, but nobody counted him with his brothers, for he was not so learned as they were, and he was generally called 'Blockhead Hans.'

'Oh, oh!' said Blockhead Hans. 'Where are you off to? You are in your Sunday-best clothes!'

'We are going to court, to woo the princess! Don't you know what is known throughout all the countryside?' And they told him all about it.

'Hurrah! I'll go too!' cried Blockhead Hans. The brothers laughed at him and rode off.

'Dear Father,' cried Blockhead Hans, 'I must have a horse too. What a desire for marriage has seized me! If she will have me, she will have me, and if she won't have me, I will have her.'

'Stop that nonsense!' said the old man. 'I will not give you a horse. You can't speak. You don't know how to choose your words. Your brothers—ah, they are very different lads!'

'Well,' said Blockhead Hans, 'if I can't have a horse, I will take the goat which is mine. He can carry me!'

And he did so. He sat astride the goat, struck his heels into its side, and went rattling down the highroad like a hurricane. Hoppetty hop, what a ride!

'Here I come!' shouted Blockhead Hans, singing so loud, the echoes were roused far and near. But his brothers were

riding slowly in front. They were not speaking, but they were
thinking over all the good things they were going to say, for
everything had to be thought out.

'Hullo!' bawled Blockhead Hans. 'Here I am! Just look
what I found on the road!' And he showed them a dead crow
which he had picked up.

'Blockhead!' said his brothers. 'What are you going to do
with it?'

'With the crow? I shall give it to the princess!'

'Do so, certainly!' they said, laughing loudly and riding on.
'Slap bang! Here I am again! Look what I have just found.
You don't find such things every day on the road.'

And the brothers turned round to see what in the world
he could have found. 'Blockhead,' said they, 'that is an old
wooden shoe without the top! Are you going to send that, too,
to the princess?'

'Of course I shall,' returned Blockhead Hans. And the
brothers laughed and rode on a good way.

'Slap bang! Here I am!' cried Blockhead Hans. 'Better and
better—it is really famous.'

'What have you found now?' asked the brothers.

'Oh,' said Blockhead Hans, 'it is really too good. How
pleased the princess will be.'

'Why,' said the brothers, 'this is only mud, straight from
the ditch.'

'Of course it is,' said Blockhead Hans, 'and it is the best
kind. Look how it runs through one's fingers.' And, so saying,
he filled his pockets with the mud.

But the brothers rode on so fast that dust and sparks flew
all around and they reached the gate of the town a good hour
before Blockhead Hans. Here came the suitors, numbered according to their arrival. They were ranged in rows, six in
each row, and they were so tightly packed that they could not
move their arms. This was a very good thing, for otherwise
they would have torn each other in pieces, merely because the
one was in front of the other.

All the country people were standing round the king's
throne, crowded together in thick masses almost out of the
windows, to see the princess receive the suitors. As each one
came into the room all his fine phrases went out like a candle!

'It doesn't matter,' said the princess. 'Away! Out with him!'

At last she came to the row in which was the brother who knew the dictionary by heart, but he did not know it any longer. He had quite forgotten it. The floor creaked and the ceiling was all made of glass mirrors, so that he saw himself standing on his head. By each window were standing three reporters and an editor, and each of them was writing down what was said, to publish it in the paper. It was fearful, and they had made up the fire so hot that it was grilling.

'It is hot in here, isn't it!' said the suitor.

'Of course it is. My father is roasting young chickens today,' said the princess.

'Ahem!' There he stood like an idiot. He was not prepared for such a speech; he did not know what to say, although he wanted to say something witty. 'Ahem!'

'It doesn't matter,' said the princess. 'Take him out!' And out he had to go.

Now the other brother entered. 'How hot it is!' he said.

'Of course. We are roasting young chickens today,' remarked the princess.

'How do you—um,' he said, and the reporters wrote down, 'How do you—um.'

'It doesn't matter,' said the princess. 'Take him out!'

Now Blockhead Hans came in. He rode his goat right into the hall. 'I say! How roasting hot it is here,' said he.

'Of course! I am roasting young chickens today,' said the princess.

'That's good,' replied Blockhead Hans. 'Then can I roast a crow with them?'

'With the greatest of pleasure,' said the princess. 'But have you anything you can roast them in? For I have neither pot nor saucepan.'

'Oh, rather,' said Blockhead Hans. 'Here is a cooking implement with tin rings.' And he drew out the old wooden shoe and laid the crow in it.

'That is quite a meal,' said the princess. 'But where shall we get the soup?'

'I've that in my pocket,' said Blockhead Hans. 'I have so much that I can quite well throw some away.' And he poured some mud out of his pocket.

'I like you,' said the princess. 'You can answer, and you can speak, and I will marry you. But do you know that every word which we are saying and have said has been taken down and will be in the paper tomorrow? By each window do you see three reporters and an old editor? And this old editor is the worst, for he doesn't understand anything.' But she only said this to tease Blockhead Hans. The reporters giggled, and each dropped a blot of ink on the floor.

'Ah, are those the great people?' said Blockhead Hans. 'Then I will give the editor the best.' So saying, he turned his pockets inside out and threw the mud right in his face.

'That was neatly done,' said the princess. 'I couldn't have done it; but I will soon learn how.'

Blockhead Hans became king, won a wife and a crown and sat on the throne. This we have still damp from the newspaper of the editor and the reporters—and they are not to be believed for a moment.